THE HORSEMAN'S WORD

The Horseman's Word Copyright © 2019 Erica Obey

Paperback ISBN 13: 978-1-948338-85-1
E-book ISBN 13: 978-1-948338-86-8
Kindle ISBN 13: 978-1-948338-87-5

ALL RIGHTS RESERVED. In accordance with the U.S. Copyright Act of 1976, no part of this publication may be reproduced, distributed, or transmitted in any form or by any means, or stored in a database or retrieval system, without prior written permission of the publisher, Encircle Publications, Farmington, ME.

This book is a work of fiction. All names, characters, places and events are products of the author's imagination or are used fictitiously, and any resemblance to actual persons, living or dead, or to actual places or businesses, is entirely coincidental.

Editor: Cynthia Brackett-Vincent
Book design: Eddie Vincent
Cover design: Deirdre Wait
Cover images ©Getty

Published by: Encircle Publications, LLC
PO Box 187
Farmington, ME 04938

Visit: http://encirclepub.com

Sign up for Encircle Publications newsletter and specials
http://eepurl.com/cs8taP

Printed in U.S.A.

THE HORSEMAN'S WORD

Erica Obey

Encircle Publications, LLC
Farmington, Maine, U.S.A.

PROLOGUE

Gramercy Park, New York City, May, 1863

Lee had just won a decisive victory at Chancellorsville, and reports swirled that the Confederate Army that was marching up the Shenandoah Valley would succeed in invading the North this time. Anxious families along the Susquehanna had already begun to bury the family silver and board their windows. Those that could abandoned their homes and fled with what valuables they could carry.

The fear, however, had not yet stretched as far as New York City. At least, it had yet to reach the sheltered enclave known as Gramercy Park. The tall windows of the lofty townhouses had been flung open rather than boarded up, and the silver sparkled, along with the guests. The lamps were lit, the champagne flowed, and the music from a string quartet wafted across the cobblestone street into the quiet of the gated park. For, tonight, the well-known philanthropist Jonathan Adair was to sign the final papers that deeded his magnificent collection to the City of New York, and he was celebrating this singular contribution to the betterment of mankind by unveiling the contents of his priceless new acquisition: An ancient casket, beaten out of ancient bronze and chased with curious figures of horses that some said was Gaulish, and some said Phoenician. Some even said it had survived the cataclysmic Fall of Troy itself.

But such tales meant nothing to the desperate Fenian that Rose Adair confronted at gunpoint in the shadows of the gated park across the cobbled street. A true-born son of the Gael, Declan Sullivan had confided his own burning dreams on that fatal trip to Jones's Wood when she had fallen in love with him. Spun yarns of a mysterious society of horsemen with powers bestowed on them by Epona, the Horse Goddess herself, as they had swung together in a gondola suspended from a massive wooden scaffold. And whispered the powers of the priceless artifact he had risked his soul to steal from the goddess' sacred spring and now sought to sell, while they giggled at the finish line of a wheelbarrow race, and a daredevil walked a tightrope high above their heads.

All of those stories no more than words, as much of a cheat and illusion as the tales he had spun of Tir Na nOg, the legendary Irish land beyond the Western Sea. Or his love for her. For like the Fair Folk that populated those fabled lands, the man who faced her now might never lie, but he was incapable of telling the truth.

"Roisin," he said. "My sweet Roisin Dubh. My dark Rosaleen."

"Please do not call me that. For I have told you my true name often enough." She swallowed hard, trying to prevent her voice from shaking as badly as the pistol she held in both hands. "But I cannot say the same of you, Captain Fallon. Captain Tamerlane Fallon, I believe it is?"

A moment's silence, during which even the music wafting from the open windows seemed to still. Then, his jaw set. "Ah," he said.

"Indeed."

She lowered the pistol and turned to go, for there seemed little more to be said. But Fallon laid a hand on her arm to stop her. "I would have you know I bade you meet me here so that I might have a chance to explain myself. In fact, I am risking my life to do so."

"Then I regret to inform you that you have risked your life for naught."

"Oh, no, that was cruel. You were never cruel to me, Roisin." Rose thought she heard a genuine note of hurt in Fallon's voice.

No, Rose *wanted* to hear a note of hurt—wanted him to be as hurt and confused as she was now. "I told you my name was Rose."

"You will always be Roisin to me. My dark Rosaleen. The one woman who ever truly believed in me." He made to draw her closer. "Please. You did not hate me when you thought I conspired against the English. Can you not at least give me a chance to explain my true motives now?"

Wrenching herself free, she raised the pistol once more between them. "The authorities have already spared you that task. They say you have plans to spread Greek fire throughout the city tonight and burn it to the ground."

"And do you believe them?"

"Would you deny it?" she countered.

Instead of answer, he simply studied her—and the silver dueling pistol that was said to have belonged to Charles II himself. "Would you do it?" he mused.

"Would you truly shoot me?"

"Why should I not? The police say you're a Confederate spy," she said.

"I am not," he said.

"Just an ordinary thief and profiteer, then?"

His face twisted. "Roisin, please. Just give me one moment to explain."

Explain what? That he had lied to her? Used her in the cruelest way possible? She shook her head. "This is no time. The police are searching for you everywhere. They seek to hang you."

And if what they said about him was true, it was no less than he deserved. She drew a deep breath, considering her options. In one hand she held the fate of Declan Sullivan, the only man she had ever loved. No, she amended herself furiously. In one hand, she held the fate of Tamerlane Fallon, liar, spy, and traitor, who had used her most abominably. In the other, the fate of New York City—or even quite possibly that of the Union itself.

She weighed them in the balance and made up her mind.

"Go," she said, lowering the pistol. "Go while you still can. Mayhap you can make it to Canada in safety if you ride all night."

He raised an eyebrow, as he studied her. Then his face softened. "Ah, my sweet Roisin. Beneath that sweet face, you have the spirt of Grainne Ni Mhaille, the Pirate Queen herself."

"My name is Rose," she said. "Now, *go*."

But her words were cut off by a flash of light that illuminated the entire gracious square in garish green. And she just barely had time to recognize the stunned shock that twisted Declan's—no, Tamerlane Fallon's—face, before the explosion was followed by a clap of sound and a gout of smoke from the shattered windows of her father's house. The music screeched to a halt. Feet pounded, men shouted. And her Cousin Preston in his evening wear flung open the front door, shouting, "Murder! Treason! The Fenians have just assassinated my uncle!"

Her father, dead? And by her own lover's hand? No, it could not be true!

She whirled on Declan—no, *Tamerlane*—who had gone sheet white. "No," he said. "No, no. This is all wrong."

Without another word, he dashed out of the park at a pace that belied the customary hitch in his gait, running so fast that, hindered by her skirts as she was, she just barely managed to grab his sleeve before he reached the park's elegant gate. "Stop!" she cried. "What are you thinking? Even if this is your doing, you cannot put it right. They will hang you, do you understand, you fool? Now, run. Run for your life."

For a moment, his face grew as wistful as her heart. Then his jaw set, and he reached under his coat and pulled out a thick envelope she incredulously recognized as her father's confidential correspondence file—the one even she was not allowed to touch. But Fallon simply ignored her outraged gasp and handed it to her, his face hardening with determination as he studied the mayhem that spilled from her own front door. "You say you want to set things right? Then I will tell you how you can best do that. Not by saving my sorry skin. Not now—although I confess I have hopes to finally explain myself to you later. But if you truly want to help me, you need to go to Jones's Wood as soon as you can, and find a man named Sammy Nunn. Tell him to give this to Declan Sullivan—in the name of the Society of the Horseman's Word."

Her eyes widened in exasperation. "Would you persist in this foolish lie, even at such a critical moment? Declan Sullivan is not real. He never was."

"Oh, Declan Sullivan is real enough. He simply is not me," Fallon assured her. The corner of his mouth pulled up in a wry smile, as he added, "And, if you have a chance to encounter the genuine item directly, would you be so good as to tell him… it was naught but a joke—my wretched sense of humor playing me one last foul trick. Or at least, so it began."

Which meant… what?

No, what could it matter right now? It cost her only a moment's hesitation before she tucked the envelope in her sleeve. "And you?"

He raised a shoulder with a nonchalance she was certain he was feigning. "I will face the fate many would say I so richly deserve," he said, then his face softened once more. "My sweet Roisin, you would do me the favor of saving my worthless neck, but I would ask another favor instead. Give me one last kiss before we part, my love, Roisin. One last kiss as a token you will not hate me when you remember me."

And without waiting for her answer, he kissed her deeply, sweetly, in a way that she knew, despite the fact that he was a liar, a spy, and her father's murderer, would ruin her for ever being kissed by any other man.

Then he sprinted across the street into chaos.

And straight into the path of a pair of New York City detectives, who were pounding down the street in a maelstrom of whistles and rattles, in response to Cousin Preston's frantic summons.

It took only a moment for Cousin Preston to recognize his quarry. "Seize him!" he cried, whirling on Fallon with a pointed finger. "For there is the spy you seek! A foul, Fenian assassin..."

"No!" Rose cried. "No, he was never..."

But as she snatched up her skirts in some last, irrational impulse to defend him, Fallon turned calmly toward the detectives and said, "Peace, I pray you, gentlemen. For I fear you are laboring under a dreadful misapprehension. For I am given to understand that you are seek to hang me as a Confederate spy, and I can I assure you that I am no such thing. I am in fact an English spy. And if I am to be hanged for that, so be it. But let us at least have our charges correct."

Roisin gasped. The detectives stopped, stymied.

"No more words!" Cousin Preston snapped. "You know your duty! Seize him!"

The policemen lunged, but Fallon stepped back easily. "Have a care, gentlemen! There is a little matter we must clear up before you kill me. For this fire is only one of a score that is set to go off around New York City tonight. And if you would not see that happen, I must speak personally to General John E. Wool, Commander of the Eastern District before my neck is to be broken."

Preston went puce. "Pay him no heed. The man is a liar who sought to sell my uncle smuggled antiquities..."

"Whose friends sought to end this war by the most reprehensible means necessary—and casting the blame for their deeds on a lot of ignorant, starving Irishmen," Fallon said, his eyes and voice suddenly cold. He turned back to the detectives. "And that is why General Wool needs to hear me—before more men die. For I promise you, it is a conspiracy so pernicious in its power, it could topple the Union."

The policemen—most likely Irishmen themselves—shuffled again, torn between displeasing a rich man and fear of the Confederate Army that was said to be drawing ever closer.

"Come, come, gentlemen," Fallon said, his voice suddenly as soft and persuasive as when he had cajoled Rose to accompany him to Jones's Wood that one fatal night. "Surely there can be no risk here. I am not denying that I am a spy and a traitor—and am willing enough to go along quietly to the scaffold. All I ask is that you clap me in irons in one of the forts in New York Harbor instead of in the Tombs. How could such a thing possibly hurt? You have my complete assurance that an Army gallows can hang me as thoroughly as a police gallows ever will."

1

Gramercy Park, 1865

Lee had surrendered. The war was over—and Rose was at last able to look down onto the peaceful precinct of Gramercy Park without seeing the shades of the soldiers who had camped there, armed with Howitzers to defend those who lived in the surrounding townhouses against the raging Irish mob. The Park's gate had been safely relocked against future trespassers, and the shadows of the soldiers had faded along with the darker memories of the riots.

But although Rose might at last be able to gaze on the park, she had yet to be able to return to strolling its paths. For other memories proved much harder to erase. Memories of exactly what it felt like to have her heart broken. And the memory of a voice that still seemed to awaken her from her troubled dreams at the breaking dawn, calling, "*A Róisín ná bíodh brón ort fár* éirigh *dhuit*. My dark Rosaleen, do not sigh, do not weep."

But what did she have to weep for? For a man who had used her and her family in the cruelest, most callous way? For the possibility he had perished on the gallows as he so richly deserved? Or for the possibility that he had not?

*****

Bridie McMann could be forgiven for her reaction to a colored man presenting himself at the front door of the Adair townhouse. It had only been two years since the draft riots, and rumors still swirled around Manhattan about the colored people taking their revenge on the Irish who had so abused them.

"Service entrance is around the back," Bridie said, with an asperity that suggested a colored man would not be welcomed there either.

The man was polite, but firm, as he stood his ground and removed his hat. "I'm no servant. No tradesman either. I have come to solicit Mr. Adair's aid in pursuing a matter pertaining to his collections."

Bridie's snort suggested how likely she thought that proposition. But Rose was more circumspect. The man might be colored, but he was impeccably dressed and well spoken. And that made him far more dangerous than looters and renegades that were still rumored to threaten the houses of decent people. Gathering her skirts, which were cumbersome enough, although certainly far less voluminous than fashion dictated, Rose hurried across the Grand Foyer, which remained cluttered with the same King's Ransom of treasures that it had on that fateful night she had seen her father struck down.

"My apologies, Mr...."

"Washington," he supplied. "Cole Washington III."

"My apologies, Mr. Washington," she said smoothly. "Mrs. McMann has yet to re-accustom herself to the wide variety of art dealers that my father was wont to receive before the war…"

"I would not introduce myself under false pretenses. I am no art dealer," Washington said. "I seek only information."

And that was what Rose was afraid of. For information was precisely what she sought to hide behind the velvet curtains of the townhouse that were drawn even at day: information about the man who remained New York City's most famous collector, despite the fact that none of his wide circle of business and social acquaintances had seen him in nearly two years.

Bridie looked ready to summon a manservant to throw Washington bodily from house. But his firm dignity suggested the futility of any such notion. Despite her misgivings, Rose could see no other choice than to invite him inside.

"I regret to inform you that my father is in ill health and rarely receives guests. But I have served as my father's amanuensis for the past several years, so perhaps I can answer your questions instead." When Washington hesitated, she smiled faintly. "Please, Mr. Washington. Do you doubt a humble woman's abilities in such matters?"

From the sharp look he cast her, that was clearly not what he was in doubt of at all. But he conceded the point with a swift inclination of his head. "My wife was a schoolteacher who taught me to read and write," he said. "So, no, I would scarcely doubt such a thing. I apologize if I insulted you."

"Then please come in, and let us find a place to discuss this matter more comfortably."

She gestured for him to precede her into the grand foyer. It was little changed since the shocked guests had crowded around her father's insensate body, felled, most said by Fenian anarchists although there were those who had already begun to whisper of an ancient, unholy curse. The Greek fire had been easily contained and the damage quickly repaired. But no-one had thought to move the objects that had been massed to impress the glittering guests before they were transported to the new museum that her father and several other civic-minded gentlemen planned to dwarf the New York Historical Society's collections. Greek kouroi, Roman sarcophagi, and a pair of winged lions from Nineveh, stood sentry beneath Titians, Van Dykes, Tintorettos, and Rembrandts rose in ranks above the gilt chairs and tables that groaned beneath the weight of the epergnes that were said to have been crafted by Benvenuto Cellini himself—all of them simply assembled, with no particular sense of order, like passengers randomly gathered in a railroad waiting room.

Washington's lips tightened as he studied the various displays. "Your father must be quite the connoisseur."

"My father champions art and beauty."

"By owning it."

Washington spoke without inflection, but Rose was obscurely roused to defend her father. "He intends to donate it. For the betterment of the masses."

"And I'm sure the masses owe him their profoundest thanks."

Rose cast the man a sharp look, but his face was as bland as his voice. Vaguely discomfited, although she could not have told you how, she threw open the doors to the library. It was a lofty room with two stories of incunabulae and illuminated manuscripts that rose behind brass grills to a ceiling decorated with frescos of mythological subjects by Fragonard. A jewel-toned tapestry hung above the massive fireplace. Glass cases displayed everything from golden torques to intricately carved chess sets. Her father's desk, where he had last sat in order to sign the papers deeding his collection to the city with a quill that had been used to sign the Declaration of Independence, held pride of place in the center of the room, but Rose ignored it, and instead, showed Washington into the alcove that served as her personal workspace.

"So exactly what information is it that you seek, Mr. Washington?"

He took his time removing his hat and laying it on the table, before he said, "I seek information on a secret society known as the Society of the Horseman's Word. They are by all accounts a Scottish friendly society of farriers and ploughmen, established to protect their interests against the farmers and landowners who would use them. I would like to know whether they have spread to the United States, particularly among the Irish community."

At least, that is what Rose might have thought he said, but she was suddenly past hearing anything but the voice of a ghost whispering, "*A Roisin Dubh*. My dark Rosaleen."

A ghost who had never been anything more than a lie, she reminded herself sharply, any more than the food of the Fair Folk, whose tales he loved to spin, had ever been anything more than acorns and dirt.

"And what is your interest in this society?" she asked. "Are you a horseman, Mr. Washington?"

"I raced down at Metairie for two decades, although my name is not as well-known as those of the horses I rode." Washington's mouth twisted. "Mostly, I was listed as Colonel Farraday's Negro."

Rose glanced at him sharply, finally registering the faint hint of an accent beneath the cultured vowels. Had this man been a slave then? Her mind went back to the man's comments as he had gazed into her father's galleries. Was he right? Was owning art—or even horses—no different from owning people?

"And do you race now?" she asked.

"I retired from racing the day Mr. Lincoln freed my people."

"Then what is your interest in this Society?"

"No longer a practical one, I admit. However, I have heard tales that the Society protects far deeper, darker secrets than the ability to coax a horse—which I can assure you is a relatively simple skill indeed. Some would say that secret was nothing less than Adam's ability to command the animals. Others would say it was the secret of Tubal Cain, the first smith—who killed his own father, Cain, in order to gain his sorcerer's powers."

"Have you come here seeking sorcerers then?"

Washington ignored her patent disbelief and studied her for a moment, his dark eyes appraising. "I have come here seeking an Irishman who offered your father a priceless artifact for his collection," he said evenly.

"A talisman stolen from an ancient shrine of the horse goddess, Epona. A cursed talisman, and yet one so powerful that some say it affected the outcome of the war itself."

Could that possibly be true? And was that the explanation Tamerlane Fallon had sought to offer that night? Could the casket that had struck down her father truly have contained a weapon so powerful that Fallon had been willing to risk his life to obtain it? But *why*? He was an Englishman. What did he care about an American war?

"And are you a folklorist, then, Mr. Washington? A collector of legends?"

"It is no legend that Mr. Adair was about to reveal that talisman when he was the subject of a savage attack."

"An attack, yes, but scarcely a magical one. My father was the victim of a Fenian plot to spread terror through New York City by means of Greek fire, not the divine justice of a secret society of horsemen."

"And yet could not the two be one and the same thing?" Washington asked. "Could not the Society of the Horseman's Word disguise a group of Fenians who sought to destroy Manhattan? Who may still seek to destroy it?"

Fenians led by a dreamer and patriot named Declan Sullivan? "You speak of the similar plot that transpired just this year? Several hotels were burned, were they not, along with Mr. Barnum's Museum?" Rose asked, playing for time to compose herself. "But those men were Confederate spies, not Irishmen."

"And what of the men who paralyzed New York City with three days of rioting scarcely two months after the attack on your father?" Washington asked, his voice suddenly very quiet. "They were Irish, were they not?"

She drew a deep breath, willing herself not to think of Declan Sullivan and his wild dreams, for what could they have to do with the mob that had run amok in the city for three days, lynching and burning until the Army had finally been called in to subdue them? Those had been no Fenian heroes riding out to save their land. They been naught but impoverished Irishmen who were being conscripted into the Union army, their fury equally targeted at the colored people on whose behalf they were expected to fight and the rich men who could afford to pay $300 to hire a substitute for their sons. Declan Sullivan's high tales of the honor and glory of the Old Ones had nothing to do with such things.

But Declan Sullivan did not exist.

A ruthless English spy named Tamerlane Fallon did.

The Horseman's Word

"To what end?" she asked.

"Some said they sought to claim Manhattan as a New Dublin. Others said they sought an alliance with the Confederacy to reclaim Ireland for the Irish. Some said they did it for no better reason than the sheer love of devilry. Whatever their reasons, I would speak with your father directly about whether the Society of the Horseman's Word played any part in his obtaining that stolen treasure."

She shook her head, firmly rejecting any other tales of Fenian conspiracies. "My father is unwell," she said. "Unfortunately, the events that you seek to investigate are what led to his indisposition. I regret to say I cannot allow anyone to disturb him with these matters."

"And who do you think you are to allow or disallow me anything? Eh, miss, will you answer me that?"

Rose froze, as a fresh, angry voice brought an end to their conversation. Two years' indisposition since he had collapsed in front of a chest that had contained nothing but Greek fire had done nothing to hamper her father's cat-like tread, even if his mind remained as broken and patched as the rest of the house. Drawing a deep breath, she turned to look at him, dreading what she might see—no, what Cole Washington might see. But today seemed to be a good day. Her father was completely—no, impeccably—clothed. And while his gaze was clearly angry, it was also lucid. Perhaps there was a chance she could brazen out this fiasco.

"Father, may I present Mr. Washington? He asked to speak to you of the events of two years past, but I feared you would find it too taxing."

"Too taxing, you think? Why? Do you think me some kind of invalid? For that would suit your purposes, missy, would it not?" her father sneered. Ignoring her, he wheeled on Washington. "Who sent you? Preston, I have to assume? Trust him to choose an illiterate to do his dirty work. Letters are too dangerous to those who can read."

Anger flashed across Washington's face, but was immediately replaced by wary appraisal. "I'm afraid I'm not entirely certain what you mean, sir. Who is this Preston?"

"It is not for your kind to play their betters for a fool," her father said sharply. "I speak of Preston Olcott. My nephew—or some such thing. He is well known about town. Said to be an up-and-coming man."

That was one way of describing Cousin Preston, her father's confidential secretary whose duties Rose had assumed ever since he had found that joining the war effort provided an ideal excuse not to answer several uncomfortable questions her father's lawyers had raised about the family accounts, and her father had found a practical use for the governesses he had grudgingly paid for ever since his wife had been inconsiderate enough to die and leave him with an unwanted daughter. Left to her own devices, Rose would have been more likely to describe her cousin as a liar and a cheat. Not to mention, lately, blackmailer.

She eyed her father once more, anxious to spot any tell-tale signs that would give him away. But Jonathan Adair evinced no more emotion than if he were going over accounts with his man of business as he settled himself opposite Washington and confided, "She schemes, you know. Schemes with him. Weakness of her sex, it is, a weakness she inherited from her mother before her. Foul woman. Treacherous woman—as is all of her kind. She thinks I have no idea, of course. But I know. Seen the letters. Seen the treasonous correspondence between them. I know, oh, yes, I know."

Washington's face set with sudden understanding and he cast a sharp glance at Rose. And the pity underlying his expression was something she was not prepared to bear. "Mr. Washington came to inquire after the Irishman who brought you that unfortunate chest," she said to her father as smoothly as she could. "He has been given to understand that he might be part of a network of Fenian conspirators known as the Society of the Horseman's Word."

As she had hoped, her father shook off the question pettishly. "Not an Irishman. An Englishman. A spy and traitor by the name of Tamerlane Fallon. A thief and a profiteer. Should have been hanged, were it not for the unfortunate madness that overcame this city two years ago. Escaped from his cell in broad daylight, they say."

Rose's heart stopped in mingled surprise and hope. It was the first time she had heard of such a thing. How had her father? But he had been allowed his correspondence, his contacts, albeit carefully screened. Rose had had no choice in that. Anything else would have raised suspicion.

"By 'madness' you refer to the Draft Riots?" Washington's voice grew preternaturally calm, just as it had before.

Her father's face stiffened in distaste. "An episode we would all do well to forget. Why, did you know we had soldiers—*soldiers*—camped inside the park to protect us?"

"An inconvenience with which the Colored Orphans Asylum was sadly unencumbered when it burned to the ground," Washington said. He spoke

The Horseman's Word

without rancor or emphasis, but his gaze grew briefly far away before he returned to the present and the matter at hand. "But to return to the matter at hand, I have come to beg you to share any information you might have on the role the Society of the Horseman's Word might have played in this… 'unfortunate madness.'"

Her father's jaw set, and he transformed into an entirely different man—a dark and dangerous one that frightened Rose in a way all his blustering contempt never had. "And were I to tell you that such knowledge could bring you nothing but danger and disappointment?"

Washington met his eyes steadily. "I have long been schooled in both. And so I would beg you, Mr. Adair, not to make my decisions for me. That has already been too long the case for my people and me."

A moment's pause. Then her father exploded into one of the rages that had plagued him ever since the events of two years past. "Your people? Do not speak to me of your puling, troublesome people, lest I suggest that they have been humored for far too long. And now you would have them demand choices, instead of counseling them to be grateful for the sacrifices their betters have already made on their behalf? Do you have any idea how much this wretched war has cost us? The kinds of plans it disrupted? Important plans, crucial to the future of this nation—all put on hold by a bunch of rabble-rousing female novelists and abolitionist preachers. Only now are we at last able to pick up the pieces where we left off, and now you would seek to block our effort again. We strove to build a repository for the world's knowledge, but the little people would not let us be…"

No. No more. Next to come would be torrent of foul words that left Rose's ears blistering, about gods and curses and unholy rituals…

She swept to her feet. "Please, Mr. Washington, in the name of humanity, I beg you."

With a swift inclination of his head, Washington followed her out to the hallway, where he paused to don his hat before he said, "For what it might be worth, Miss Adair, I apologize. I give you my word that if I had had any idea, I would have gone elsewhere…"

Alas, that was exactly what she feared, especially now that Washington had paid first-hand witness to the broken workings of her father's mind. Cole Washington seemed to be a decent and honest man—unlike most of her family, frankly. But that didn't make him any less dangerous for having seen what he had seen.

"And I apologize for my father as well. Obviously, at times, he has no idea what he is saying..." She drew a deep breath, as she forced herself to think like Tamerlane Fallon: analyzing alternatives, weighing options. "Forgive me for being direct, but it is clear to me that you are a very determined man. Unfortunately, it is also clear to me that, given what you have heard, if my father cannot give you any satisfactory answers, you might think it logical to turn to my cousin Preston instead. And I, for one, could not blame you. However, I feel it incumbent upon me to warn you, my cousin is not a particularly scrupulous man."

"Nor are most of the men in the horse world," Washington acknowledged.

"Be that as it may, I can only speak to my cousin's character. And I would be deeply remiss if I failed to inform you that my cousin is deeply in debt and has no money or prospects beyond those with which my father might gift him," she said, warming to her theme. "And so I would warn you that if you are here at Cousin Preston's instigation, I would sever that connection as quickly and thoroughly as you can. Anyone who joins him can only lose his good name, as well as whatever money he might have been persuaded to invest. And if you are not, I would still urge you, Mr. Washington, to have nothing to do with him, lest you be tarred with the same brush he is when the enterprise fails. Or worse. For I can only warn you that my cousin has a peculiar knack for allowing others to shoulder the blame for his misdeeds."

A moment's pause, before Washington nodded gravely. "I thank you for your frank advice. But I am here at no-one's behest but my own—certainly not your cousin's."

"I believe that, Mr. Washington," she said, "but I also understand that my urgings may not be enough. And so I would offer you a compromise. Pledge me a week before you approach my cousin. Pledge me a week to find out what I can about this secret society. And if, in the space of a week, you are not contented with the answers I can provide you, then I cannot fault you for taking any actions you might choose in pursuit of this sad affair."

2

Saratoga Springs, N.Y.

Despite the soft song of the fiddle and the steamy scent of boiling potatoes that spilled from its kitchens, the neighborhood known as Little Dublin was no Jones's Wood. Nor was it a Five Points slum either. Instead, it was an unexpected bit of Irish heaven sprung up in Saratoga Springs, N.Y.: a solid neighborhood of modest frame houses, in a town where men could find better, safer jobs than in the quarries to the south or the tanneries to the north. The Irish had come here at first to work on the railroad and the Erie Canal, but as Saratoga had grown into what many called America's finest resort, many were finding work as the trainers, jockeys, waiters, touts, faro dealers, and cooks without which John Morrissey's newly-built racetrack could not survive.

As dreams went, it was the complete antithesis of the glittering ones spun by Saratoga's most famous Irishman, John Morrissey, a Tammany Hall enforcer and convicted thief, who had set himself the improbable task of using his talent for fighting and faro to force his way into the first circles of society and transform Saratoga Springs into America's most famous resort. And against all odds, he seemed to be succeeding. The gaming house that Morrissey had established conveniently near the railroad station was now joined by a racetrack complete with a newly-built grandstand where America's elite could gamble away their fortunes by day, before turning to his lavish new casino for amusement at night.

But although the men and women of Little Dublin might work in Morrissey's Saratoga in order to feed their families, their souls belonged to another John: John Costigan, who a quarter century ago had founded the Church of St. Peter in a disused theater. Now the church's spire rose in proud acknowledgement of the fact that, in addition to a full belly and a warm bed, Little Dublin also offered that final piece of the Irish dream: freedom to worship one's own God in the way one chose. Not that the last had not been a hard-won victory: tales still circulated of men coming home from a day's work on the Erie Canal to spend the night mounting guard armed with shotguns against those who would not see papists come to Saratoga. But the sons of those men had been the first to have places in the newly constructed parochial school, and their daughters now had their own school as well. So, while Little Dublin had none of the fairy tale magic of the resort it served, those who had braved the perilous journey across the sea in order to live there could be justified in believing they had truly reached the fabled Western Isles at last.

Sullivan could no more bring himself to believe in the Catholics' Risen God than the goddess whose curse had chased him first from Ireland and then from New York City, but he had found, if not a home, a safe haven in his room above the livery stable and the nearby inn where he took a warm meal nightly. But it was a tenuous peace, arguably as much ascribable to the whiskey that lubricated his food as to Sullivan having found any real place where he belonged. He had always accepted it would never last, long before the voice of Sammy Nunn's red-haired lass drifted out from the open door of the shabby clubhouse that served those who could not afford the richer pleasures on the other side of the railroad tracks.

> *The Pale Queen, oh, she lost a kiss*
> *Out in the bonny heather.*
> *The Pale Queen, oh, she lost her mount*
> *When he broke her tether.*
> *The Pale Queen oh, she lost her Knight,*
> *Then came death and slaughter.*
> *The first Queen nurses*
> *The next Queen curses*
> *But the Red Queen is her Father's daughter.*

Sullivan froze. The last time he had heard that song it had been crooned by a mother he had never known until a grim-faced priest had angrily overridden his father's furious objections and summoned Sullivan to her deathbed. He had been no more than fifteen at the time, and frankly terrified by the vacant-eyed crofter whose bloodless lips repeated and repeated the meaningless old ballad—a sure sign, the neighbors who sat the death watch whispered, that she had been pixilated when he had been born.

> *The Raven Queen, she lost a kiss*
> *Out in the bonny heather.*
> *The Raven Queen she lost her mount*
> *When he broke her tether.*
> *The Raven Queen, she lost her Knight,*
> *Then came death and slaughter.*
> *The first Queen nurses*
> *The next Queen curses*
> *But the Red Queen is her Mother's daughter.*

They had eyed him askance as well, as he ducked his head beneath the croft's low ceiling, as if his height and fine clothes might be a sign that he was as dangerous as his mother. Had crossed themselves and spat, as the dying woman had grabbed his wrist, with a claw-like hand that was at once cold as the grave and dank with sweat. "He sought to dispossess you. He sought to cheat me of the reward he swore was yours," she said, her voice low and cracked. "But the Goddess will prevail, the Virgin will be delivered to your bed, and you will have your rightful inheritance. So I do swear by the three sacrifices for the three ways, the three paths of the Goddess's crossroads, the very oath by which he sought to cheat me."

Sullivan believed in the crofters' rude superstitions no more than in Costigan's papish ones, but he still shivered against the song as a bad omen. And so it was, for a message awaited him along with his first glass of whiskey. "Man's been around here," the barman said. "Asking for a horsewhisperer."

Sullivan took a careful sip. "Not sure what you're talking about."

"A sorcerer. A wizard. An Irishman that had a way with horses that defied belief, who could tame the most savage horse with a single word. Some said he went by the name Daniel Sullivan."

"A Newmarket legend forty years past," Sullivan snorted. "A man who's worked with horses as long as I have, learned long ago not to listen to any horseman's tales except for amusement."

The barman's face darkened. "Still, we need no such rumors around here. Bad enough they still think we're a bunch of papists."

"Then you'd be best off not spreading such stories further," Sullivan said.

"Spilling them to a pack of men already in their cups."

"He asked for you by name," the barman said.

"A courtesy surname bestowed on a fatherless boy, and not an uncommon one at that." Sullivan spoke casually enough, but his voice had taken on a warning edge. "A lot of Sullivans in Ireland. Here in America too. *Súileabháin* means the dark-eyed one, and the Good Lord knows the Irish have had plenty to darken their gaze over the past few centuries."

Deliberately, he moved to take the steaming bowl of stew that the innkeeper's wife had placed in front of him to a table, but the barman wasn't finished.

"This man said Sullivan was not the only one. He spoke of an entire race of such men. Worshippers of the Old Goddess, Epona, and practitioners of a secret craft of charming horses that has been passed down all the way from the first sorcerer, the first smith, Tubal Cain."

"Some kind of folklorist, then," Sullivan snorted in disgust, before he drank off the rest of his whiskey and pushed the glass back to the barman for a refill. "We suffered a plague of them back on the Auld Sod. Professors and clergymen looking for Curing Priests and Fairy Doctors and the Bean Sidhe and half a dozen other creatures that a man in Holy Orders has no business believing in." He met the barman's eyes. "Nor should any God-fearing man who renounced the devil and all his works and ways when he was received into Holy Mother Church."

For was that not what the priest had said to him, when his mother had at last been lowered into the ground, and few final prayers had been whispered with such unseemly haste that Sullivan might have wondered if the priest secretly planned to return in the dead of night and thrust a stake through her heart just to make certain? Renounce the devil and all his works and ways, and trust only in Holy Mother Church and God's infinite goodness…

Even if that infinite goodness had bestowed on Sullivan a fate he never asked for, and a father who he wished never to see again. He had fled to the New World the next day.

"Be that as it may," the barman said. "He left this for you."

From under the bar, he pulled out a curiously knotted fetish that seemed to have been braided out of horse hair, and laid it on the counter. But Sullivan made no move to reach for it, his jaw clamping as he watched the peace that he had fought so furiously to believe in shatter once more.

It was not right. What peace he had found, he had paid for with his own two hands, buying his way across the Atlantic with his back, unwilling to even indebt himself to his father by selling off his fine clothes to pay the price of his passage. And for some time he had found it. The farmlands of Fordham were as abundant with horses as with the hay to feed them, and the men who owned them were willing to pay handsomely for a man with Sullivan's way with a horse. Even at fifteen, he was too tall to be a rider, but he had had a way of making a horse run so effortlessly, it could have won with a sack of flour up in the saddle—and word got around quickly enough.

But his cursed fate had not forgotten him, and soon enough an entirely different kind of word had spread as well: Of secret societies and smuggled talismans with unholy powers and a conspiracy of Fenian sorcerers who sought to hone their skills on American battlefields and American soldiers, before they returned to liberate the Auld Sod, and replace the hated English with the ancient order of druid-kings, riding at the head of an army of the Aes Sidhe, the Shining Ones, the Tuatha de Danaan, risen to reclaim their land from the mortals who had stolen it.

Sullivan believed in none of it. Indeed, Sullivan believed in little beyond the soft, sweet truth that was the language of the horses he so well understood. But Sullivan had learned quick enough that what he might believe in mattered little, when a fantasy as airy as Meagher's plans to raise an army to reconquer Ireland had suddenly and sickeningly turned into a very real conspiracy that had cost very real men their lives. And Sullivan had had no choice but to run again.

This time, he had kept his head as low as he had in the croft. He knew no work, had no skill other than horses, but he dared not venture close to the racetrack, afraid, now, of word getting around about his abilities once more. He lived in a livery stable. He mucked stalls. And still his cursed fate would not leave him in peace…

His eyes went back down to the fetish, and in that moment, you might have noticed that his eyes were in fact not black, but the darkest of blues, as he picked up the charm and pocketed it. "Did the man leave any message, or just the token?" he asked.

"He said, 'A debt is owed. A debt will be paid.' And that he can be found at Congress Spring almost any night." The barman cast Sullivan a worried look. "We don't need any trouble with Fenians either."

A considering pause, then Sullivan's face darkened in a way that might have had you believing in witches and sorcerers, even if you did not believe in horsewhisperers. "Neither do I," he said. And, his meal uneaten, he strode back into the night, where the voice of Sammy's red-haired lass still echoed:

> *The Red Maid, oh, she gave no kiss*
> *To none she did not choose.*
> *The Red Maid, oh, she needs no Knight,*
> *Her maidenhead to lose.*
> *The Red Maid, oh, she needs no mount,*
> *She runs freely as the water.*
> *The first Queen nurses*
> *The next Queen curses*
> *But the Red Queen is her own son's daughter.*

3

No sooner had Rose closed the door behind Cole Washington than she found herself bitterly regretting her offer. She had no desire to revisit the events of two years ago, any more than she had any desire for the lying man who had purported to be Declan Sullivan. But Cousin Preston was already a constantly-looming threat. She simply could not afford to put information such as Washington's in his hands.

"Girl!" her father's voice rang down the hall. "I have need of you. Now!"

Rose's shoulders slumped as she turned back to the library, where her father waited, his face livid.

"You will tell me the truth, and you will tell me immediately," he enunciated. "Have you been in touch with that man?"

"What man? Mr. Washington?"

The question only served to redouble her father's rage. "Do not play me for the fool! I mean your Cousin Preston, of course."

"Why, of course, I have, Father," she said wearily. "It was my impression you desired me to handle all the family correspondence."

No matter that said correspondence largely consisted of her cousin sending her his increasingly extravagant bills with more and more frequency. That was the price she had paid to keep Cousin Preston safely away in Saratoga, far from the courthouses here in New York.

"I warned you! Do not play me for a fool! Weak-brained as you are, your sex can be cunning enough when you need to be."

"Father, please." Refusing to react to his cold contempt, she forced herself to keep her voice steady. For that was the mistake her mother had made, and it had carried her off as surely as the consumption ever had. "I fear you are working yourself into one of your attacks."

"Attacks? Is that what you would call them? Or is that what Preston would?" Her father's face grew cunning as his voice dropped to a whisper. "He wants to have me locked up as a madman, you know. Keeps sending his cursed doctors to examine me. But I think you already know that, don't you, girl? *Don't you?*"

And Rose suddenly found herself too tired to keep the truth off her face. For, not only did she know about Cousin Preston's schemes, he had invited her to participate in them with the same directness that he had first proposed the obvious solution to the family's tangled finances on Rose's sixteenth birthday, when she had reached something that might be considered marriageable age.

"He's quite insane, you know. Has been for years," Preston had urged. "Fancies himself some kind of latter-day magus. That's the true purpose behind his collection, you know. Talismans and amulets, unholy treasures looted from forbidden tombs."

"Collecting may be a singular obsession, but it is scarcely a mania," Rose objected.

"Squandering the family fortune in order to found a museum is!"

"Father understands his responsibilities, and has made adequate, if not extravagant provision for us."

"We'll see how adequate that provision sounds when the truth is known about your diary. With a sum like that, you'll be lucky if you have a spavined schoolmaster as a suitor."

She stiffened, containing her fury. "Well, seeing as you're the only suitor I have ever had, I must thank you for presenting your motives so clearly."

Head held high, Rose had turned to go, but Cousin Preston caught her arm. "A judge will never sign an order of commitment based on my word. Not without some kind of substantial proof. But they would never doubt the word of a gently-bred young lady. Just a hint of... unnatural practices inflicted on his dutiful daughter in the name of Devil worship, and they would never press you for details..."

She had dismissed his plan in cold disgust. But two years of dealing with her father's uncontrollable rages and watching him roam the hallways in the dead of night, kneeling in front of the various objects he had collected and muttering inchoate prayers in languages she didn't recognize, was swiftly pushing her toward the conclusion that Cousin Preston was right.

She drew a deep breath. "Please, Father, if you have an accusation to make against me, I would prefer you do it directly."

"If I have an accusation to make? *If?*" he mimicked her, then shook his head in disgust. "Having been able to mold you into some kind of serviceable amanuensis, I had hoped that you might be above the foibles of the rest of your sex. Alas, I see that I am wrong."

"Please, Father, I fear Mr. Washington's visit has upset you…"

"Enough with your Mr. Washington! What do I care for some man's slave? *This* is what upsets me." He snatched up a sheaf of papers from his desk, and waved them at her. "Do you know what these are, girl? Do you?"

She forced herself to keep her voice even. "I would never examine your private papers except in your presence."

"Ha!" He flung them into her face. "Then please examine them now, and tell me, are these not all the papers I had drawn up for my museum? Papers that, to this day, remain unsigned?"

The papers scattered to the floor, but Rose made no move to retrieve them—only partly out of respect for her own dignity. For the truth was, she had no need to examine those papers in order to know exactly what they were, just as she knew they were unsigned. She also knew that the fact that those papers remained unsigned was her most crucial weapon in the fight to keep Cousin Preston at bay.

Her father slammed a hand down on the desk, sending the priceless inkwell and several seals scattering. "Your Cousin Preston," he said, with careful emphasis on the possessive, as if there were no blood tie between the two of them as well, "should have informed me about this immediately. Can you explain to me why he did not?"

"You were ill, Father," she said. "The doctors advised against any excitement…"

"I was not ill! I was nearly murdered!" He dismissed her stammered protest with a wave of his hand. "Do not humiliate yourself by lying. That Irishman was never a Fenian, he was a common cutthroat, a paid assassin…"

"I confess I find myself confused, Father," she said, struggling to keep her voice even. "Are you accusing me of conspiring with Cousin Preston or Declan Sullivan?"

"Do not be pert! That cursed lying Irishman seduced you into betraying me, when your scheming cousin could not. But why should I have ever hoped it would be otherwise? Do not think I did not see what he was up to almost immediately. It was my fault entirely to have trusted you, to have clung to the hope that you would rise above the weaknesses of your sex."

It was the same refrain that had sent Rose's mother in the welcoming arms of death as if she had been eloping with a lover. But there was no such kind escape for Rose as her father unleashed the full fury of his towering rage.

"But when has a Daughter of Eve been unable to resist the temptations of the flesh? Why should my own daughter be any stronger than her Mother was? It was my folly entirely, my fault to believe you could be molded into a satisfactory amanuensis. But, girl, do you have any idea the destruction your folly has wrought?"

Rose was not given to losing her temper easily—especially when it came to her father. She had paid no heed to the protests of the phalanx of female relatives and concerned friends who had protested at how ruthlessly he had used his daughter, not out of any sense of filial duty, but because she had rapidly discovered that she preferred the simple tedium of handling her father's correspondence to the restless tedium of making polite conversation over tea or taking the air in Central Park or strolling the newly fashionable Ladies Mile. But at this moment, her temper exploded at the sheer *unfairness* of her father's accusations. It was not just that Cousin Preston had wanted to have her father declared mad. It was that he saw the threat of doing so as a means to systematically enrich himself at her father's expense—and one that cost him far less effort than courting her. She had spent every waking hour of the past two years keeping Cousin Preston at bay in Saratoga Springs and her father out of a lunatic asylum. And now she was being accused of colluding with him?

"You have my word—for what the word of a Daughter of Eve may be worth—that I have no idea what you are talking about, but I will enquire as to Cousin Preston's activities immediately," she said tightly.

"You will do no such thing," her father said. "It is clear you are incompetent to handle this matter, and so I am forced to do it myself."

No! Her stomach clenched. If there was one risk she could not afford, it was the prospect of her father walking into his business offices and demonstrating to the world at large what she and Cousin Preston already knew.

"If you have instructions as to how you wish me to pursue your enquiries, I will of course follow them to the letter," she said.

"My instructions are for you to engage passage to Saratoga immediately, so I can have matters out with that perfidious pup for once and for all."

In other words, he proposed to deliver himself and control of the family fortune straight into Cousin Preston's hands. She shut her eyes, fighting to steady her breath. She had always known it would come to this, had always been aware that she had never been doing anything but buying time—and to what purpose, she asked herself bitterly. Matters were never destined to end any other way. But like Madame du Barry, pleading with the executioner, *encore un moment, monsieur le bourreau,* Rose heard herself trying anyway.

"But, Father, consider your health… I'm sure the doctors will never permit…"

As soon as the words crossed her lips, she knew she had made a fatal mistake.

"Permit? Am I prisoner in my own house?" her father demanded.

No. Not yet. But it was quite likely that, by the end of this journey, he would be something far, far worse. "Of course not, Father."

"Then you will arrange for us to travel to Saratoga immediately."

*****

It was said that when Commodore Vanderbilt took an interest in a place, the first thing he did was build a railroad line to reach it. And it was well known that the Commodore had taken an interest in Saratoga Springs. Nonetheless, the train trip to Saratoga was enough to make Rose bitterly wish that she had yielded to the impulse to simply lie to her father and tell him no train tickets to Saratoga were available. The seats in the first-class carriage may have been upholstered in velvet, but the lush fabric seemed specially made to capture the smell of coal. The air inside the car rapidly grew stuffy, and then stifling, but any attempt to open the rattling windows admitted only smoke, rather than fresh air. The thick carpets on the floor did little to relieve the jarring jolts each time the wheels passed over a joint in the track. Worst of all, there were no private compartments, so Rose had been forced to endure the entire journey in an agony of anxiety that a clumsy porter or an awkward fellow passenger might cause her father to erupt into one of his rages.

Things were little improved when they finally reached Saratoga. Commodore Vanderbilt may have taken enough of an interest in Saratoga Springs to run a railway there, but he had not taken such an interest in the Saratoga Railway Station. The depot was as thick with dust as the train had been with smoke. Carriages jostled side by side on the unpaved road that lay beyond the stationhouse, some passing by, some arriving for passengers or luggage, but all of them fighting in a crush of noise and dirt that was little different from Manhattan—at least outside the quiet confines of Gramercy Park.

Her father had consumed the better part of a flask of brandy by the time the train finally wheezed and whistled to a halt, forcing Rose to remove his travelling desk from his grasp and steer him down the narrow aisle of the carriage. Nonetheless, he swayed embarrassingly as soon as they reached the metal steps on the rear platform, and a solicitous porter immediately sprang to help him.

At the same time, Rose felt the awkward weight of the traveling desk plucked from her hands, as a man said, in a broad, Irish accent, "Now, miss, you just leave that all to me. Your Cousin Preston sent me, and you can be certain a proper carriage will be along quick enough for you and your father."

But as Rose gratefully turned to relinquish her burden, she paused in puzzlement. Surely, she knew this Irishman.

"You blackguard!" her father cried, wrenching himself free of the porter. "What do you think you're doing?"

Rose spared the man a second puzzled glance, before she sighed, "I'm sorry. My father can be particular when it comes to business matters…"

"Apologies, I'm sure, miss," he said hurriedly, then vanished into the crowd.

She stared after him another moment, then shook her head. She was being carried away by her nerves. Why shouldn't the man be familiar? Cousin Preston had sent him.

"Come, Father," she said, her soothing voice intended as much for herself as for him. "Your desk is quite safe, I promise you. Shall we try to find the carriage Cousin Preston sent?"

They did find their carriage in quick order, but that was the only quick thing about the rest of the trip to their hotel. Driving in Saratoga Springs was nothing short of an impossibility. Broadway was so crowded with landaus, buggies, curricles and four-in-hands, that the dashing young gentlemen in phaetons who wished to show their whip hands were forced to drive at the same plodding pace as the dog-carts they squeezed next to cheek-by-jowl. Clearly, if you wanted to get anywhere, the most sensible means of travel was by foot—but only if you were willing to brave the dust that rose everywhere—churned up by the traffic on the road.

The people that risked the noise and dirt to stroll beneath the porticos that fronted the grand hotels were no more to Rose's liking—although she instantly understood how Cousin Preston might have found a congenial home here. They were all fashionably dressed, and yet Rose couldn't help feeling there was something *sporty* about them. The cut of the ladies' walking dresses, the angle of their hats a touch too daring; the gentlemen's tailoring just a trifle *sharp*.

It went without saying that Cousin Preston had taken rooms at the grandest of the grand hotels, Union Hall. Said to be the world's largest, its front stretched 400 feet along Broadway, and soared four stories into the air—above a piazza that rose three stories itself. Rose's shoulders slumped as she saw that every inch of those stories seemed to be as crowded as Broadway had been. With an exhausted sigh, she relinquished both her father and his desk to another porter, and remained to consult with the major-domo about their luggage. But as soon as she was handed down from the carriage, her nostrils curled. "What is that disagreeable smell?"

"Oh, that was the United States Hotel. It burned just a few weeks ago," the major-domo said casually. "Caused quite a scramble for rooms, let me tell you. You wouldn't believe the lengths the Hall went to in order to accommodate you and your father at such a moment's notice. But anything for Mr. Olcott, that's what they say. Your cousin is an up-and-coming man."

A scramble for rooms? What about injuries or even deaths, God forbid? Had anyone been harmed?

To be fair, no-one else in Saratoga Springs seemed to be taking any more notice of the burned-out remains of the building that loomed over Broadway than the major-domo did, as he went on, "I tell you, the crush has been enormous. It has scarcely been a week since General Grant opened the Lelands' new Opera House, and the meet season is right around the corner…"

And indeed, she could see that the patriotic bunting still hung from the white colonnade of the newly built Opera House.

But a crash and pounding footsteps drew her attention from the serene heights of Orpheus to the wild marsh that was Congress Park, just beyond. Suddenly, policemen seemed to be swarming everywhere. "Is something amiss?" she asked.

The major-domo's mouth twisted. "Wretched business altogether. A man was found drowned in Congress Spring. Probably stumbled while he was in his cups, but the police are taking no chances. No effort is too great when it comes to ensuring the safety of our guests. And the spring has been shut down indefinitely—until the health-giving properties of its waters are assured."

Safety of their guests? What about the safety of the streets? "But what of the drowned man?" Rose demanded. "What steps are being taking to apprehend the miscreant?"

The major-domo smiled soothingly. "Well, now, I will not lie and say there are no miscreants in Saratoga, but trust me, the police have persuaded the majority of them to submit to the quieting effects of the water and the disciplining of Mr. Morrissey—as they like to put it. Those that don't, are chalked and ordered away soon enough."

"You make it sound rather like some town in the Wild West."

"Well, now Miss, we're not in New York City, where the militia must be called in to control its citizens. Here in Saratoga, we prefer to take it for granted that no improper conduct will be tolerated, and the happy result is that the best of order prevails, despite the lack of numbers in our police force."

Any further questions were cut short by a triumphant shout from Congress Park. The major-domo placed an anxious hand on Rose's arm, attempting to draw her into the safety of the lobby. But it was too late. Already, officers had wrestled a dazed, bruised man out into the street. And Rose's world stood still. Even from here, she recognized the familiar limp, although now it was a lurching stagger. He wore what passed for the uniform of a Union officer, but this was no American soldier finding his way home from the army.

This was Declan Sullivan…

No, she corrected herself sharply. Declan Sullivan had never existed. This man was the liar, spy, and traitor, Tamerlane Fallon. And once more, he appeared destined to be dragged off to prison and hanged.

4

The war was over. The time had come to put the past where it belonged—along with the shabby wraiths who had the bad taste to sully the serene peace of Congress Park, where they could only serve as a reminder of an unpleasantness everyone would do best to forget. But the past had no such gentle plans for the shabby wraith named Lane Fallon. Instead, the past was quite clearly determined to catch up with him and exact its full measure of vengeance. All Lane could wish was that it had managed to do so without ruining what little clothing he still owned.

He didn't remember much about last night's meeting—little beyond the fact it did not go well. At the very least, the hot-blooded bastard might have had the courtesy to hear him out before Lane had found himself knocked out cold by a wild roundhouse he had never seen coming.

And when the shouts and whistles of what seemed to be an entire army of police detectives had finally brought Lane back to himself—shivering, groggy, and nearly half-drowned in the Park's marshy undergrowth—he had stared straight up at a hulking man, whose eyes lingered on the insignias on Lane's patched and mended officer's coat.

"Irish Brigade?" he asked.

"Afraid not," Lane said pleasantly. "Not for some time now."

"More likely you stole it off a dead man's back."

A fist slammed into his ribs before Lane could stammer out a protest—cracking them, Lane thought with disbelieving expertise. The bastard must be wearing brass knuckles. He doubled over immediately, giving the man no excuse to swing for his face, for when a man was possessed of a wardrobe as limited as his, bloodstains were a disaster of the first magnitude. As he did, his hands were swiftly and painfully manacled behind him, and then the world went dark once more.

He came to in a cell, still manacled, empty cells surrounding him. Apparently, someone was determined that whatever happened to him remained private. He assumed the next step would be to leave him there for several hours in order to let hunger, thirst, cold, and fear take their toll, but in fact the bars swung open with an immediacy that suggested he was being observed, and the Irishman stepped in, accompanied by a man in a dark coat who immediately receded into the shadows, as the Irishman availed himself of the chance to land a smart backhand across Lane's face, before he hauled him to this feet and pulled off the manacles, none-too-gently.

"Have a care!" Lane protested. "This is my second-best shirt."

"Stolen off a dead man's back as well, for sure," the Irishman said. "And now ye've moved on from thieving to murdering."

"Murder?" Lane's fingers moved reflexively to the sore spot on his jaw. Everything about the last night was a blank from the moment that the hard fist had collided with his face, but he was certain that the blow had knocked him out cleanly—to his shame, he would be the first to admit. Still, he was willing to offer his bruises as proof positive that, whatever else may have transpired, he had been in no condition to kill a man the previous evening.

"Dinna play the fool with me. If I had my way they'd hang you on the spot. But apparently you've got friends in high places. Just as your types always seem to."

Lane frowned, suddenly on far more familiar ground. For this was a refrain Lane had heard in varying keys all his life—from his schoolmates, from his fellow-officers, from the Irishmen who farmed his father's land when they thought the quality was out of earshot—and it was not unjust or even untrue. But this had a feeling of playacting about it, Lane thought as he massaged his wrists—even though he was certain the Irishman wasn't playing at all. No, the dumb bastard was being played as much as they hoped to play Lane—using the man's class hatred to set the stage for the conversation that was to follow. It was the man in the shadows that was in charge here, his ramrod straight bearing proclaiming him a military man, despite the fact he was wearing carefully non-descript civilian clothing.

Lane's eyes narrowed appraisingly. "Army intelligence?"

If the man noticed the ironic inflection that suggested that in Lane's mind such a thing was an impossibility, he was too well trained to react. "Seconded on special assignment," he said, not bothering to hide his English accent. "Colonel..."

"Please," Lane cut him off. "You know and I know that both name and probably rank are both a lie, so let's not waste both our time."

His sparring with the man was reflexive, something to keep him distracted while Lane did his best to calculate what was really happening here. An English officer and an American Irishman working together? Admittedly, neither seemed happy about their enforced cooperation, but Lane could only think of one man even capable of persuading them to remain in the same room without launching themselves at each other's throats. And if that possibility were truly the case, it was even more of a complication than the matter that had drawn him to Saratoga in the first place.

"It seems to me that a man facing the justice of both Her Majesty's Government and that of the United States would consider the possibility of avoiding both something more than a waste of time," the Colonel said.

Lane raised an eyebrow, as matters grew a shade less opaque. "You speak of the charges leveled against me in New York City two years ago?"

"You know exactly what I speak of."

And perhaps Lane did, but this man certainly did not. He could have been reading from a dispatch for all the understanding he displayed as he went on, "Which is why I have a warrant for you to stand trial for spying and profiteering, and I will ask the Detective's Bureau to execute it unless..."

"Ah, now we come to it," Lane said gently. "Unless..."

The Colonel's face tightened with distaste. "Make no mistake about it. You are a disgrace to Her Majesty's Service, and if it were up to me, I would see you bear the full force of the law..."

"Full force of the law for what?" Lane asked. "Being an Englishman in Saratoga?"

"A man is dead," the Colonel said. "Found drowned in Congress Spring."

Well, that at least explained the Irishman's talk of murder—as well as the army of detectives whose shouts and whistles still echoed through Lane's throbbing head. But this was a new development—and not a welcome one. "And I stand accused?"

"You were found in Congress Park."

"Unconscious, the victim of a savage attack myself. Scarcely in any condition to kill a man."

"Nonetheless, it would clarify matters if you could explain what you were doing there."

A brief pause, as Lane weighed how much of the truth to tell him. "I came to Saratoga to find a man…"

"You mean, your half-brother…"

"Oh, la. Now, you're dragging my father's good name into this as well. Bad form to acknowledge sons born on the wrong side of the blanket, you know, even if you do take responsibility for their education and upbringing…"

"Enough with your babble. They always said you had the Devil's own tongue," the Colonel snapped. "Let us not fence. It is already being said around Saratoga that the dead man was seen in several of the less-savory gambling establishments, claiming to have information about a terrible conspiracy that involved some of the world's most powerful men—information he sought to sell to the highest bidder."

Lane gestured at his worn coat. "And you think I was the one that won that auction?"

"I think a man who sought to preserve that information and could not afford to buy it might be forced to… alternative measures."

"Such as killing him? Why?"

"I was sincere when I said, let us not fence. You know as well as I do that you arrived in New York City under questionable, if not downright false, pretenses: an Anglo-Irish officer of uncertain antecedents and an even less certain rank in the Ordnance Survey, obviously sent away from England to hush up some scandal—the details of which, no-one was rude enough to pursue once word got around about the quality of the antiquities you were offering for sale." The Colonel's jaw set, before he added, "Just as most of your buyers were unwilling to press you for details of your loyalties in the Anglo-Irish conflict."

So the Colonel was a little better informed than he had first seemed. "You'd have me a closet Fenian then?" Lane asked with a shrug. "'Tis not much of a conspiracy, even if it were true. Half the Fenians who escaped to New York have made no secret of harboring such dreams. Men like Meagher have made an entire career or it."

"Men like Meagher do not stand accused of selling stolen Irish antiquities to wealthy collectors to finance their cause," the Colonel pointed out.

"And do I stand so accused?" Lane shook his head as pettishly as if he were a don critiquing a failing exam. "Why should I? If an officer in the

Ordnance Survey was willing to loot the treasures the English army sent him to protect, why would he not see to his own profit instead of placing both the profit and his life in the hands of a ring of Irish scum?"

The Irishman took another swing, almost casually, and blood began to trickle from Lane's nose.

"Have a care, I tell you! Break my ribs if you must, but try not to get blood on my linen." Lane dabbed at the blood with the back of his hand, then wiped it off on a wall with ostentatious care, before he added, "But you may set your mind at rest, Colonel. The entire notion is ridiculous. I may well be a thief and a profiteer, but I have never once been accused of idealism."

"And as for your brother?" the Colonel asked. "The one you came to Congress Park to find?"

Lane had to clench his fist to keep himself from touching his jaw again, for this was a particularly tender sore spot that he dared not reveal. "Was the man found dead in the fountain my brother?"

A pause. Then the Colonel conceded, "As yet, he remains unidentified. But by his own word, it seems unlikely that he was a committed Fenian." The Colonel met Lane's gaze and held it. "Instead, he claimed to have knowledge of a far darker conspiracy—one that nearly delivered New York City into the hands of the Confederacy."

Lane grew very still. "An Irish conspiracy?"

"An *English* conspiracy. An ungodly alliance with a group of powerful Americans who sought to influence the course of the War Between the States—and not to the Union's benefit."

A fraction of a hesitation before Lane raised a shoulder. "Why should England be forced to conspire? It is well known that England favored the Confederate cause. Indeed, there were many in Leeds and Liverpool referred to as the Confederacy's bankers."

"Quite so. Yet it is said that the American government remains a touch volatile when it comes to issues of seditious conspiracies—so much so that they might not hesitate to string up the spy without considering such logical niceties—especially if some powerful men brought pressure to bear."

There was naught for Lane to do but nod and concede the point. "It does sound like powerful motivation for your spy—if he actually existed—to kill such a man."

"*If* our spy actually existed," the Colonel allowed. Suddenly, his voice went back to those clipped, artificial cadences. "Then again there is one other possibility. The dead man might be the English spy himself…"

A pointed silence followed. Then Lane cast the Colonel an ironic look. "And apparently, Her Majesty's Government would prefer that was the case. Why? Why shield me from the justice I so richly deserve—unless, of course, you don't think I am?"

"Fleeing to Canada seems to be a rather significant admission of guilt." The Colonel's face hardened. "But it is not your guilt or innocence that concerns us here. The war is over. Her Majesty's Government is anxious that no embarrassment arises over England's activities during the War Between the States. Her Majesty is especially eager that there be no hint that England attempted to influence the outcome of the war."

Lane raised an eyebrow. "From that am I to infer that Her Majesty is willing to pardon a known profiteer and murderer in order to prevent a diplomatic incident?"

The Colonel's jaw tightened. "As I said, it is not the choice I would make. But unlike you, I respect my orders. A merchant vessel awaits us at Albany. We can set sail for England within the day. No-one ever need know that you returned to America. No-one even need know that you were ever here. Word is already being quietly spread in London that you have been in Canada for these past three years, conducting a private mission on her Majesty's behalf, which you have only now brought to a successful conclusion. All that remains is for you to depart immediately and let this poor soul be buried as an English spy and profiteer. Content yourself instead with escaping the hangman's noose."

Lane nodded ruminatively. "And if I prefer to simply stand my trial?" he asked.

The Colonel stiffened. "I'm afraid that is not an option."

Lane raised an eyebrow. "Somehow, I didn't think it would be," he said. "So I'm afraid that leaves us at something of an impasse. I am perfectly willing to stand my trial. In fact, if you press the matter, I'd rather insist on it. I've always had a rather unfortunate weakness for causing diplomatic incidents. So, unless you intend to leave me here with your thug to see if he can beat me into acquiescence—which I can assure you, he will not, for frankly the man is sadly unimaginative—I suggest that you allow me to accept your apologies for this unfortunate case of mistaken identity and let me go on my way—while I still have a chance to salvage my second-best shirt."

Lane rose to leave, suppressing his sudden gasp of pain only by sheer force of will. But the Colonel stepped stubbornly into his path.

"You were born with gifts most men can only dream of. Gifts that some say exceeded the bounds of nature itself. Your schoolmasters said you had the makings of a brilliant scholar; your riding and fencing masters foresaw a glittering military career. Instead you were sent down not just from Oxford, but from Trinity College and the Royal Military academy as well—only to wash up on the shores of America nothing more than a common thief. You could have bestrode the globe. Instead you chose to throw Heaven's gifts straight to the Devil. Does that not even trouble you?"

"Apparently not half so much as it troubles you."

Lane braced against another swing, but the Colonel was made of sterner stuff than the Irishman. "You don't trouble me at all," he said, his voice dripping with contempt. "If I had my way I'd let you rot in the gutter, where you so richly belong. But there are others… higher up… who have forced me to give you a chance to redeem yourself…"

Lane's face hardened as his suspicion became certainty. "Higher ups such as my Lord Wolverton?" he enquired. "Do I detect his fine Italian hand behind all this?"

"Your father is as stout an English gentleman as ever was," the Colonel said without any apparent irony.

"I was speaking metaphorically," Lane pointed out.

The Colonel's jaw tensed, and Lane found himself wondering whether he had at last succeeded in pushing the man into taking a swing at him, but the man's discipline won out one last time. "Be that as it may. Your father is offering you a chance to redeem your good name. Why will you not seize it?"

A strange look fleeted across Lane's face and then was gone—and his expression was blandness itself, as he asked, "So it is true? It is my father who is offering me this undeserved chance at redemption?"

"Does it matter?" The Colonel leaned closer. "You have just been offered a chance to return to the comfort and safety of your old life in England—which is far more than the poor wretch we found in the spring can claim. Seize your chance, and get out of America. Leave this matter alone. How much more do you want?"

For a moment, Lane just stared at him, looking for all the world like it was all he could do not to burst out into incredulous laughter. Then he raised one shoulder lazily.

"Well, seeing as you asked so nicely, I'll certainly give that suggestion all the consideration it's due." He turned for the door, gingerly feeling his bruised face. "Now if there is nothing else…"

*****

The gentleman who was watching from the adjacent room had remained completely impassive, his hooded green eyes unblinking, as he watched his son walk to the door, his military bearing offering no hint of the pain that must be constricting his ribs and his breathing.

"Well, that went well, wouldn't you say?" he commented to the attaché that was doing his best to hide his anxiety at being a firsthand witness to the techniques of the White Wolf.

Until now, the man had been as much of a legend as his son—whose mother, it was said, had thrown herself from the tower of the family castle in a frenzy when she had discovered the truth about the child she was about to bear. If it was possible, the man who sired him was even more frightening—even if you did not believe the rumors that his white hair and deathly pallor were the result of being struck insensate for nearly a year upon the news of his wife's death.

The White Wolf had no known official capacity, but it was said of him that he only had to move a pawn on a chessboard in Whitehall, and a government would fall half a world away. Others said he commanded a secret society whose operatives were everywhere, more powerful than even the Illuminati or the Rosicrucians. But all those tales did nothing to prepare the attaché for the spectacle of a man who had ordered his eldest son and heir seized, beaten, and then released—to no apparent purpose other than to put his life at risk.

If it were possible, the attaché writhed with even more anxiety. "With respect, sir," he finally brought himself to say, "rumor has it that your son hates you and would do anything to thwart you—so much so that if he knew an order came from you, he would disobey it entirely. Abominable misunderstanding, obviously. Have no idea how such an idea might have gotten around…"

His voice trailed off as he was subject to the full force of the Wolf's sardonic amusement. "Sons, actually," the White Wolf corrected him. A ruby glinted on his forefinger, as he reached for an ebony walking stick set with a curiously wrought silver head, and rose to leave. "And quite on the contrary, it's the absolute truth—in both their cases. As a matter of fact, I'm rather depending on it."

5

Katie O'Grady was a girl who knew how to hold her head high. She was Nunn's Irish Rose, after all, and old Sammy Nunn had schooled her how to bear herself like a true flower of Erin, ever since he had caught her skinny hand as it had closed around his purse, and, instead of shouting for the coppers or even cuffing her aside, had studied her matted ginger hair as if he had been sizing up horseflesh, then asked, "Ye think ye can learn to dance instead of thieve, lass?"

He had started by partnering her with angelic-faced Mikey, whose carroty hair matched hers perfectly, as the Twa Wee Half-Jiggers—and Katie had practiced herself to near collapse for four weeks straight to learn the steps, before Sammy had pronounced her fit, then baptized her with a scalding scrubbing that made her hair shine like polished copper in the footlights. From there, Katie had painstakingly scaled the ladder of Nunn's Select Pantomimes and Irish Revue, until she had reached the pinnacle, and knew Nunn's Irish Rose need bow to no-one. But even Katie was rapidly coming to the conclusion that Saratoga Springs was no Jones's Wood, and that neither she nor old Sammy had no business being here.

She still did not understand the stroke of luck that had caused Sammy to trade their trailer gaily painted with harps and shamrocks for a casino run by his influential friends in Saratoga Springs, where, he promised, not only did the Irish live in peace and prosperity—but an Irishman ran the town. "*Tiocfaidh ar la*, the old men say," he assured them. "Our day will come. Well, I say our day is here. It's only blue skies from now on."

But the glittering casino Sammy had dreamed of had been little more than a shabby gaming hell, and the gentlemen who frequented it were only interested in one kind of entertainment from Sammy's girls. And while Katie was well aware that most of the men who had crowded in front of the trailer back in Jones's Wood were more captivated by a glimpse of the comely ankle that flashed when she stepped out the old reels and jigs than any vocal talents she might be said to possess, well that stopped at the stage door, where old Sammy informed the gentlemen proffering bouquets of shamrocks that all his girls were convent-bred, and had taken to the stage only out of loyalty to their Irish cultural heritage. Which was a facer, but old Sammy took care of his girls—at least until the point where they told him they didn't want taking care of any more.

But Sammy showed no such protectiveness here, fawning on his new friends like an overeager dog, and urging his girls to show a little friendliness to the gentlemen—in order to encourage them to play deeper. Even worse, unlike the crowds in Jones's Woods, who understood the difference between a good-natured frolic and the depravities of Five Points, the Irish here shunned Sammy and his girls, the good wives of Little Dublin ostentatiously turning their backs on all of them, as if they had stepped straight out of the stews. The only ones that were more insufferable were those who felt obliged to reach out a hand to help their less fortunate countrymen—like the tired-eyed priest who offered Katie a chance to earn her room and board as well as an education by cleaning the new parochial school for girls, under the gimlet supervision of the Sisters of St. Joseph.

Just that morning, she had once again refused the offer he repeated every time she went to pick up their wash from the laundry the nuns ran. And so it felt like nothing short of the Divine Retribution the nuns were always going on about, when she walked into Sammy's private office to discover herself alone with the worst of Sammy's new gentleman friends: Preston Olcott, Sammy's chief partner in the gaming hell, who simply took the friendliness of Sammy's girls as an additional return upon his investment. It was almost enough to make her wonder whether the priests and nuns were right and the God they wanted her to waste her life praying to, really did want her to repent and change her sinful ways.

Hastily, she backed for the door. "I'm so sorry to disturb you, Mr. Olcott. I was unaware there was anyone in the office."

Katie spoke with exactly the right measure of aloofness to indicate that while she was a young lady on the stage, she was not one *those* kinds of young ladies on the stage. As usual, Olcott refused to take the hint. "Always a pleasure, Miss O'Grady," he said, never lifting his eyes from the packet of papers he had casually extracted from Sammy's strong box. "The only greater pleasure would be to hear that you are finally willing to grant your permission that I might consult Mr. Nunn about ways we might further your career to *all* our profit. A beautiful girl like you is wasted in these circumstances."

It was his usual refrain, and there was no doubt as to the type of career Olcott foresaw for her, but today he was so preoccupied with whatever he had found among Sammy's papers, he made the offer absently at best—giving Katie the chance to drop a neat curtsey and beat her retreat by offering to go fetch Sammy.

But Sammy was already otherwise engaged—with a tall, harsh-faced man who hadn't even bothered to brush the straw he must have just finished turning from his dusty clothes, mayhap because there was a none-too-clean bandage wrapped around one hand.

"A man came to the inn, asking for me by name," the stable lad said. "Now, another man is dead."

Stable lad was only a description of the man's work; there was in fact nothing of the boy about him. Katie supposed he could have been well-enough looking in a black Irish way had he bothered to try to smile or make himself agreeable. But those dark eyes and scowling brow beneath his half-combed hair made him look like one of Finn's old warriors stumbled fresh out of the wild woods, as he loomed over Sammy, who suddenly looked old and small.

"And what's that to me?" Sammy's voice was strangely weary.

"It is said the dead man was selling information. Information about a Fenian conspiracy down in New York City that nearly killed a man."

Sammy's face set. "I know nothing about any Fenian conspiracies."

The stable lad studied him. "But you do know something about the man who came looking for me."

For a moment, Sammy seemed to crumple even deeper within himself. Then he swelled with righteous indignation. "And what if I do, ye traitorous bastard? 'Twas you that brought that curse with you."

"Thrice cursed by the triple goddess I betrayed? Cursed with the loss of my sight, the gift of the Crone, the clear-seeing. Cursed with the loss of my name, by the Mother who first gave it to me. Cursed with the loss of my freedom by the first Virgin I bring to my bed, for she will destroy all that protects me and deliver me into the hands of the man I hate most…"

The lad grinned, and for a moment, he was almost attractive. "Fortunately, there's a simple enough way to avoid the last. Saves on awkward situations with inflamed fathers as well."

"I was speaking of the English bastard that followed ye here."

"As well we should." The brooding menace was back on the lad's face so quickly that Katie could only wonder if she had imagined the fey flash of humor. "What do you know of that? Were you the one set him on my trail?"

"No," Sammy said flatly.

"Then who? Preston Olcott?"

Sammy stiffened. "What know you of Preston Olcott?"

"Enough to know that if you involve yourself in his plans for long enough, you're liable to end up like the poor fellow they found in the spring."

"Preston Olcott is simply a business acquaintance," Sammy snorted. "I am scarcely privy to his plans."

The stable lad nodded, and the harshest edges of his menace seemed to recede into something that in another man might have been sympathy. "In other words, you're nothing but a pawn to be used at will, then discarded."

"Sammy Nunn is no man's pawn."

"Then why do you not run? Leave right now before you meet the same fate as the poor bastard drowned in the spring."

For a moment, the stable lad's words hung with the force of prophecy, and his eyes glittered with a weird light that made them seem more blue than black. Then Sammy shook his head. "Word was, you had lost the Sight."

The weird light faded from the stable lad's eyes. "There is no need of the Sight to see what's plain as a pikestaff. You cannot stay in Saratoga. You need to flee—tonight. Go somewhere they cannot follow. Chicago. San Francisco. Back to Ireland, if needs be. Why spend a moment longer in service to these blackguards?"

"Why?" Sammy asked with a shrug. "If you see death behind me, it can follow me as easily to Dublin as Saratoga."

"Listen to me, you fool! I'm trying to help!"

"Then I'll thank ye to help yourself and leave me to manage my own affairs," Sammy said. "I give ye my word 'twas not I that gave out your name, and let matters be done between us."

But that wasn't true—although old Sammy might have no idea he was lying. Katie's mind went back to how Preston Olcott had not bothered to hide the fact he had been leafing through old Sammy's papers. Sammy made a fuss about those papers, telling anyone who'd listen that even John

Morrissey didn't have documents with the power that these did. But the fact of the matter was, Sammy couldn't read a word in them—which was probably the only reason why Olcott allowed him to keep them.

And judging from the way he had not tried to hide them from her, Olcott had obviously assumed that if Sammy could not read, what was the chance a lowly girl could? What chance indeed? For, before there was Sammy, there had been the nuns, and they had taught her enough letters to read her prayer books—and in Latin too. It was enough to drive any girl to run away and try her luck picking pockets in the street instead. Katie smiled angrily, but not unhappily. The world would do better not to underestimate Nunn's Irish Rose.

6

The lobby of the Union Hotel was even more imposing than its façade, if such a thing was possible. Crowded with both exquisite furnishings and even more exquisite racegoers, who had paused in the Grand Saloon for a brief refreshment after the morning's concert on the piazza and the afternoon's garden party, before retiring to their suites to prepare for that evening's dinner and ball, the lobby's five stories of balconies stretched up to a rotunda that spanned eighty feet. But it was not the lobby's dizzying heights that caused Rose to pause the moment she stepped through the front doors. Instead, her gaze was immediately drawn to the object that held pride of place on a velvet-covered table that stood directly beneath the center of the rotunda. It was an ancient casket, beaten out of bronze and chased with curious figures of horses. Beneath it, a card in a gilded frame read "Presented to the Saratoga Association by Mr. John Morrissey, on the Occasion of the Completion of the Racetrack Grandstand." The last time Rose had seen it, the chest had hung soot-blackened and gaping above the inert figure of her stricken father. Now, it had been meticulously mended and polished to a sheen that sparkled more beautifully than gold, but it was impossible for her not to recognize it—any more than it was impossible not to be overcome by a superstitious dread that her father's inert figure once more lay at its feet.

But in fact, there was no sign of her father in the lobby—beyond the bewildered porter who stood, clutching his traveling desk, as he babbled, "I'm sorry, miss. But he stormed right out of here as soon as he saw it! I could do nothing to stop him."

"By 'it' you mean this chest?" she asked, fighting to keep her voice steady.

"Said it was his own and would have satisfaction from the man what stole it from him. All I could do to stop him from seizing it there and then."

Well, she supposed that was some kind of faint mercy, although she was hard-pressed to see it as such. "Thank you for that," she said, tamping her rising horror beneath a courteous calm she distinctly did not feel. "Did he perhaps say to whom and where he proposed to press his case?"

"No, Miss." The porter held up the desk. "He only bid me see this safely locked in his room before he raced out of here as if the Devil himself was chasing him."

More like the demons that had haunted him for the past two years had finally caught up with him. But did she dare join in the chase as well? Surely, even here in Saratoga, the prospect of a daughter racing out on the street to recapture her escaped lunatic of a father would cause more a scandal than whatever scene her father's uncontrollable tantrums might create. It might be far wiser to accompany the beleaguered porter up to their suite and at least make certain he did not deliver her father's traveling desk—and the unsigned papers within it—into Cousin Preston's waiting hands.

But when the porter unlocked the oak double-doors and ushered Rose into a suite every bit as crammed with elegant furnishings as the lobby, she found no-one waiting on the gilded and embroidered settees beyond Cousin Patricia, Cousin Preston's tight-lipped mother. She was a woman who inspired in Rose impatience and sympathy in equal parts. She certainly had just cause for the pursed lips with which she brushed Rose's cheek in greeting. The first American Adair, a Scots-Irishman who had fled England to make his fortune in the Colonies—and some would say to save his neck from the hangman—had been a canny enough businessman to leave the whole of his fortune to the one son he deemed capable enough to increase it, providing only a competence for his other descendants. And Rose's grandfather had fulfilled his father's trust, so much so that no member of the Adair family would ever have cause to complain of the competence they received. But while her own father was an astute enough hand when it came to money, even Rose was forced to admit that his plan to devote the bulk of the family fortune to founding a museum for his collection was folly, if not sheer madness—as Cousin Preston loudly insisted.

But manners were manners, and Cousin Patricia greeted Rose's arrival with brittlely feigned enthusiasm, as she pressed Rose to join her on the settee. "I confess both my son and I delighted—if, I will admit, more than a little surprised—at your father's sudden inclination to join us on our summer sojourn." Her voice dropped confidingly. "For, frankly, cousin, I cannot tell you how much it has pained me to witness the way your father used you. Squirrelling you away for his own selfish purposes at the very moment when you should have been stepping forward to take your place on the great stage of society..."

"There was a war that stood in the way of any such plans," Rose pointed out as neutrally as she could.

"Of course, of course. I am by no means casting blame. Still, I cannot help but wish that your father had cast a kinder eye on my willingness to guide a poor orphan through the treacherous shoals of a *debut*."

"I am no orphan," Rose said sharply. "I may be motherless, but I have a father."

"A fact to which your wardrobe only too sadly attests," Cousin Patricia agreed, casting a long look at Rose's simple cotton travelling dress, with its modest crinolines, and few decorations beyond a lace collar and a single flounce at both hem and sleeves. Her voice suddenly grew stern. "For if you intend to join us, you must understand that we are speaking of *Saratoga*, my dear. You scarcely want to promenade on Broadway looking like a lady's *companion*."

And perhaps it was the sudden resurrection of Declan S—*no,* Tamerlane Fallon, but Rose suddenly felt an unaccustomed stab of regret that she had paid so little attention to the details and accessories of the ladies who strolled the newly fashionable Ladies' Mile. Was it some impossible hope that if Sull—*Fallon* had in fact cheated the hangman once he might do it again that inspired this unusual interest in fripperies and furbelows?

If it was, it was a thought best put out of her head. Better by far to concentrate on how unusual it was for Cousin Patricia to demonstrate any concern for Rose's appearance. Hitherto, she had sought to further her son's interests by being at least as much of an impediment to Rose's formal introduction to society as the four years of war—as persistent in her own way as

Cousin Preston who had renewed his suit with metronomic precision every time their paths had crossed.

"Unfortunately, my father was most adamant." Rose dropped her voice to match Cousin Patricia's confiding tone. "In all frankness, I must mention that my father is more than a little troubled by the recent bills from Cousin Preston's recent ventures here in Saratoga. Is it true he proposes to enter the meets this year?"

Cousin Patricia smiled indulgently. "Now, you must allow a man his little pleasures."

"But these are scarcely little pleasures. Why, I was studying the programme myself during our railroad journey, and I must confess myself as concerned as my father. Why, the fees for entering the races are almost enormous as the prizes. Could it possibly be true that the Sweepstakes cost $200 per owner?"

Cousin Patricia lifted a shoulder. "In racing circles, it goes without saying that an owner must be prepared to stake his own horse. They don't just allow any riff-raff who can climb into the saddle to approach the starting line. But a sum such as $200 is a trifle to men like Jerome and Vanderbilt. It is said that the Commodore stakes that much nightly at whist."

"But Cousin Preston is scarcely the Commodore. And this is not for just one race. The race fees continue, race after race daily. And it is said Cousin Preston has three horses! How on earth does he propose to afford it?"

One look at Cousin Patricia's face, and it was perfectly clear exactly how he proposed to afford it—the same way he had afforded all his bills during the past two years. But Cousin Patricia managed a well-bred smile, and said, "Well, now, the members of the Saratoga Association would never be so vulgar as to press a man for his money up front—at least, not a gentleman who can so clearly afford his sport."

Perhaps. But Cousin Preston clearly did not belong to that category. And Rose was hard-pressed to think that men like Commodore Vanderbilt and Leonard Jerome, who traded shares and railroads as casually as farm wives traded cabbages and fresh eggs would be so obtuse not to arrive at that conclusion immediately. Which could only force her to wonder whether maintaining the façade of her father's sanity was her most pressing problem. Should she be more concerned about her cousin bankrupting the family instead?

Perusing that evening's dinner menu offered little reassurance. Vermicilli for soup; chicken pie French style; Ficandeau of veal; broiled pigeons a la Americaine, and Charlotte Russe. Clearly, the privations of the recent war had not reached Mr. Morrissey's Saratoga. Tossing it aside, she settled at a gilt harpsichord and paged through a book of ballads that had been left there for the ladies to divert themselves. Then she recognized the slow, sad melody she was picking out on the keys.

Roisin Dubh. Dark Rosaleen.

With a muffled exclamation, she sprang to her feet and gathered her wrap and reticule. Cousin Patricia had issued dire warnings about the dangers facing an unescorted young lady in Saratoga, but if Rose had to sit here and do nothing any longer, she would go mad. Congress Spring was barely 200 feet from the hotel's grand entrance, and she was scarcely some country girl unaware of the dangers of a bustling city. Still, she snatched a letter knife from the desk and hid it in her sleeve.

It was still daylight, but the shadows were lengthening, and the fashionable guests were all preparing for dinner and the evening's entertainment now. Only a few stragglers remained in the park, and most of them seemed to prefer the privacy of the surrounding trees. The pavilion itself was empty save for one shadow, who was scouring the ground around the stone fountain where the water spilled from iron pipes. He stooped with a swift cry of satisfaction, and slipped something into the pocket of his coat.

And as he straightened, Rose saw it was a Union officer's coat.

She slid the letter knife out of her sleeve and stepped into the pavilion. "Good evening, Captain Fallon," she said. "Dare I ask whether you still have a price on your head?"

He looked up, and for a moment, he seemed as lost in the memory of long ago as she was. Then, his mouth twisted into the ghost of a smile. "That remains to be seen," he said. His gaze moved curiously to the knife she held. "Would you truly use that against me?"

"That remains to be seen," she answered him. Holding the knife carefully in front of her, she took a moment to study him. The past two years had not been kind. His linens, formerly so impeccable, were threadbare, his cuffs and collars twice-turned, both coat and trousers mended. The past few hours had apparently been worse. Livid bruises were swelling across his face, and he moved carefully, almost tentatively, as if something pained him beyond his customary limp. Was this truly what she had been willing to betray her family and her country for?

She felt the knife lower, as if of its own accord.

"What are you doing here?"

A long pause, and then he raised a shoulder. "I should think the same thing as you are. I'm here to seek answers."

"To what questions?"

He met her eyes, his face suddenly sober. "We could begin with the question of those papers I stole from your father. Did you deliver them along with my message?"

"Yes," she said. "I kept my word. Although for the life of me, I could not tell you why."

She could not keep the bitterness out of her voice—and Fallon's face softened. "*A Róisín ná bíodh brón ort fár* éirigh *dhuit*," he said gently. "My dark Rosaleen. Do not sigh, do not weep! For I assure you that I am not worth your tears…"

And she was back in Jones' Wood the night Declan Sullivan had first kissed her. The park had been crowded with the Irish, although it was scarcely the "Monster Irish Festival" of 1861 during which Thomas Francis Meagher had delivered his famed address, recorded word for word in Beadle's Dime Patriotic Speaker. Still the fiddles played on every side, and red-faced women and men cut the elaborate figures of reels, while their children laughed and squealed at wheelbarrow races. Then the red-haired waif in a gaudy green dress who had been step dancing on a wagon that touted Nunn's Select Pantomimes and Irish Revue, instead began to sing in a thin, youthful voice, and silence fell.

"*A Róisín ná bíodh brón ort fár* éirigh *dhuit*…"

"They call such a poem an *aisling*," Sullivan explained softly. "It is love song, a vision quest, a poet's mystic journey to find his own heart and soul. But this is not just any *aisling*. This *aisling* sings of heart and soul of Ireland herself." His green eyes had met hers just before his lips had. "Alas, those of us who are not gifted with such loftiness of vision are condemned to content ourselves with simply finding the woman who owns our heart and soul."

Not gifted with loftiness of vision. At the time, she had thought it a modest disclaimer, for she had never met a man with such high honor and heroic dreams. Now, she knew how truly he had spoken. "My name is Rose," she said. "And right now, I have no intention of either sighing or weeping. Instead, I would like the answer to my questions. They say a man was found dead here this morning. Did you kill him?"

Fallon shot her a sharp look, not untinged by humor. "The police are satisfied I did not."

"Which is scarcely an answer," she pointed out. "Any more than you have offered me any sort of satisfactory explanation as to what are you doing here at the spring."

"What the police ought to be doing," he said simply. "Searching for clues."

"Such as whatever I just saw you slip into your pocket?"

Another sharp look. Then he reached into his coat and wordlessly held out a curious object—a fetish that seemed to have been braided out of horsehair and twisted into an elaborate knot.

"What is it?" she asked. "And please waste no time spinning tales of Fenian conspiracies or magical weapons that can chart the course of human events."

Fallon raised an eyebrow. "Even if they are the absolute truth?"

"I have believed you many things, Captain Fallon, but never a madman."

"And what of what your father believes?"

She froze. Had word of her father's condition reached him somehow? "I can assure you, my father is not a man given to credulity."

Which was, in fact, an utter and complete lie. But not one she dared see discredited, no matter how justifiably. All she could do was to steer the conversation away from such treacherous shoals. "Two years ago, you said you would explain yourself to me. Perhaps the time is come for you to do just that. Would you truly have me believe that there is a connection between my father and the unfortunate man who died here?"

"I cannot say for certain, but this charm suggests there is."

"What kind of connection?"

"I have yet to determine that, but I would beg you to take me seriously when I tell you that your father's mania for collecting may have placed him in the power of some very dangerous men."

"And what men are those?"

"A secret society that seeks to control the course of human events…"

"Naturally. As it so often seems to be."

"I am telling you the truth!" he said, his voice suddenly earnest. "Two years ago, I stumbled upon a conspiracy of men who may well have sought to influence the outcome of the War Between the States…"

"Two years ago, you sought to sell my father smuggled antiquities to benefit the Fenian cause."

His jaw set. "It may have begun that way, but I assure you that matters swiftly grew more complicated. *Far* more complicated."

There was no mistaking the meaning beneath his words. But Rose could not afford to understand it. Dare not *want* to understand it. "My father is a collector, not a conspirator."

Fallon raised an eyebrow. "You do not believe in the power of objects?"

"Objects such as the chest you once proposed to sell my father?" she snorted. "Would you have me believe it contained a genie?"

"Objects can have the power to inspire men to a greatness they never knew themselves capable of, and that is in itself a kind of magic." Fallon's face briefly grew distant, before he shook his head and recollected himself. "The chest was never important—at least not until someone tried to use it to kill your father. Now, it is the key to a vile conspiracy. As were the names that I once gave you."

She nodded slowly, inclined to believe him despite herself. But it was too easy to trust him, far too appealing to think that she might have any kind of ally in the weary, hopeless game she had been playing for these past two years. "And what is your interest in this conspiracy? Why has it drawn you back from the safety of England or Canada or wherever it was that you fled?"

"I wronged you," he said simply. "I would make it right."

"You wronged my father."

His face hardened. "No. Your father wronged both Ireland and his own land, arguably along with the gods and any vestigial sense of decency he might possess. And given that much, I would happily leave him to the fate he has brought down on his own head. But you are a different question altogether. I wronged you. And I will not rest until I set that right."

The conviction in his voice would have convinced even a hanging judge—and most likely it already had. "Why?" she asked. "And pray spare me any cant about saving your soul. If that is your goal, I suggest you address yourself to a priest."

For a moment, he looked genuinely hurt. Then he smiled—the familiar insouciant smile that could have once persuaded her to do anything. "Alas, I was lost to the priests at birth. Lame foot, caul over the face—doubly marked as the Devil's Own. It is said the Holy Water spit and boiled when they baptized me."

"As if that is not a rather convenient way to justify your bad behavior," she snorted. "After all, if you're destined for Hell, why deprive yourself of the pleasures you can find along the way?"

The moment the words were out of her mouth, she wished she could have them back.

"So cruel, Roisin?" This time, there was no mistaking his hurt.

"My name is Rose…"

"Where is that confounded girl? Dinner has yet to be ordered and my desk is scarcely unpacked!"

Fallon tensed as her father's voice rang across the lawns that separated them from the hotel. Then he said hurriedly, "Please trust me, Roisin. I may not be a good man, and I am certainly not the man you believed you loved, but I am a gentleman. And a gentleman always fulfills his pledges—especially here in Saratoga Springs. In fact, many would say it is the only law of the land in this place."

But before she could answer, her father was upon them, his towering rage redoubling the moment he recognized Fallon. "You… you thief! First you proposed to steal my property. Now you propose to steal my daughter?"

Fallon stiffened. "I beg you, sir, insult me as you will. But if you would besmirch the good name of your daughter, I *will* call you out…"

"Please," Rose hissed. "This cannot help…"

"Would you claim otherwise? You think I did not watch you, did not see how you eyed her, see how you looked for the moment you could spirit her away?" her father cut her off as he leaned closer to Fallon with a fey smile. "Hid yourself in that chest, did you? Just like you learned to do in Troy. Folded yourself up, so quiet, so secret—hush, hush—while you whispered to her, begging her, cajoling her, turning her weak woman's mind to your purposes. Betraying me. Betraying her family. And all for what? A stolen kiss?"

Fallon's lips whitened, and for a moment, she was certain he was about throw himself at her father. Then his eyes flared in sudden understanding that was a thousand times worse. For it had been difficult enough to keep the truth about her father out of Cousin Preston's hands, but for a man like Fallon to be possessed of such dangerous knowledge was unspeakable.

Her father's smile turned to a giggle. "Reverse the puzzle. Horse on the *inside*. Men on the *outside*. Did you think you would fool a true adept like me? I saw your schemes then, and I see your schemes now. Carry off the woman as your prize, carry the virgin to your bed…"

Rose's face flamed, but Fallon's face suddenly set in a way that made him an entirely different man—a man Rose was forced to admit she had never truly known. There was no rich, Irish passion, no heroic ideals in his expression, as he turned to Rose. No poetic lies. Simply calm calculation, as if he were laying down a hand at whist. "I think it would be best if you let me bring him in through a service entrance," he said. "The staff are used to gentlemen in their cups using the mews in the name of discretion. You can await me in your suite, and we will see him safely to bed together."

"Please," she sighed, "allow me to manage this. You have wreaked enough havoc in my life already."

"Arguably." He grinned. "But you are a highly intelligent woman—which is only the first of many reasons I fell in love with you. I never could abide a fool. And so I trust that you will understand my next actions spring from necessity, not anger."

Before she could react, he spun and dealt a single blow to her father's jaw that sent him staggering. "At least for the most part," Fallon added, as he deftly caught her father and began a lurching path toward Union Hall, bursting loudly into a drinking song whose unspeakably bawdy lyrics seemed to increase in outrageous inventiveness with every step he took.

7

This time, when Sullivan's cursed fate arrived to pay its respects, it was in the form of a gentleman in a top hat and opera cloak that better belonged in the grand hotels on the far side of the tracks than here in Little Dublin. Nonetheless, he made his way unerringly to Sullivan's table in the corner of the inn, and sat down uninvited, laying his hat carefully on the bench beside him, before he straightened his cuffs and cravat with elaborate care, before he said, "My name's Preston Olcott. And I'm looking for a horsewhisperer."

Sullivan evinced no reaction. Simply unstoppered his whiskey bottle, poured with the careful neatness of one already well on his way to being drunk, and spent a few meditative moments staring past Olcott, as if the man didn't exist, before he said, "There's been a lot of you lately. What's your interest, then? You one of those folkloric gentlemen?"

"I regret to say I am no scholar."

"I dinna think so." There might have been a flash of humor deep in the Irishman's eyes. "A sporting man, then?"

"I have an interest in this season's meet," Olcott conceded.

"As well as an interest in a horsewhisperer," Sullivan sighed. "Why? Or do I really need ask? The meets are nearly upon us. What end does a sporting man ever seek? He wants a horse to pull up mysteriously lame? A favorite to shy at the start, so that a spavined nag wins against all odds?"

"I have heard you can do such things."

"Heard from who?" Sullivan asked sharply. "Sammy Nunn?"

"Who told me doesn't matter," Olcott replied. "The question is can you do the things they claim?"

A long moment's silence. Then Sullivan raised shoulder. "As can any man. You scarcely need a horsewhisperer. All it took in the case of Thunder two years ago was an apple with the seeds removed and filled with an unknown substance that tasted hot and bitter to the trainer. Thunder might have gone like the blazes in his morning workout, but Sympathy didn't need Gilpatrick up to win the two-mile heat that afternoon.

"But there are far simpler cheats than that. Easy enough to bribe a boy to pull his mount up short. Even easier to lame a favorite by cutting a tendon. All you need is a tin of shoe-blacking to color a tell-tale stocking and disguise a champion so you can enter him under a different name. You need no wizard to do that. It's practically part of the rules, as some would say."

Sullivan turned back to his drink, a clear signal he was done talking. But Olcott merely nodded. "Yet the word is around the track that you have an uncanny way with a horse—although you do not choose to use it."

"Rumors are rumors," Sullivan said. "The only talent I possess is the one I get paid for—mucking out stalls."

"Ah, yes. I heard it said you work at a livery stable now." Olcott shook his head. "A terrible waste of a valuable talent."

Sullivan's eyes grew darker. "Waste or no waste, what trouble is it of yours? There are plenty of talented horsemen around Saratoga, especially this time of year."

"I'm not looking for a talented horseman. I'm looking for a horsewhisperer."

"Well, I wish ye the best of luck in that search. Now, if there's nothing else?"

Olcott raised an eyebrow. "It is said that you fled Ireland to escape being hanged for witchcraft," he said.

If he had hoped to goad Sullivan, he did not succeed. "Then I guess I should count myself lucky to be in America, where they gave up on hanging people for witchcraft more than a century ago," Sullivan said with a shrug.

"But they do still hang people for murder."

The night suddenly seemed to fall silent. "I'm not sure what you mean," Sullivan finally said.

"I am merely pointing out that it would be very easy to kill a man if one were possessed of such power," Olcott said. "And it would be well nigh impossible to be arrested and tried for the crime."

Sullivan's jaw set. "Horses bolt. Men die. And they don't hang horses in the United States either, as far as I can tell."

"Indeed." Olcott agreed with a faint smile. "And yet a man has been recently struck dead in Congress Springs, by all accounts by a sudden blow—as hard and sharp as that of a horse's hoof. I hope the Pinkertons will not be reduced to seeking out the horse responsible."

Sullivan met Olcott's gaze, the dark blue glint in the depths of his own eyes the only sign of his rising fury. "If you have an accusation to make, I would prefer you do it directly."

Olcott nodded, glancing only momentarily at the bandage on Sullivan's hand. "Of course, no reasonable man believes in hell horses any more than hell hounds. The odds are the man was killed by someone skilled with his fists. Now, the rumors have begun to swirl around Saratoga, that those fists belong to a member of a secret society, whose secrets the dead man sought to betray. Worshippers of the Old Goddess, Epona, and practitioners of a secret craft that has been passed down all the way from the first sorcerer, the first smith, Tubal Cain…"

"And you would seek such men?" Sullivan asked. "To what purpose? Are you trying to save them from the gallows or are you recruiting your own assassins?"

"Scarcely mutually exclusive propositions," Olcott pointed out.

"And neither one I can help you with," Sullivan said. He tucked the bottle of whiskey beneath his worn coat and began to rise. "Now, if you'll excuse me, I have an early morning ahead of me…"

"Now that's a pity," Olcott said softly. "Because I was hoping not to have to go to the Pinkertons with my information."

Sullivan subsided back onto the bench. "And what information is that?"

"I have heard that members of this society might be right here in Little Dublin—and that they were drummed out of Ireland not as witches but rather as very real and very dangerous ring of Fenian rebels."

A long pause. Then Sullivan shrugged. "As were half the Irish in America. My reasons for leaving Ireland are my own. But most of the others who fled make no secret of the reason. Take Meagher, for example. In his case, I believe the precise penalty being hanged, drawn, and quartered, but Her Majesty did not have the blood lust of her forebears when it came to treason and sedition, and contented herself seeing him transported instead." Sullivan made to rise again. "Condemned as criminals in the old country, hailed as heroes when they escaped to the new, such men have never tried to hide the fact that they joined the Union cause in order to hone the fighting skills they need to launch a new rebellion against the English."

"Nonetheless, we don't need such troublemakers in Saratoga."

"After the debacle of the Irish Brigade and the horror of watching their sons die in another country's war, I frankly doubt there are many in Little Dublin who would want them here either. But to clean out all the Fenian sympathizers from Little Dublin right at the beginning of the meet?" Sullivan smiled with genuine amusement. "You'd best ask Morrissey what he thinks about that."

"You think the old bruiser will remember his Irish roots now that he rubs elbows with Vanderbilts and Jeromes?"

"I think the man that aims to build Saratoga Springs into America's greatest racetrack would not look kindly on you rounding up half the boys, trainers, cooks and waiters a scarce week before the meet is scheduled to begin." Abruptly, all humor vanished from Sullivan's face, as he added, "What is it you really want?"

A moment's hesitation, then Olcott inclined his head. "Very well, I will not insult your intelligence with further circumlocution, Mr. Sullivan, for you seem to be a surprisingly well-educated man."

"My sainted mother had ambitions for me, despite my unfortunate birth."

"I may be new to Saratoga," Olcott went on as if he hadn't spoken, "but I aim to make my mark. In doing so, I could use some powerful friends."

"Then I suggest you start with something better than the Irish," Sullivan snorted.

"I said I would not insult your intelligence, and I will not," Olcott said. "I know why you fled New York City, as well as why you live in hiding, scraping out an existence as a stable boy when you were once the fastest rising trainer in New York City…"

"Sammy Nunn telling tales again?" Sullivan shook his head. "I would suggest there are more reliable sources of information."

"The most recent of which now lies dead in the Saratoga Springs mortuary." Olcott leaned close. "And it is not only Sammy Nunn who is saying that he was killed because he knew the truth about the chest Mr. Morrissey recently presented to the Saratoga Association: that it had been looted from an ancient tomb by a gang of Fenians and smuggled into New York, where they sought to sell it to raise funds to support their cause."

Sullivan's face set. "And would you say those sacred treasures better served Eire by attesting to her glory in galleries and universities while her children starved? Yes, children, Mr. Olcott, rooting up rotting offal from the sewers of Dublin as if it were a prize, and following the English cavalry like birds in order to scoop the remains of their horses' grain from their droppings.

Could you blame a man for thieving a sacred treasure any more than a loaf of bread?"

Olcott raised a shoulder. "You speak with sudden passion, Mr. Sullivan."

"I speak no more than a truth even a blind man could see." Sullivan eyed Olcott narrowly. "But as for you, Mr. Olcott, I would still like to understand your interest in the case."

"My cousin, Jonathan Adair, was nearly killed when he attempted to purchase this chest two years ago. From an Irishman who called himself Declan Sullivan."

Sullivan's mouth curled. "And you are here to demand satisfaction on his behalf?"

"Of course not. It is no secret that my cousin and I are at odds over his squandering the family fortune over his obsession for collecting. Whoever disrupted that purchase did me a considerable service." Olcott met Sullivan's eyes. "Which is why I feel I should return the courtesy and warn him that his history with this unfortunate chest may see him straight to the gallows this time."

"Why should it? Even if antiquities were stolen and smuggled out of Ireland, surely that is a problem for the Irish government, not the American one."

"But if these antiquities were used as part of one of the many seditious conspiracies to betray New York City to the Confederacy, it would be very much the concern of the American government." Olcott's gaze grew hard. "The penalty for spying is hanging, Mr. Sullivan, no matter whether it was in service of American ideals or Fenian ones."

A thunderous pause. Then Sullivan shook his head. "Poor men have no ideals beyond filling their bellies—or the bellies of their families, if they are unfortunate enough to be blessed with one. And although I am happily spared the burden of a family, I assure you that I am still a poor man."

"Nonetheless, poor men can and will be hanged."

Most likely Sammy Nunn first among them. But Sullivan had tried to warn him. How much more was a man expected to do? And suddenly Sullivan was tired of fencing. It didn't matter whether you dressed them up with smuggled treasures, tarot cards, family curses, or the cause of Irish freedom, when did it ever come down to anything but this: Rich men using poor men as pawns in some chess game that mattered only to them?

"Be that as it may, Mr. Olcott, I know nothing about what you speak of."

Which was not entirely true, but Sullivan had settled that matter to his own content the previous night.

"But you are called Declan Sullivan?"

"A common enough name." His eyes suddenly flashed blue, and his voice darkened with a wyrd that he denied he ever possessed and rarely allowed anyone to witness. But when they had witnessed it, most men were loath to speak of it further. "So while I appreciate your courtesy in trying to warn me, I assure you it is entirely misplaced. You are speaking with the *wrong man*."

And although he put a brave enough face on it, Olcott could not withstand the force of those words any more than any other man. He took his time carefully replacing his top hat, but his step was quick enough as he did his best to stroll out of the inn. The blue light faded from Sullivan's eyes as he glanced around warily. But if the other drinkers had witnessed anything amiss with this strange, silent man about whom they had always cherished hidden doubts, they did the wise thing and turned to study their drinks with an ostentatious care that signaled they had seen nothing untoward. Still, their collective shoulders seemed to settle with relief when Sullivan rose and followed Olcott out the door.

In time to see Olcott step out into the street. And straight into a still steaming pile of horse droppings.

Mayhap, Sullivan thought with a small smile, as he turned to head toward his shabby quarters in the stableyard, the goddess truly did defend her own.

8

Morrissey's Club House was still on Matilda Street, where he had originally built it to be conveniently close to the railway station, although it was said that the ambitious Irishman had already put plans in motion to build a far grander one closer to his influential friends at the Saratoga Association. It was ten in the morning, and the gaming house was barely waking up from the previous night's excesses. Rose glimpsed maids busily dusting and mopping the card rooms they were airing, while kitchen boys hauled spilled wine and spoiled food out into the alley, as she and her father were shown to John Morrissey's private office.

John Morrissey was not an old man, but he looked like he'd lived a thousand lifetimes. A self-made man, who, it was said, had taught himself to read and write while he was in prison, he dressed impeccably, his unruly hair smoothed back with pomade and his curly beard hiding the scars he had won as a bare-knuckle fighter. He bent over Rose's hand courteously as they were introduced, but he did nothing to disguise his disbelief as she introduced herself as her father's secretary. His courtesy never wavered, but his expression shifted to hard appraisal when he turned to Jonathan Adair and said, "I've been told you wish to speak to me about a matter involving stolen property."

Rose glanced at her father anxiously. It had been difficult enough to insist on accompanying her father when the invitation had arrived along with their breakfast tray; now, there was little she could do to control an outburst beyond mouthing a prayer beneath her breath. But mercifully her father sounded lucid as he replied, "If you will not take my word for it, I can have my *bona fides* cabled instantly. I *purchased* that chest that is now on display in the lobby of Union Hall—for a not-unsubstantial sum, I might add."

"For the price of feeding a starving village for a month," Morrissey corrected him. "From a gang of Fenians who looted it from a barrow in Tipperary and smuggled it into the United States in order to raise money for their cause."

"What does that matter?" Again, a reasonable-enough answer, but her father's face was beginning to harden in a way Rose knew only too well could signal no good. "If you would like to take your claims to the United States legal system, I would beg you to do so, for I can assure you that I am not the only one who would stop at nothing to bring it to this country and ensure that it remains here."

Morrissey nodded. "You are not the first to suggest such a thing," he ruminated. "Indeed, the poor wretch who was found dead in Congress Spring approached me claiming that he had evidence of just such a conspiracy..."

"You must forgive me," Rose cut in anxiously, afraid to so much as glance at her father, "but I must beg you to desist from any such talk of conspiracies, for such matters are still very painful to my father. You may not be aware that he was nearly the victim of another conspiracy involving this unfortunate chest..."

From the look in Morrissey's eyes, not only was he was more than aware of that fact, he was manipulating it deliberately. But his voice betrayed nothing but bland curiosity as he asked, "Why? What is so important about this chest?"

"What is important is that it is mine." Her father's voice took on a dangerous, petulant edge. "That is all a man like you need know. What can you possibly understand of my plans to bequeath my collection to the people of New York City as a gift?"

Rose stiffened. It was said that Morrissey had killed a man with his bare hands over far less of an insult. But his voice remained blandly polite, as he agreed, "Indeed, you are correct. In my limited understanding, most men would prefer bread and a warm place to sleep. In fact, many of my countrymen risked death crossing the Atlantic for nothing more."

"The masses don't know what they should prefer. But educated men see what they need. Educated men that include your new friends and supporters in the Saratoga Association—who will cut you dead if you propose to test their friendship in this matter." Her father leaned across Morrissey's desk, his voice softening to a whisper. "The old world is finished. The future belongs to America now. And so is it not fitting that the old world's treasures should be brought to America to serve the rise of the new world? Is it not right that a society of visionary gentlemen should dedicate their time, money and power into achieving this task and leave a legacy for the country they have truly founded?"

Her father's face was alight with fanaticism now, but Morrissey merely smiled, as he mused, "You call them a society. In Five Points, we called them gangs. Just as we call them thieves, while you prefer the term robber baron." He broke off abruptly, and spread his hands. "But what do I care about idealists, Irish or American? I'm a practical man. Take the box. Consider it my gift to you. A token of goodwill."

No, Rose thought as her mind went back to the fetish that Fallon had uncovered at the spring. This, too, was a token of a debt. One that was owed and would be paid in full when the right time came. For she believed Morrissey when he said he was a practical man.

She also believed that behind that bluff exterior was a mind as subtle and cunning as any she had ever met—even that of Tamerlane Fallon. Every word Morrissey had spoken had been calculated to push, to goad her father, to test his very fragile limits. The question was, she thought as she forced a smile and took as pleasant a leave of John Morrissey as she could, how much had he truly understood? And what price would he demand for his knowledge?

*****

Little did Rose suspect that by the time they returned to Union Hall, John Morrissey would be the least of her concerns. The first hint of trouble came as their carriage drew to a halt and she found herself handed down not at the grand front portico, but instead at one of the discreet side doors which Fallon had made use of the previous evening. And instead of their being greeted by a major-domo, Cousin Preston awaited them, along with a dark-suited man whose black bag proclaimed him to be a doctor.

Rose froze on the tiny ornate step the driver had folded down for her. "What is happening?"

"Nothing you need to concern yourself with," Preston assured her, as he reached to hand her down the rest of the way with an unctuous smile. "Please, dear cousin, trust me when I say how much I admire your dedication to serving your father during this trying time when he has been so terribly afflicted, but I must now beg you to shed the burden that has so cruelly overtaxed your slender shoulders and allow me to handle matters from here."

It was a speech he must have been preparing ever since he had received word of their arrival, and it was enough to make her recoil from his proffered hand. Instead, she looked over at the dog cart that she had just noticed was being piled with her father's baggage by a group of suspiciously burly porters. "What matters?" she asked. "Where are you taking us?"

"We are taking *you* nowhere," the doctor said reassuringly. "And have no worries, your father will be very comfortable. Indeed, we were lucky to procure one of the cottages for him at such short notice…"

Cottages? Was he referring to the newly-built clusters of private homes that flanked the Opera House? "But those are reserved for the most exclusive of families," she protested. "We can hardly afford…"

"When it comes to your father's comfort, no expense is too great," the doctor said. "But I fear your father may not understand our concern of his welfare, and so I would spare you an unpleasant scene. It would be best if you retire to your suite until we can resolve matters as discreetly as possible. I assure you, you will be able to visit your father as soon as we have him settled."

"Dr. Mitchell is a very discreet man," Cousin Preston supplied.

More likely he was a very well-paid man. But Cousin Preston had taken her hand once again, this time so tightly that she had no choice other than to allow him to hand her down, unless she wanted to engage in an undignified tug-of-war on the carriage step. Still, she balked at simply allowing herself to be sent indoors like some errant schoolgirl dismissed before the adults walked in to dinner. Icily removing herself from Preston's grasp, she turned to the doctor. "May I at least be informed as to exactly what medical concerns you believe warrant such an action? For if this is in reference to my father's behavior of last evening, surely overindulgence is not a medical concern, especially not here in Saratoga…"

Or was it? Her mind flashed back to Tamerlane Fallon's drunken singing. His extremely *loud*, unmistakably *noticeable*, drunken singing. Had she been wrong to trust him? He had already as much as admitted that he sought to destroy her father on one occasion. Was he using her again?

No. Even if it were true, she could not afford to be so distracted. For, just that moment's inattention had caused her to miss her father slithering down from the carriage with a madman's rapid cunning and lurching toward the dog cart with cry.

"You blackguards! What do you think you're doing?"

Dear God, no. Rose gathered her skirts to run to stop him, but Cousin Preston stepped into her way.

"This is no place for a lady."

"And *this* is scarcely discreet," she retorted. She turned to the porters. "This is my father. I know how to manage him. Please allow me through."

"Rose, please!" Cousin Preston protested.

"I really must insist you not interfere," the doctor added.

But the porters hesitated.

"*Now!*" Rose commanded—in the voice Bridie had taught her to use to banish unwanted tradesmen from the door.

The porters shuffled aside. And Rose's heart sank as she saw her father crouched by the side of the dog cart, his eyes wild, a trickle of spittle coursing out from the corner of his mouth, as he clutched his travel desk to his chest. There was no question of further resisting the doctor's plans. Seeing her father like this, no man would pronounce him sane.

But there was one thing she could do. "Please, father," she said, "give me the desk. You know your lawyers are arriving in a few days. Allow me to place it in the hotel safe until then."

Her father's lip pulled back in a feral smile. "Bitch," he hissed. "You think I have not seen your schemes. You think I do not remember your meeting your lover last night, by the cover of the spring… plotting, plotting. Did you think to run off with him then?"

"Enough!" Cousin Preston snapped. "I cannot allow a woman under my protection to be so addressed…"

Under *his* protection? But that was nothing but another distraction. Rose fought to keep her voice calm. "If you will not trust me, then please, trust the hotel. You can see your desk into the safe yourself, you can watch Mr. Leland secure the combination. All you need is to give it to me… or if you will not trust me, then give it to one of Mr. Leland's porters…"

"Excellent plan!" Cousin Preston said. He snapped his finger at one of the porters. "Sammy!"

But with a feral howl, her father thrust the desk at her instead, hard enough to send Rose staggering backwards, into the arms of a porter—no, *the* porter who had seemed so strangely familiar back at the railroad station. "Miss," he pleaded, his Irish brogue redoubling with the strain. "Allow me to escort you inside, I beg you. There's no need for you to see this."

"See what? What is the doctor doing?"

She twisted back toward the dog cart in time to glimpse the medical man wielding an ugly hypodermic needle.

"No!" she cried.

But this time, a curt word from the doctor caused the porters to close ranks around her father—with a grim expertise that could only make Rose wonder whether they were even porters at all.

"Please, miss," the Irishman said. "There are others who can best help him now. You've had a shock. I think you'd best go inside and sit down, and leave them to do what they can."

It was sound advice, but what about the Irishman nagged at her, warning her not to trust him? No, what did that matter? It was nothing but a distraction as well. For, she would not help matters at all by succumbing to the megrims. Instead, she must focus on the fact that she at least had possession of her father's traveling desk. "You will escort me to Mr. Leland's safe," she said.

"Please, miss. I'd be happy to take it for you."

"That will not be necessary," she said. And, heavy and cumbersome though the desk might be, she hefted it to hold it more securely. Only to stop as a splinter dug into her finger.

"Wait!" She frowned at the two ugly scratches next to the burled brass lock that marred the rosewood's smooth surface, then turned to the Irishman. "What's this? Who did that?"

His face set. "I'm sure I don't know what you're talking about, Miss."

"This desk has been tampered with! Did you do that?"

"Of course not, miss. Perhaps it fell when your father climbed on the wagon."

"This was no fall. These scrapes are right by the lock. As if someone were trying to break into it." Her voice was growing shrill, but strangely, her mind was not. It could well have been a hysterical reaction, but it was actually a relief to think about the problem that now confronted her, rather than wonder what was happening to her father. "Did you leave it alone for any period of time?"

"Naturally, miss, I had to set it down while I loaded the other bags," the Irishman said.

"So someone could have tampered with it?"

"Well, it's a possibility, of course, miss."

"Did you see anyone suspicious? A tramp, maybe?"

"Plenty of tramps around Saratoga during the meets," the Irishman allowed, but his face set with a strange cunning that made Rose freeze. Something was wrong…

No, something was *very* wrong! A burst of activity among the porters revealed Cousin Preston hurrying toward her, pale-faced, with the doctor striding furiously beside him. And Rose could read the grim truth in their eyes an eternity before the doctor said, "I fear I have some distressing news. I think it best that you sit down."

9

It was only when Rose had finally rid herself of Cousin Patricia's irritating fluttering, and begged to be allowed to retire to her room, where she stared numbly at one of the myriad crystal glasses of sherry that had been pressed on her from every side, that she realized she had yet to weep for her father. And even now, the tears would not come. She still had too many questions that people simply refused to answer. If she were to cry now, it could only be from sheer frustration that everyone simply dismissed anything she said as a symptom of her overset nerves.

It all began when she had thrust her father's desk at Sammy and wrenched herself free, dashing straight toward the worried knot of porters. With an oath and a grunt, one stepped forward to stop her. "Miss, please," he snapped. "This is no place for a lady."

But the mishap had opened a narrow gap, through which she glimpsed a blanket-covered lump—and a limp hand with gold signet ring she immediately recognized as belonging to her father. "Please," she breathed. "I must get through."

"I'm afraid that would hardly be wise," Dr. Mitchell hurried to intervene with practiced soothing and a flask of brandy that seemingly had materialized from nowhere.

She whirled on him. "I'm not a child! If he is well and truly gone, then I need to close his eyes. To kiss him goodbye. Would you deny a daughter her final duty?"

"He is gone," Dr. Mitchell said. "You have my word he is gone."

"No need for you to see him like this, miss," the porter that had tried to stop her agreed. "We'll lay him out nice and proper for you, I give you my word. Just let us do our job."

"What job? Who are you? Where are you taking him? Are you the police?"

"Now why would the police have anything to do with this?" Dr. Mitchell patted her arm in a way that suggest that if she'd been a year or two younger, he would have patted her head. "Your father's death was sudden and shocking, but it is hardly a matter with which to trouble the authorities. You must be strong and resist succumbing to hysterical fancies."

She pushed aside the flask he pressed on her. "I am not in the least inclined to hysteria, I assure you, Dr. Mitchell. I am merely asking, should not the manner of my father's death be a matter for the police to decide?"

"Well, of course, of course. As are all deaths—in the abstract, that is. But you have my assurances that the police are happy to cede their authority to a medical man when there's no sign of foul play."

"But there *were* such signs…"

Dr. Mitchell stiffened. "Would you insinuate…"

No. Not in the least. That was not what she had meant at all. But why such fierce objection? What had been in that needle the doctor had plunged into her father? Had it a medicine that had gone horribly awry? Or something far darker and far more dangerous?

She forced her voice to calm. "My apologies, Dr. Mitchell. I was of course not implying anything about your professional competence. It was just that… all this… is so sudden, so unexpected…"

"It was an apoplectic fit. I'm willing to stake my professional reputation on the matter."

"Be that as it may. There were marks on my father's desk. Scrapes that clearly suggest that someone was attempting to interfere with my father's papers. I must insist that a police officer examine them before my father is carried away."

Mitchell's patience deserted him, and his soothing turned stern. "Insist as you will, Miss, we're not in New York City, where the militia must be called in to control its citizens," he said. "It is my authority that holds sway here. And Saratoga Springs does not need to be troubled by an hysterical rumor that seeks to inflate a completely natural, if tragically unfortunate, occurrence into a murderous conspiracy."

Nor did she seek to do so. But why did the doctor seem so afraid she might? "I have no such intention," she said. "But certainly the simplest way to put such rumors to rest is to allow the police to pronounce on the matter."

"You forget that this is Saratoga. And I can assure you there would be no faster way to spread such rumors the length and breadth of Broadway than to go to the police. Better far simply to accept the will of the Divine." Mitchell's voice dropped pointedly. "Or some might even say the gentle Mercy of the Divine. For it is no secret your father was unwell as of late—so much so that many would say his passing was naught but a kind release. So why would you wish to promulgate gossip and scandal that can serve no purpose but to taint the family's bereavement? Most families would see it that way, if you don't mind me saying so. I can only suggest that it is your overset nerves that are keeping you from thinking clear-headedly…"

Once more he proffered the flask; this time she pressed it aside with unseemly force. But before she could reiterate her demand for a policeman, Cousin Preston appeared, and to her furious disbelief she saw that he was now carrying the desk she had left in the hands of the Irishman, Sammy. Her anger only redoubled when the doctor immediately pulled her cousin aside for a murmured consultation, during which she heard the words "hysterical accusations," and "overset nerves" repeated more than once. Cousin Preston nodded gravely as he listened.

"Thank you for your advice. Pray allow me to handle this." He turned to Rose and held out a hand, as if he were coaxing a frightened child. "The doctor has informed me of your concerns, and I understand them completely. I shall arrange for Sammy to take that unfortunate desk to the police station, where it can be thoroughly examined. In the meantime, please allow me to remove you from a scene which you can only have endured for too long."

He spoke in a soothing sing-song—as if he were talking to a madwoman, she realized in horror. And if she weren't careful and persisted in making a scene, she might reasonably fear being carted off as one. For, it would certainly suit Cousin Preston's purposes if she were confined to a doctor's care just as he had sought to do with her father. She drew a deep breath, forcing herself to reconsider. Insistence was not getting her anywhere. Perhaps it was time for her to concede that the doctor was right and her delicate nerves had been overset.

Widening her eyes in what she could only hope was an overset fashion, she snatched the desk from Cousin Preston's grip before he had the wit to resist. "You are quite correct. I do need to withdraw and rest," she said. "But I couldn't possibly relinquish this desk at this moment. You were there when I made my father a promise—on his deathbed, although none of us knew at the time. You must allow me to honor my word, at least until I can return home and see my father properly buried."

Cousin Preston's jaw set, but he conceded the point—and the desk—with ill grace. And Rose surrendered herself to her cousin's care with equal reluctance—forcing herself to be content herself with a last backward glance at the burden the porters were loading onto the stretcher and a whispered promise she would not give up on seeking the truth as her final farewell to her parent.

*****

Cousin Preston may have ceded the field over the matter of the desk, but he clearly considered himself bound by no such promises when it came to the rest of her father's baggage. As soon as the string of sheepish porters hauled it back into to the suite, he left the task of plying Rose with restoratives to his mother, and started toward her father's room, barking orders about how the men should unpack.

Rose was on her feet in an instant. "What are you doing? Do you dare to violate my father's personal property at such a time?"

To judge from the exasperation with which Preston's shoulders set, he was about to do nothing less. But he forced a smile and turned back to take her hand, his palm unpleasantly warm, unpleasantly damp against hers. "I merely seek to assume my responsibilities as the man of the family. A sore burden many would say, but I would have you know that I consider it both an honor and privilege to cast myself in the role of the protector your father should have been, and I only aspire that you will give me a chance to repair the wrongs your father's selfishness has caused you…"

It was not an unfair accusation. Yet it was all Rose could do to simply withdraw her hand, and moderate her voice, as she said, "I beg your pardon, cousin. I am very aware of my father's limits as a parent—as well as his value, which you seem to be determined to ignore. But I would point out that we are a house of mourning now, and I can hear no ill spoken of him under the circumstances."

"Of course, of course." Cousin Preston's smile grew as warmly unpleasant as his touch. "And given the circumstances, I am unhappily aware that I must put aside any selfish, secret hopes I might cherish between us for the indefinite future. I pledge to devote myself solely to my role as your guardian until a suitable period of mourning has passed."

Guardian? No! Surely, her father had made other provisions. And yet Rose felt a tell-tale lurch of her stomach at the possibility—for if her father had been too lax to secure the future of his beloved museum, she doubted he would have troubled himself over something as trivial as making provisions for his daughter.

"How dare you? How could you? You... unfeeling *monster*! To speak of cherished hopes at a time like this…" Rose allowed her voice to ratchet up into a near shriek. And she was prepared to keep on screaming all night if need be, until her cousin finally allowed her to lock her father's door and deposit the key in her bodice. Let them dismiss her as hysterical and overset if they would, she was gambling that even here in Saratoga Springs, Cousin Preston would never survive the scandal of being discovered making love to a recently-bereaved lady—especially one under his protection.

And her ploy worked. Ignoring Cousin Patricia's fluttering remonstrances, Preston had angrily withdrawn to spend the night at his club, and Rose was finally, mercifully, left alone with the hotel maid who proposed to draw her bath and see her to bed. She would have thought that it would have been impossible to sleep, but at last the sherry and fatigue conspired to draw her into a restless slumber—in which she was suddenly, safely home, as if the events of the past days had been nothing but a passing nightmare.

Her father was suffering one of his episodes again, and had slipped from his bed to prowl among the silent sentinels of his collection, and she had donned a wrapper and slipped silently after him, as she had always done, as he held up his flickering light to statues, paintings, and sarcophagi, as he demanded over and over, "Was it *you*?"

But no answer was forthcoming until at last, she recognized the curiously chased chest that held pride of place among the others, before her father's candle exploded into brightness that illuminated Tamerlane Fallon's head inside the chest, his tongue protruding, a noose pulled tight around his neck…

With a shriek, Rose sat bolt upright in bed.

And stared straight at the stealthy shadow that had awakened her.

Her maid was bent over her father's desk, pressing the lid back, and peering inside.

"Stop!" Rose cried. "What are you doing?"

Too late, a vestige of her dream caused her to fear that the maid might have been sent to assassinate her, just as her father had been. But instead the girl just dropped a sullen curtsey. "Nothing, I'm sure, miss. I just thought to lay out your clothes for the morning."

"There is no need," Rose said with an icy calm she did not feel. "I am accustomed to dressing myself."

"Of course, miss. I meant no harm, miss."

The girl scuttled out the door, closing it behind her.

Rose waited for the girl's footsteps to fade, then slipped out of bed and firmly locked the door behind her.

*****

She took the first steps she could in the morning, informing the maid that her services were no longer required and cabling for Bridie McMann to come to Saratoga as a replacement, long before Cousin Preston arrived to pay his morning call.

"I fear you are still overtaxed by your father's unfortunate demise," he reproached her with what grace he could muster. "I had hoped a good night's sleep would cure you of these senseless fears."

"My night's sleep would have been much better had I not awakened to find the maid that the hotel supplied rummaging through my belongings."

"My dear girl, the Union Hotel is one of the finest establishments in Saratoga. I trust you are not suggesting there is a ring of thieves operating inside it."

"In fact, I am suggesting something much worse," Rose said, as she forced her voice to a calm she did not feel. "I am suggesting the girl may have been in the employ the Society of the Horseman's Word."

Not only were the words a calculated risk, they were ones that she had been contemplating all morning. She had had little doubt who had directed the maid's actions, but she needed to know whether her cousin was behind it.

"I must confess myself uncertain as to what that might be," Cousin Preston said carefully.

"I believe it a secret society," she said promptly. "A network of horsemen who covet the chest that may well have succeeded in destroying my father, and will stop at nothing to obtain it."

A long pause before Cousin Preston managed to force a supercilious smile. "Oh, come now, you will not have me believing your poor father was felled by some kind of curse?"

"I would have you believe that my father was nearly felled by a Fenian conspiracy two years ago," she retorted calmly. "Is it so very illogical to believe they might still have cause to pursue him, even now? Even as far as here to Saratoga?"

And it was a logical question. But that did nothing to stop Rose from thinking of last night's very illogical dream. Some of the more advanced theories suggested that dreams allowed you to see truths you could not, or would not, see during waking hours. But was she to believe last night's dream showed who she truly believed was behind the attack on her father? Not a Fenian society, but rather Tamerlane Fallon?

Admitted adventurer. Traitor. Profiteer.

But was she to believe assassin as well?

She looked up from her ruminations in time to see the shock on Cousin Preston's face be replaced by swift calculation, as he came to a sudden decision, and said, "I had attempted to spare you any unpleasantness in deference to both your sex and your recent bereavement. But I am rapidly reaching the conclusion it would be better to have complete honesty between us."

In Rose's opinion, such a thing was as unlikely as a unicorn galloping around Morrissey's racetrack. But she inclined her head and said, "I'm afraid my father has bred me to prefer forthrightness."

"Then I shall be frank," Cousin Preston said. "I fear these Horsemen may be coming after me."

That was not answer she had expected. Indeed, it took all Rose's self-control to preserve her calm, as she exclaimed, "You! Why surely I am not to believe that you are an initiate of their Society?"

"Of course not! But where there are horses, there are inevitably such blackguards. And I very much fear that they may have cause to threaten me in the hopes of influencing the outcome of the races at the upcoming meet."

She met his eyes. "Fear?" she asked. "Or know?"

Preston jaw tensed in a way that suggested he was about to lie, before he conceded with a shrug, "These are matters that are most likely above a lady's understanding, but we have agreed on complete frankness between us. As you may be aware, the stakes for entering a race are quite high." His face hardened petulantly. "So high that I was certain there would be no point in approaching your father to back my venture. And so I was forced to take the advice of… other interests, who suggested I play for other stakes as well. Other stakes that promise to more than recoup my promised entry fees."

The puzzle pieces were falling into place all too damningly, but she forced herself to feign a bewilderment she did not in the least feel. "But would not hazarding your entry fee on your own horse simply redouble your risk?"

"There are certain wagers," he said. "And then there are even surer wagers."

Her stomach sank, and she turned her face away, avoiding his gaze. So it was as she had feared: Her cousin had not been content simply to overextend himself; he had embroiled himself—and with it, the family—in a full blown cheat.

But what, if anything, did this have to do with a Fenian conspiracy and smuggled treasure?

She drew a deep breath as she considered before she made her next move. "And what would you have me tell Mr. Washington?" she asked.

It was a gamble—arguably as risky as any her cousin had undertaken. But the blank puzzlement on her cousin's face suggested it was a good one. "I don't know that I'm acquainted with such a man."

"He is a horseman, but hardly an Irishman. Rather, he is a former slave who rode down south. He approached my father seeking information about this Society just a few days ago, and I gave him my word I would discover what I could. And so I must ask, in the spirit of perfect frankness between us, is there any information I might unearth on his behalf that might run counter to your interests in the upcoming meets?"

Instead of answering, Cousin Preston merely nodded. "Clever fellows those Negro jockeys," he mused. "Why, it was One-Eyed Sewell who dominated the opening meet at Saratoga, just these two years ago. Billy Burgoyne made as good a stand as he could, given he had a broken leg, and Gilpatrick himself came out of retirement to ride. But it was the Negro that won three races, not the Irishman, and him with only one eye at that…"

"Clever enough to have been offering my father some kind of veiled threat? Or perhaps a warning?"

Cousin Preston met her eyes and held them. "I'm afraid only examining the contents of your father's desk could offer any answer to that question."

She drew a deep breath, congratulating herself on her foresightedness in summoning a porter to remove her father's desk back down to the safe, even before she had dismissed the maid. "Unfortunately, I fear you are too late," she said. "The porter has taken it downstairs along with the rest of my father's private papers with explicit instructions that it remain locked in the hotel safe until my father's lawyer arrives to examine it. As I should have done yesterday—had my wretched nerves alas not been quite so overset."

10

Katie misliked old Sammy's mood that morning, just as she misliked his demand that she accompany him to Congress Spring in order to take the waters. She misliked traveling to the scandalous part of town that lay on the other side of the railway tracks even more. She had learned to hold her head high and ignore the cursed nuns and housewives who eyed her half in pity and half in contempt whenever she walked out in Little Dublin. But there was no way she could hold her head high enough not to know she and Sammy were fathoms beyond their depth when they proposed to stroll among the fashionable crowd on Broadway. Not that Sammy didn't do his best to put a brave face on it, nattering on about how the champagne would flow like water in Morrissey's newly-built grandstand, and pointing out the Vanderbilts, Belmonts and Jeromes who managed their fortunes by cable as they played euchre on the piazzas along Broadway. Such men always had an eye out for the next sparkling protégée they might champion, he dropped his voice to inform her. For was it not common knowledge that Jerome had named his daughter Jennie for Jenny Lind, the Swedish Nightingale herself?

As if men who paid their attentions to opera divas were likely to take notice of a tatterdemalion Jones's Wood singer like Katie. Old Mary, the dresser, might have done her best, sprucing up Katie's frock with what ribbons and bits of lace she could scrounge from the ragman, but Katie's freshly decorated bonnet looked more tatty than rakish and the flounce along the hem of her skirt did nothing to hide the fact it had been intended to display her shapely ankles when she danced onstage. Not that the dresses of the fashionable women on Broadway were any less flash—or their rouge and mascara any less obvious. They were just more expensive. Which only confirmed Katie's initial impression that the sins and sinners here were no different from those of Five Points—just better dressed.

Her wariness only increased when she and Sammy arrived at the white colonnaded Congress Spring Pavilion, and Preston Olcott detached himself from the fashionable crush that had been little diminished by the reports of the recent drowning in those health-giving waters. "Good afternoon, Miss O'Grady," he said with a tip of his hat—which she saw had been freshly fitted with a black crepe band.

"Mr. Olcott," she said, forcing a smile worthy of the Irish Rose. "Are we to enjoy the pleasure of your company on our promenade?"

"I regret that propriety forbids such a thing," he said, "as well as my joining Mr. Nunn's regular game tonight—or for some time, I fear. We have had an unexpected death in the family."

"My condolences," Katie said automatically, although she was frankly not in the least bit sorry. Indeed, she had to fight down a decidedly unseemly urge to throw her arms around whoever had been so gracious as to die and rid her of Olcott's unwelcome advances for the foreseeable future.

"As a matter of fact, I'm taking a tremendous risk even being seen talking with you—especially in this place—for the rumors are already swirling about my unfortunate cousin's death." He turned on Sammy with an angry glare. "Rumors about witchcraft and a cursed chest that has claimed its second victim. Of course, no good Christian would believe in such heathenish nonsense, but my fair cousin, alas, suffers from the susceptibility of her sex. And since you were the last man to speak to her during the unfortunate incident, mayhap you can tell me who might have put such fancies into her fragile head?"

Sammy's tongue flicked across his lips. "Now that's just Saratoga for you. Everyone enjoys a good gossip. What does it matter how she came by the rumor? Leave it alone, that's what I say. It will be a nine days' wonder, but eventually people will move on to other tales, and the tragedy will be laid to rest."

"Unfortunately, my cousin is of a sterner mind than most of her sisters, and seems determined not to let that happen. She has taken a mad fancy that her father was killed—and by the Society of the Horseman's Word, no less. She claims the proof is concealed among her father's business papers." Olcott cast Sammy a long, pointed look. "Which, she says, you may have interfered with."

Sammy swallowed hard. "Indeed, the lady did so accuse me on the spot."

"And yet you failed to put her mind at rest."

"I couldn't, sir! The lady, she was… firm-minded."

"Pity you could not be firmer-minded. Or perhaps you were not averse to her finding the proof?"

"Why would I of all people…"

"It makes no matter," Olcott drew a deep breath, controlling his temper. "You'll need to take care of this—as quickly and as quietly as possible."

"Me, sir? This had naught to do with me, I give you my word."

"Which is about as good as the promises your girls whisper in your gamblers' ears to coax them to buy a bottle of bad champagne."

"Sir!" Sammy said. "I would point out that one of those ladies is present!"

"And I would point out this is Saratoga," Olcott said. His eyes sharpened as Katie was too slow to disguise her rising fury. "Still, there are some matters that would be best kept from a lady's ears. Girl! Go fetch us two glasses of water."

As if Katie were naught but a common serving wench. She lifted her head with all the haughtiness Nunn's Irish Rose could muster. "I regret to inform you that I am otherwise engaged," she said, and, ignoring Sammy's startled protest, she opened her parasol with a snap, even if it was sprung out and covered in crochet rather than lace, and strolled away with an insouciance she certainly did not feel.

But Katie didn't go far—just around the back of the colonnaded spring, and into the shelter of a rolling cart where an enterprising farmwife sold more substantial refreshments than the spring's health-giving waters. Katie pretended to take her time examining the baskets of late strawberries and newly-ripened peaches, as she strained to hear Sammy and Olcott's hushed, angry conversation.

"You have failed me, Sammy. You have failed me badly," Olcott said. "You were supposed to discover the contents of that desk without attracting any notice, not frighten the man into his grave."

"It was an accident! I did nothing."

"Yet the man is dead. And his death causes me no end of trouble. For the love of God, this is no time for me to be in mourning. In fact, it's damned inconvenient. I suppose I should be thankful that this is Saratoga and not New York, where men such as Vanderbilt understand that the wheels of commerce do not grind to a halt for the death of one man, but how the deuce am I supposed to put in an appearance in the grandstand next week?"

"I couldn't say, sir. But it was not my fault. A terrible accident, nothing more."

"And as for the contents of the desk?"

"I never saw them. The girl forestalled me before I could open it, I give you my word."

"We've already discussed what your word is worth to me." Olcott shook his head. "Still, perhaps it is best if I explain things simply—in terms you can understand. Consider it a token of my trust. My cousin, Jonathan Adair, was possessed by a singular obsession. Not content with frittering away the family's wealth on amassing an art collection, it was his intention that when he died, what remained of the fortune with which he had been entrusted would found a museum to house it. His monomania nearly cost him his life two years ago, and it certainly cost him his reason. But madmen can be cunning, and it is not impossible that he managed to sign a will bequeathing away the family fortune, despite my having his daughter's assurances to the contrary. So I need you to ascertain whether that desk contains such a will, and if it does, obtain it and destroy it."

"But… that is nothing short of thieving, and I'll have no part of that."

Olcott raised an eyebrow. "Well now, if that is truly the case, you should have thought of it two years ago, should you not have?"

"That was different. Those were Fenians!" Sammy swallowed hard. "There are rumors going around that the man found dead in the spring might have been a Fenian too."

"Then you'd best find out if that is true. As well as what brought him to Saratoga."

"Please, sir. I had no desire to get tangled up in that—then or now."

"And yet many would argue that is exactly where you find yourself. And as I look around, I see no other man who is willing to help you out of your predicament." Olcott's voice hardened. "A wise man trusts his friends, Sammy. An even wiser man knows exactly who those men are."

A long silence. Then Sammy said hoarsely, "There might be some that call Meagher a hero and a patriot, and his Irish Brigade, too, but the Fenians are no different than any other gang when it comes to interference in what they consider their private affairs."

Olcott's voice grew gentle—almost kindly, as if he were talking to a child. And it was a thousand times more frightening than his anger. "You should be far more concerned about what I can do to you. You failed me, Sammy. And now two men are dead—under circumstances that could well involve blackmail along with murder. And I can assure you John Morrissey does not like either in his town—unless it is he himself who is doing it. So find the will for me, Sammy, or prove to me that you have destroyed it." He moved to go, then stopped and turned back. "And by the way, I shall have need of the exclusive use of your club tonight for a meeting. Even Saratoga society would frown on my being seen meeting with my investors in a private parlor at Union Hall so soon after my tragic bereavement."

*****

The sinners that were Preston Olcott's friends were not even better-dressed than old Sammy. Their watch chains were pinchbeck, not gold, and dangled with too many fobs and seals to be quite nice. They may have been drinking port rather than whiskey, but their only interest was in Katie keeping their glasses full. And their hard eyes as they called Preston Olcott to account were no different from those of the Dead Rabbits and the Whyos as they circled a lad they suspected of betraying them in a Five Points alley—even if Olcott's friends wielded fancy words instead of cudgels.

"Your investors are anxious."

"Some have called for a vote of No Confidence."

"At the very least, we want an explanation."

"Another man is dead."

"And this one not some nameless shanty Irishman."

"We want to know why."

But Olcott showed none of the raw fear that men usually displayed when confronted with a mob. "I assure you, gentlemen, the matter has been handled," he said calmly. "Your money remains perfectly safe with me."

But the mob was not to be so easily placated. "Investing in horseflesh is always risking. But investing in a criminal enterprise is a mug's game."

"There are many who would say that investing in Saratoga is itself investing in a criminal enterprise," Olcott replied.

"Be that as it may. We have no desire to be mixed up with murder."

Olcott's lips curved into a smile. "Murder, gentlemen? And who shall we hang? A ghost?"

"Adair wasn't the first. There was a man drowned not a fortnight ago."

"Some said he was an assassin."

"Some say he was Morrissey's man."

"Just as some say he was sent by Morrissey's enemies."

"And others say the fire at the United States Hotel was no accident."

"Quite possibly so. And what of it?" Olcott raised an eyebrow. "Saratoga Springs as John Morrissey dreams of it is a fat goose ripe for the plucking. Of course, men will stop at nothing to win it. Rich men. Ruthless men. But I give you my word, I am the one with the means to emerge victorious." Olcott leaned across the table, suddenly intent. "Listen to me, gentlemen, and listen well. Shares in my stable are shares in much more than blood horses. Shares in my stable are shares in power—the kind of power most men dream about. The kind of power John Morrissey seeks to wield in Saratoga. And the kind of power I, and those who are with me, will wield instead."

They made no effort to lower their voices out of Katie's earshot—as if she were invisible—or even worse, naught but a tavern wench. Well, tavern wenches had ears just like any other woman, and Katie was busy using them as she poured their cursed wine and did her best to stay out of reach of the occasional hand that carelessly reached to squeeze her.

"And do you have any proof to offer of this power you claim—beyond the word of an embezzler and a thief?"

The question was thrown down like a gauntlet, and there was a moment's silence before Olcott nodded. "I see the old rumors are surfacing."

"Jonathan Adair claimed you took advantage of your position as his confidential secretary in order to steal priceless objects from his collection. Do you deny it?"

"On the contrary, I plead guilty as charged," Olcott said. He held up his hands to quell the angry protest that erupted. "If you know who my cousin is, then you should also know that he was a monomaniac. Even worse, he was collector. He scoured the earth and spent a fortune to bring back the most priceless antiquities from around the globe. Price was no object to him. And yet when it came to paying the relative whose fortune he sought to squander in this mad pursuit, he felt I should be grateful to have a roof over my head and food on the table. Can you really blame a man for seeking to right the balance?"

"Blame is not the issue here. Who had better motive to murder Jonathan Adair than you?"

"With a centuries-old curse? Hardly an efficient way to go about the task." Olcott's face hardened. "Although I admit no little satisfaction in seeing my cousin well-served for doing me this wrong. But there are many men who have far better motive than I. Think, if you will about my cousin's collections. Consider what all the objects he has gathered have in common. Why he stopped at nothing to obtain them."

"We have no time for riddles."

"Or fairy tales. Tell us and make us believe you or begone."

Olcott took no notice of the threat. Instead, he held up his fingers in order to enumerate. "Assyrians statues, Egyptian papyri, Greek vases, and medieval chalices. Trojan gold, Hindu idols, and the jade masks of the Maya and Incas. Codices, incunabulae, sarcophagi. A magpie collection acquired without discernment or system. Why?" Olcott lowered his voice. "I will tell you why. All of the objects my cousin collected are said to be objects of power. Objects that were once sacred talismans that protected entire peoples."

The thought was enough to make a superstitious chill run down Katie's spine, but the mob that confronted Olcott was made of sterner stuff.

"And what if your cousin was a madman? What does that matter to us?"

"Do you propose we join him in his insanity?"

"Alas, other men have forestalled us in that particular project." Olcott's mouth curved into a smile. "Other, powerful, wealthy men. For believe me, Jonathan Adair was not alone in this madness. He had a circle of friends who not only share the same ambition, but have put their fortunes in service of his cause."

"To rule the world by magic?"

"To cement the power of our fledgling republic by acquiring the most sacred artifacts of the world's greatest civilizations, and imprisoning them to our country's service in a grand museum in New York City. There, the gods of the great civilizations will be forced to bend the knee to the only true god of America: Mammon. Power and money, gentleman. That is the only god our nation worships."

An angry murmuring silence. And then the nearest man shook his head. "Even supposing this tale was true. Why should we risk ourselves over a rich man's dream to build a museum?"

"Because our knowledge of their plans will allow us to compel their obedience—and persuade them to put their fortunes to… better use."

"How? Do you expect us to believe in the power of some magic artifact?"

Olcott smiled. "Oh, I have something much more important than any magic artifact," he said softly. "I have information. Information that could see them all hanged."

More like information that was locked in Sammy Nunn's office drawer. Katie's hand trembled, spilling some wine, and she had to bite her lip to keep from gasping out loud. Fortunately, the others were too intent on their questions to notice.

"Why should we believe you?"

"How can you not?" Olcott asked with a shrug. "It matters not how or why my cousin died. Clearly someone in Saratoga is desperate to protect something. And I know exactly what it is."

A moment's silence. "What kind of information do you purport to hold over them?" a man at last asked.

"Now that would be telling," Olcott said. "And it's well-known that two men can keep a secret only if one of them is dead."

"So you propose we simply take your word on the matter?"

"I propose you consider the names of the men my cousin was seen meeting with before his unfortunate demise…"

"Van…"

"Jer…"

"*Consider*," Olcott cut them off sharply. "Not mention. And when you are finished considering, I propose you ask yourself why these men would drop everything—to meet with my cousin in person. Surely not over the matter of an upstart stable. Or even the matter of a stolen artifact for their precious museum." Olcott smiled, cat-like. "No, these men are very afraid of the information I possess. And I have every intention of keeping them so."

Slowly, the accusation in the other men's eyes turned to speculation. "Even if 'tis true, 'tis a dangerous game you're playing," one muttered.

"Then I'd best needs win it, should I not?" Olcott spread his hands. "But any man who has no stomach for the fight is welcome to leave. I need take no pains against a deserter betraying us, for I can assure you, gentlemen, my cousin's friends will be far more ruthless in protecting their secrets than I could ever be. Simply leave now, and let it be quits between us."

He paused, then went on, "But as for those who would run the risk to reap the rewards, I promise you power beyond your wildest imaginings. Now, is there any man here who would like to cash out of their interest in my barn right now?"

11

The next day passed in a merciful blur of activity. Overwhelmed as she was by anxiety, uncertainty, and yes, sadness, Rose was forced to allow that making arrangements for her father to be transported back to New York City, in order to be properly interred in the family vault, was actually a far simpler task than the constant cajoling, hiding, and lying that had been her life with her living, complaining father for the past two years. In fact, she found composing the myriad letters and cables to everyone from her father's men of business to the Rector who would bury him, a welcome relief from what had felt like an endlessly spun web of secrets and evasions.

Even Cousin Preston had proved himself remarkably considerate, withdrawing once again to his club for the evening, and leaving Rose with no more upsetting company than Cousin Patricia, whose anxious twittering Rose had learned to ignore long ago. It was, Rose was certain, the calm before the storm, but she forced herself to accept whatever small grace she had been afforded. Trouble would come of its own accord quickly enough.

And so it did, in the form of Cousin Preston's courteous offer to meet Bridie at the railroad station and personally drive her to the Union Hotel. But no sooner had Rose accepted his offer and addressed herself to signing the first of that morning's stack of cables, than an anxious lad tapped on the door to their suite, with an urgent message from the desk. "The gentlemen said that you were on no account to be disturbed," the lad told her. "But the manager was uncertain, seeing as you gave your instructions so specific-like."

Gentlemen? What instructions? Snatching up the skirts of the grey walking dress that was as close to proper mourning as she could come on such short notice, Rose hurried down to the lobby after the lad.

And saw that instead of driving down to the train station to meet Bridie as he had promised, Cousin Preston was alternately threatening and cajoling,

The Horseman's Word

not the major-domo, but one of the Leland brothers, one of the Union Hotel's new proprietors. And standing by Cousin Preston, as if as his second, was the odious Dr. Mitchell.

"I insist you relinquish my unfortunate cousin's belongings immediately," Cousin Preston's repeated demand rang above the voices of the guests who were convening in a flurry of parasols and walking sticks for the morning's stroll down Broadway to take the waters.

"But his daughter's instructions were quite exact," Mr. Leland protested.

"Miss Adair is in no condition to give anyone instructions."

How *dare* he? First her father and now her? In her eagerness to give Mr. Leland *ample* opportunity to judge for himself, Rose flew off the grand staircase and pressed herself through the throng with a singularly unladylike haste, the lad hastily murmuring her excuses in her wake.

"The young lady has sustained a severe shock," Dr. Mitchell said. "There is more than a little reason to fear for her wits in my considered medical opinion."

"In the meantime, I am Miss Adair's guardian," Cousin Preston said. "Surely you must see that my wishes must supersede hers—even were her nerves not in such a delicate state…"

"My nerves will be decidedly improved if I did not have to worry about you lying to me!" Rose cried, not troubling herself to modulate her tone. "Why are you not on the way to the railway station as you promised?"

Saratoga took pride in being impervious to scandal, but a good piece of gossip was just that. Several of the well-dressed guests about to make their exit instead turned their heads, suddenly evincing no interest in embarking on their morning promenade.

Cousin Preston did what he could to force a fatherly smile. "My dear cousin, there is of course ample time before the train arrives. I merely sought to spare you from an unpleasant task when I found myself with a few moments leisure."

"By 'unpleasant task,' I am forced to assume you mean carrying out my father's last wishes?" she snapped. "Devoted cousin that you are, I would scarcely think your nerves would be any more up to the task than mine, so may I suggest instead that you spare us both, and wait for my father's lawyers to examine his belongings, for surely their extensive professional acquaintance with such matters has inured them against any such childish fits of the vapors."

Cousin Preston's face hardened. "Sarcasm does not become you."

"Then perhaps you should withdraw yourself from your role as my guardian if you find my presence so uncongenial."

"I will not have it said that I allowed my personal feelings to interfere with my duty to the family."

"And I would suggest that you assume no duties until my father's lawyer informs you as to what they are."

Mr. Leland glanced back and forth between them with ill-concealed anxiety. For here in Saratoga, men were certainly known to call one another out in *affaires d'honneur*. And wives were sometimes summarily dispatched to rest cures, just as sons and heirs were packed off to the Continent with unseemly haste. But there was a difference between whispering of such dramas and playing them in full dramatic detail beneath the great rotunda of the Union Hall lobby, where, God forbid, they might scare the horses.

"Now, Miss Adair!" the odious doctor leapt into the fray. "I have warned you against overexerting yourself!"

"I am not over-exerted! I am angry!"

"Which is why I must insist you return to your room before you lapse insensate just as your father did. And I must insist that you confine yourself to your room until I decide otherwise."

"Insist. Confine. Do you suggest I am a prisoner here?" she demanded.

"A patient, not a prisoner." The doctor's face grew grim. "But in my professional medical opinion, I must pronounce myself extremely concerned. Such paranoid accusations about those who have your best interests at heart are scarcely healthy."

"I think I would prefer to consult my own physician on this matter."

"My poor child, you have no idea what you might prefer. I must insist that you return to your room and leave these matters to us—lest I be forced to hire a nursing sister to enforce my instructions."

Rose's jaw set. "I will not go upstairs until I have Mr. Leland's assurance that the desk will remain locked in the hotel safe until my father's lawyer arrives to open it."

"I'm afraid you are in no condition to make such decisions."

"And I'm afraid that I have no intention of taking your word on that matter..."

"This argument is only counterproductive. You are ill. You must take rest. If you will not go willingly, I will be forced to call for attendants...!"

The Horseman's Word

Mr. Leland suppressed a sharp gasp, and Rose froze, suddenly unsure of herself. The justice of her position was inarguable, but was it proof against Mr. Leland's more than reasonable fears that his elegant lobby might prove the scene of the capture of a woman escaped from…

A madhouse?

Or perhaps even the cottage to which they had planned to confine her father? Was it still available, with a contingent of nursing sisters to replace the hulking porters—discreetly located just beyond the side door?

"Come, my dear cousin," Cousin Preston said, reaching to take her arm. "Trust us to know what is best for you."

"By all that's holy, man! I will thank you to unhand my wife."

For a fleeting moment, Rose could only believe the doctor was right and her nerves had at last given way beneath the strain, for the haughty English accent that echoed all the way to the top of the lobby's great rotunda, could not have shocked her more if her father had risen from the dead to rescue her. But the aristocratic command that froze even the most hardened of racegoers, was immediately belied by the sight of Lane Fallon limping through the crush, his worn officer's coat even shabbier in the clear light of morning than in the shadows of Congress Spring.

Cousin Preston's face set with fury, and his grip tightened on Rose's arm as he turned on the hapless Leland. "What kind of establishment is this that it allows tramps and beggars to march right in through the front door? I demand you remove him immediately. My cousin is in no state to find herself harassed by such types along with everything else."

"A man can scarcely be accused of harassing his own wife," Fallon protested, his eyes alight with reckless energy. "But I fear I cannot say the same for a man who proposes to manhandle a female under his protection."

Own wife? What on earth did he mean?

What did it matter? Liar, traitor, and thief though he might be, the man was offering her a chance. "Captain Fallon," she said, seizing the opportunity to pull herself from Olcott's grip and offer him her hand. "I'm afraid you have arrived at a very difficult time."

"Of course," Fallon agreed, sobering instantly. "My sincerest condolences on your sad bereavement. However, I must be selfish enough to own that your family's tragedy had at least one happy effect, for it has afforded me the opportunity to announce our relationship openly and honestly. And to think I was about to leave Saratoga on the morrow."

Relationship? What relationship?

"Captain Fallon? Captain Tamerlane Fallon?" Olcott cut in before Rose could even think to answer. His fury mounted visibly as he made a show of inspecting Fallon's shabby clothes and bruised face. "Why yes, I see now that it is you. I must apologize for not recognizing you sooner, but you are altered sadly since the time I knew you as New York City's most famous profiteer."

"Apparently reports of my profitability were somewhat exaggerated," Fallon said with a shrug.

"Apparently." Olcott's eyes hardened. "So is that what brings you to Saratoga? Are you here to recoup your fortunes?"

"What greater fortune can I recoup than my lost bride?" Fallon asked.

"Quite literally, many would argue," Olcott snorted. "So let us have done with this nonsense. There is no question that you and Miss Adair are wed."

"'Twas a clandestine affair, and I admit not to my credit, but I will hear no word of dishonor against the lady," Fallon admitted. "An impulsive idyll in Jones's Wood, a midnight elopement born out of wartime desperation, but I can assure you that Miss Adair would never have consented to grant my fondest wishes without a true and proper wedding."

"You're mad," Olcott dismissed him.

"Well, now that seems to be an accusation that you and your pet medical man have been making a bit free with of as of late, if I dare say so," Fallon said with a dangerous smile. "So, instead, might I propose we frame our discussion in absolutely rational explanation? What else save his daughter's honor could drive Jonathan Adair to risk a dangerous journey to Saratoga that he could only know must be, if not fatal, injurious to his fragile health?"

"Ridiculous. My cousin was well-known to be a monomaniac on the subject of his collection..."

"And yet I'm certain more than one man might be willing to step forward to testify to his launching foul accusations at me last night at the Spring—in terms that could only lead a hot-tempered man to call him out," Fallon went on, nothing but rational, nothing but reasonable. "And I'd be the first to admit, that while his terms were foul, the accusation was not, and so I did not engage in a scene that could not possibly be palatable to a lady whose good regard I cherish. But I warn you that I may not be so circumspect with those who clearly seek to abuse her."

Despite the clear threat in his voice, he made it sound so logical.

Reasonable. So much more plausible than the grim charade Rose had been living out for the past two years.

But plausible lies were Lane Fallon's stock in trade—as she of all people had cause to know. What was he playing at here? He had spoken last night of setting right the wrong he had done her. But why should she believe him? Why should she trust him any more in that matter than in anything else?

As if she had spoken the thought aloud, Fallon turned to her, his gaze sharp with warning. Then he smiled gently and his voice grew as caressing as when she had believed he was nothing but a poor man named Declan Sullivan, whose only fortune was the passion of his dreams, as he said, "Ah, sweet Rosie, I've been seeking you for these two long weary years. Will ye nae now come home with me?"

Well, now, that was laying it on a bit thick. Surely, he did not think to fool these men with his feigned love-making…

Any more than he had teased her and coaxed her and more than once kissed her? She forced herself to push the honeyed words aside and concentrate on the present. Whatever his motives, Fallon was offering her a way to avoid an unpleasant—and possibly losing—battle to wrest back control of her father's belongings, along with her own independence, from Cousin Preston. A husband's authority would supersede that of any real or fictive guardian.

But what did she truly know about the man into whose hands she proposed to deliver that control instead? Nothing beyond the fact that he was the most convincing liar she had ever met…

And that he had already used her cruelly once before.

The doctor found his voice. "Nonsense," he snapped. "This man is nothing but a rank imposter; this whole scene nothing but a scheme to take advantage of a young lady who has tenuous control of her wits at best. He's here to scoop up a fat prize and you'll see nothing more of him once he gains control of her money."

She wasn't certain whether it was the "fat prize" or the "tenuous control of her wits" that made up her mind. She might have no idea what Lane Fallon was playing at—or even what kind of man he really was—but he had said he was here to set things right. And she had no such doubts on either count about Cousin Preston. If nothing else, Lane Fallon was offering her the opportunity to be free of her cousin's clutches while she sorted out this nefarious business of the horse races and whether there might be any connection to her father' death. Once her father's lawyer arrived, it should be simple enough to repudiate Fallon if he persisted in his claim—which her instincts told her he would not. She knew little enough about the man she remembered—and even less about the man he had become—but she believed she knew him well enough to be certain that his coming to her rescue was at worst nothing but a moment's lark, the sort of mad, daring impulse he could never resist, at best, an attempt to put right a wrong he believed he had done her. What she was less certain of was whether she was relieved or disappointed at the thought.

But time enough to answer that question later. She gasped and fluttered her eyelashes, then opened them wide, her entire face alight with what she hoped was newlywed devotion. "My husband! My own true love, returned to me at last! I confess I was beginning to despair of ever seeing you again—not because I ever believed you were the faithless dastard they accused you of being, but out of fear that the curse of the deconsecrated chapel in Jones's Wood, which was the only possible place we could be wed, had claimed you as we were warned."

Fallon raised an eyebrow, and his mouth quirked. "Best not to dwell on the details," he warned her. "Such painful memories might still overwhelm you and cause a relapse."

"And that is precisely my concern as well!" the doctor snapped. "Miss Adair is still in a highly suggestible state—and what more evidence do you need of it than she has bought into your tissue of lies?"

"Perhaps because they are the truth?" Fallon suggested.

"What proof have you of that?" Cousin Preston asked. "Do you have the marriage lines, perhaps?"

"Alas, the only priest we could find who would wed us was a drunken Papist, who disappeared straight back into the bowels of Five Points from where we had managed to unearth him the moment the ceremony was concluded."

"Bad luck seems to dog you," Cousin Preston said with ill-disguised sarcasm.

"But no longer," Fallon said, holding out his hands to Rose. "My bride is restored to me! Come my love, return to my arms at long last."

"Enough! I demand an end to this farce immediately! If you cannot produce your marriage lines, I'm afraid I must insist that you withdraw your claim—and yourself—until you can offer proof…"

Feeling herself possessed by what could only be described as an imp of the perverse, Rose cut off her cousin's diatribe in sudden inspiration. "Oh, but there is one simple form of proof," she said, turning to the doctor. "I refer of course to the proof husbands in the mysterious east provided after their marriage night—often presenting the sheets themselves…"

The doctor's expression when he finally took her meaning was nearly matched by that of her would-be husband, but it was Fallon who was the first to recover himself enough to choke, "Surely you do not propose a medical examination, my love? In your fragile condition?"

"Of course, she does not!" Cousin Preston's voice had ratcheted steadily upward, until he was shouting—his voice echoing three stories upward, past the balconies that were now lined with an avid audience of everyone from porters and chambermaids to millionaires with their wasp-waisted wives and daughters. Self-consciously, Preston lowered his voice. "Such a discussion is not suited to a public place."

"I quite agree," Fallon said smoothly. "May I suggest that if a separate room could be secured for me in the family suite, so that I may reassure myself of my wife's continued safety and well-being without imposing my presence further during this time of mourning, we can sort this matter out to all our satisfaction in private?"

Cousin Preston cast him a long look. "I assume you would demonstrate your disinterest in this matter by insisting you take this room at your own expense?"

"My fortune is her fortune," Fallon acknowledged with an easy smile. "As we so swore when we plighted our troth."

The color that rose on her cousin's face suggested he was about to shout again, but he was a wise enough man to know when he was bested. "Is there somewhere I should send for your baggage?" he asked.

"Alas, all my belongings were lost during the recent war. I have little more than a single spare shirt."

"Another singular misfortune," Cousin Preston said sourly.

Spinning on his heel, he ceded the day with a flurry of muttered instructions to Leland, then stalked up the grand staircase toward their suite.

"Cousin Preston! You seem to have forgotten your promise to meet Mrs. McMann at the station. I believe her train's arrival must be imminent by now," Rose forestalled him sharply, before she turned to Leland, her voice suddenly as haughty as Fallon's when it first rang out across the lobby. "In the meantime, my husband and I need to avail ourselves of one of your private parlors. We clearly have much to discuss."

Obviously relieved at any clear way to remove them from the lobby, Leland hastened to show them to one of the many luxurious parlors the hotel provided so that business, as well as not a few high-stakes card games, were conducted with utmost discretion—closing the heavy oak doors behind them with a haste that suggested he might have preferred to lock them inside.

As Leland's footsteps receded, Fallon studied Rose with wary humor. "A medical exam?" he said. "What would you have done if the doctor had insisted?"

"A drunken Papist vanished with our marriage lines?" she retorted.

"Who else would consent to conduct a midnight wedding in a deconsecrated chapel?" The amused glint in his eyes deepened. "And would you not say the words 'faithless dastard' were a trifle harsh?"

"I never claimed to believe that!"

Abruptly, he sobered. "And there would be many who would ask, why should you not? But truly, Miss Adair, I confess I had hoped you would have a better opinion of me. I told you I was here to right the wrong I'd done you, and by whatever gods rule this earth, holy or unholy, I will do so."

He had hoped she would have a better opinion of him? Why should she? And what were these wrongs he spoke so passionately of righting?

She drew a careful breath. "You once said you would explain yourself. May I suggest that now might prove an excellent time. What really happened that night? Why did you lie to me about who you really were? What were your dealings with my father?" She had been fighting to compose herself, but once the angry questions began to pour out, there was no stopping them. "Were you truly an English spy? Or merely a fortune hunter who sought only to use me?"

Her voice cracked on the last words, and Fallon's face set with such weariness that for a moment she could only wonder why she was putting her life in this…madman's hands. Then he smiled, and his lean features lit with the indescribable charm that had made her fancy herself in love with him in the first place. "Being as we have both just committed ourselves to the notion of a secret elopement followed by a tragic separation on the winds of war," he said, "I think we'd best save our attention for that particular story for the moment. For it does seem a bit pointless to muddy the waters with other explanations at this juncture, would you not agree?"

12

It did not take long for the rumors of a scandal that was shocking even by Saratoga's standards to reach Little Dublin, for, although it was railroad jobs that had brought the Irish north in the first place, and railroad wages that had paid for the steeple on the Church of St. Peter, these days more men preferred to work in the hotels or at the racetrack, which kept them closer to home. But the people of Little Dublin were little wont to repeat the stories about a midnight elopement and a fabled collector struck down in his prime by a smuggled treasure stolen from a pagan shrine, for there was already enough suspicion swirling about the strange witchcraft practiced by John Costigan's papists. Still, the tale reached Sullivan's ears soon enough, and its meaning was as unmistakable as the charm that had been left for him at the bar. Matters had not been settled back there at the Spring. Trouble still dogged him, demanding the debt that was still owed be paid. Not to the goddess he had offended; she had a greedy enough taste for blood, and the deaths of a few Americans in New York City would not concern her overmuch. No, this was trouble of a very human kind. Trouble that already brought down a price on Sullivan's head and blood on his hands. Trouble that had not in the least been dissuaded by the none-too-gentle persuasion Sullivan had administered back at the Spring.

Trouble that stepped through the door of the inn, as Sullivan was mopping up the remains of his dinner, in the form of a compact dark man in an impeccable suit who paused in the doorway to remove his neatly brushed derby, before he walked straight over to Sullivan's table.

"Mr. Sullivan," the man said. "My name is Cole Washington III. May I join you?"

A wary silence descended over the inn, where moments earlier fiddle music had spilled out into the cool Saratoga evening. The riots that had left no New Yorker immune—not even rich men like Leonard Jerome, who, legend had it, was forced to defend the offices of his *New York Times* with a Gatling gun—had not reached north to Saratoga. There was money enough and work enough to go around, the two groups circled each other with careful respect, maintaining an unspoken truce of two peoples who had learned early that safety came in sticking with their own. The Irish lived in Little Dublin. The other waiters, cooks, and riders that served the great hotels and the horsemen, lived in their own neatly tended cottages on Washington Street, in such peace and prosperity could almost make one forget that not that long ago a local fiddler named Solomon Northup had been kidnapped and endured twelve years as a slave before his distraught family could finally persuade the government of New York to secure his release.

"It's a free country," Sullivan said.

"So they like to say," Cole agreed.

The other drinkers decided that a brawl was not imminent and turned back to their whiskey, allowing the two men to discuss their business in peace. This was Saratoga, after all, and horses and the gambling that officially never took place here made plenty of stranger bedfellows than those too.

Sullivan eyed the other man curiously. It had long been said that if there was anyone that could rival an Irish lad's way with a horse, it was those that came up from the South. But Sullivan had no personal experience of those horsemen beyond a series of names like Abe and Billy and Dick, whose lineage was more poorly documented than the horses they rode. For there was little reason for Southern horsemen to travel north and risk their slaves bolting to freedom when there was plenty of rich racing down in Metairie. But in the wake of the war, the numbers of those riders were rapidly swelling and names like Hawkins and One-eyed Sewell were routinely appearing in the bookmakers' notebooks, often outriding even such legendary Irish lads as Gilpatrick himself.

Washington studied him in return, then said, as if coming to some conclusion, "I'll have you know I don't much like Irishmen."

Sullivan raised an eyebrow. "Well, that's your prerogative, and there'd be those who would say you had every reason, but with respect, this might not be the best place to announce that fact."

"I am telling you so that you understand how serious I am."

"About?" Sullivan sighed, before his mouth twisted with unwilling humor. "No, wait. I'm said to have the Sight. Allow me to hazard a guess. You seek a horsewhisperer."

A moment's pause, before Washington said, "Actually, I am looking for an entire society of such men. I believe it calls itself the Society of the Horseman's Word." He eyed Sullivan narrowly. "There have been others before me?"

"There are always others," Sullivan said. He pushed aside his plate. "To what end do you seek such a Society? Do you believe joining them would further your career here in Saratoga?"

"I've retired from racing. But even if I had not, I can assure you that I do not need, nor have never needed, the help of a friendly society in winning a horse race."

Sullivan eyed him narrowly. "Then why are you here?"

"My search for the Society led me to the home of Jonathan Adair in New York City, tracing a rumor that this Society nearly cost him his life two years ago. Now, I have followed the Society's trail to Saratoga, only to discover that Jonathan Adair has died—suddenly and shockingly, it is said."

"Killed by a horsewhisperer?" Sullivan asked, with an ironic disbelief he did not entirely feel. The memory of those terrible last days in New York, when he watched the life he had fought so hard to build shatter into the howls of the mob and the screams of dying men, was still too fresh. Then had come the tramp of boots and the ratcheting of arms, as Pinkertons, police, and the militia had spread throughout Five Points, throughout Jones's Wood, throughout the farms of Fordham, and anywhere else the Irish could be found, searching out men with Fenian sympathies and a way with a horse, and appeaching them of sedition and treason.

"The legends have it that the Society would kill those who betray its secrets," Washington said. "And, while Mr. Adair could be accused of no such indiscretion—indeed, the memory of that tragic night was such that he was too agitated to speak of it at all—his daughter was kind enough to promise to discover what answers she could. I would not like to think that I have unwittingly put in her in any sort of danger."

Sullivan drank off the last of his ale. "So you're the one stirring up trouble."

Washington shook his head. "Not I. I have only just arrived in town."

"Then if you have an ounce of common sense you will turn around and leave."

"I cannot," Washington said. "I have no choice."

Sullivan's jaw set as once more the screams of two years ago rose to his ears. He had tried his best. He had run out onto the street like one of the

Wild Men of yore, pleading with the beasts when men turned a deaf ear, begging the horses, the goddess' own, just as he was meant to be, that they wanted no part in this carnage… "There is always a choice."

"Maybe for your people," Cole said. "The majority of mine have very little experience of having any choice at all."

A pause before Sullivan conceded the justice of the point. "So what do you want from me?"

"I want names, Mr. Sullivan. Names of those who belong to the Society of the Horseman's Word."

Sullivan's face set. "I'm sorry," he said. "But I can tell you nothing beyond the fact that they are not people who will thank you for penetrating their secrets."

Cole remained unimpressed. "Then you do have experience of these people."

"Jonathan Adair is dead. Should that not be experience enough for anyone?"

"And if I care nothing for such threats?"

Sullivan's patience with such fencing, tenuous at best, vaporized. "Why?" he demanded. "What could possibly be so important to you that you would sacrifice the rest of your life to such a lost cause?"

Another long pause. Then Cole said quietly, "A woman."

Sullivan shut his eyes. "When is it ever not?"

"This woman worked at the Colored Orphans' Asylum. She perished when your kind decided to burn it to the ground…"

"'Twas not my kind chose to burn it!" Sullivan cut himself off with a quick shake of his head. "Even if it were, what do you seek? Revenge?"

"I seek justice."

"Why?" Sullivan sighed. "Why waste the rest of your life on no better purpose than seeing a bunch of ignorant Irishmen hanged? Half of them have probably perished buying your freedom already."

"I have already admitted I dislike Irishmen," Washington said, his voice carefully level. "But no, those are not the ones I seek to bring to justice."

"Then who?"

"It is said that there were those who wanted the riots to happen. It was said that they were caused by agitators who preached the riots in taverns and streets. And these agitators were not simply disgruntled Irishmen in fear for their lives. These agitators had networks."

Sullivan's face flattened. "Such as the Society of the Horseman's Word?"

"Most likely they were not the only one. But they are the only one whose name I know."

"Why would they do such a thing? What end would it serve?"

"Not their own ends, to be sure. Such men were catspaws every bit as much as the men that killed the woman I loved. All of them the unwitting pawns of men that were as capable of manipulating a friendly society as they did worldwide markets." Cole paused to control his voice, which had suddenly begun to tremble with anger, before he went on, "It is said there were more than a few in New York that were sympathetic to the Confederate cause, who had invested their fortunes in cotton. Those who would have not been dismayed to see the unpleasantness between the states resolved in the South's favor. Men who proposed on more than one occasion that New York City declare itself a sovereign state and remain neutral in the War Between the States. Men who had made their money in cotton. Rich men. Powerful men. Men who did not in the least mind seeing the Union army distracted from fighting Lee's army and marching to save Manhattan instead. Men who not only believed the draft riots would further their ends, but had the power to make them happen. Men who were not in the least displeased when the Irish finally had enough common sense to ask themselves why they had fled their own war only to fight in another man's and rose against the Draft."

Sullivan just stared at the man's calm face, which had not changed a jot as he had spoken, trying to decide whether he was speaking to a madman or a hero as great as any whose tales had been spun to him beside the fire. Then again, had not all the greatest Irish champions gone mad at one point or another? Why should any other race find themselves more fortunate?

"You are suggesting the Irish conspired with the cotton kings to betray New York to Lee?" he asked.

"Poor men don't have time to conspire," Washington said with a shake of his head. "It is the rich men who used them I seek."

"And you propose to bring such men to justice? With what? Your talent for winning horse races?"

"If not me, who?"

Sullivan drew a long breath as he strove to remember the days when he had been this determined, this certain, this convinced. But there had never been such a day, for he had never been such a man. Even when he had mustered the rare courage to turn his back on his father and all the easy privilege his birth might have bought him, his only object had been to flee, not to right the cruel injustice that had been done to those he should have avenged.

"It's a fool's quest," he said. His face darkened. "And if you will not take my word for it, allow me to offer you a word of warning. Perhaps you have heard the famous story of Commodore Vanderbilt's cable to those who tried to seize control of one of his enterprises while they thought him safely occupied in Europe: Gentlemen, You have undertaken to cheat me. I will not sue, for the law takes too long. I will ruin you. Sincerely yours…

"And as for Morrissey…" A smile played around Sullivan's mouth as he warmed to his theme. "I assume you are aware of how he got the nickname Old Smoke. But if you are not, it came from a grudge match with a Tammany Hall enforcer named Tom McCann. McCann had Morrissey cornered—pressed back against a coal stove that seared his flesh. Any sensible man would have given up. But not Morrissey. No, Morrissey fought his way back, then proceeded to beat McCann senseless—the whole time his flesh burning so badly, the onlookers could see the smoke rising from his back while he fought.

"Those are the men you seek to threaten, Mr. Washington. And those are the kind of men I would propose any sane man should not."

"Perhaps," Cole said, "you'll do me the courtesy of allowing me to judge for myself."

Sullivan's mouth twisted as he once more breathed the scent of blood, once more heard the screams of dying men—only to have their agony drowned out by the whispered croak of a dying woman spelling out the curse that had driven him from every home he had hoped to have known. "Or perhaps you would do me the courtesy of believing I know whereof I speak and take a lesson from the Irish who have sought to rid themselves of the yoke of English oppression since before this land was even discovered. The recent war has at least bought you freedom from the men who enslaved you, while Ireland remains crushed beneath the heel of her overlords' boot. So may I suggest that you be content with what you have, rather than emulating the poor doomed madmen who have sacrificed their lives and sanity in the name of Eire. For how has she ever rewarded their efforts? With famine and pestilence, nought more."

Cole studied Sullivan, and for a brief, superstitious moment, Sullivan could believe Cole was staring straight into his soul. "Do you consider such men fools? Do you truly value freedom so lightly?"

The Horseman's Word

"What is freedom beyond a full belly and a warm bed? If it were up to me, I'd wager there is nothing more for which a man should reach."

Washington drew a deep breath. "You offer me platitudes and cheap cynicism, Mr. Sullivan," he said. "I would far prefer names."

Sullivan took a moment, then raised a shoulder in concession. The man would not go away until he had gotten what he came for. Sullivan preferred to finish what little was left of his dinner in peace.

"I give you my word of honor that the Society of the Horseman's Word had nothing to do with either any Fenian gangs smuggling treasures out of Ireland or any conspiracies to deliver New York City to the Confederacy. And if you would seek further proof, rather than simply accepting my word, I suggest you address your questions to a man named Lane Fallon. He is just recently arrived in Saratoga Springs—to what purpose, I do not know, although I would suggest that it is most likely something other than taking the waters. But I never knew him to show up anywhere without trouble following right behind. The correct form of address, by the way, is 'The Honorable,' but I would warn you not to take it as descriptive."

"I rarely do."

Sullivan paused to draw a deep breath. He owed Lane Fallon nothing—except perhaps a second, more effective, beating. But Sammy was different. Sammy was one of his own, even if he had remained deaf to Sullivan's warnings. Maybe the voice of this quiet, determined man would penetrate where Sullivan's could not.

"There's also a man called Sammy Nunn. He runs a gambling club down near the railroad track, and many say his backers might be the kind of men you seek," Sullivan finally said heavily.

Another disconcertingly penetrating gaze from Cole. "A friend?"

"A man I have already tried to talk sense into, to no avail. Perhaps you will be more fortunate."

"I understand. And I give you my word it is the chess masters I seek to destroy, not their pawns." Cole got up from the table, replaced his hat, and touched his fingers to the brim briefly before he turned for the door. "Thank you, Mr. Sullivan."

"Mr. Washington!" Sullivan's voice rang harshly after him.

"Yes?"

"I may have given you names, but my opinion has not changed. Give up this mad quest. Forget about this. The past is the past. Put it behind you.

Start over again."

Cole favored him with a long look. "Is that advice you would take yourself? Would you prefer to simply forget about the past? Everything that made you what you are and brought you here today?"

Sullivan's face grew bleak as he heard once more the screams of the horses, and beyond them, the screams of the men dying beneath their feet. "If I could, in an instant."

A pause, then Cole said, "Then you have my sincere sympathy."

"I don't need your sympathy," Sullivan said. "I need you to walk away from this fight. It's taken too many lives already. It's not worth it."

Another long look from Cole. And then he said, "Maybe for a man in your position. But for a man in mine, it has to be."

13

It had long been said that Lane Fallon could talk himself out of anything—far, far beyond a mere threatened date with the hangman. It had equally often been said that he could talk himself into anything, especially when it came to the ladies. But right now, Lane reflected as he gazed unhappily at the woman he had just claimed as a bride, he had talked himself into a scrape that he doubted that even the Prince of Lies, who many claimed was his true father, could talk his way out of. Explain himself to Rose Adair? He could scarcely explain Declan Sullivan to himself—at least not without blushing.

For what was Declan Sullivan but the name of a half-remembered brother, whispered in a hurried plea on the eve of Lane's departure by a father most would have said was incapable of begging? Find Declan Sullivan. Find him and tell me what became of him. Assuming his half-brother's name when he had arrived in New York City had been naught but a moment's impulse, nothing more than one more example of Lane's wretched sense of humor, exactly as he had said…

No, that was a lie as well. And if there was any truth to the vows he regularly breathed that he had learned a valuable lesson from this episode and was intent on giving up lying forever, what better place to start with than ceasing to lie to himself? Assuming his half-brother's name had been more than a matter of convenience or even a jape. It was an obscure desire to… what?… *be?*… the son that had brought a flicker of emotion to the White Wolf's fathomless eyes.

The motives that led to this disaster with Rose Adair were equally murky. It had been natural for a rogue and renegade such as Lane had purported to be, to amuse himself by flirting with the daughter of the house—a passing amusement for both of them, a delicate bit of shading to the sketch of

Fenian he was impersonating. How was he to know that Rose Adair would fall in love with Declan Sullivan.

Or that Lane Fallon would fall in love with Rose Adair.

Fool that he was, he had never seen it coming. She was not at all the kind of woman he had fancied would lead him to perdition. Sweet-faced and pretty, she reminded him of the vicar's daughter from whom he had stolen his first kiss at the annual Church fete. Her simple dresses and softly gathered dark hair could have stepped straight out of a rectory or even a school room—for there was more than a hint of the bookish about her. What he could never have predicted was how that quiet containment could have inflamed him: The calm competence with which she managed her obsessed, ill-tempered father, along with her wastrel cousin and his silly mother. The way she had not so much as batted an eyelash when her father bade her explain to the Ladies' Aid Society the decidedly improper tray of fetishes collected by the Rector of Trinity Church during his mission to the mysterious east, but had simply pointed out the similarity of the knots to those tied by anglers, and had diverted the discussion to the joys of salmon fishing on the River Tweed. And when, on their first trip to Jones's Wood, a man in his cups had offered to buy her straight off Lane's arm like the most common of trollops, she had smiled and declined with about as much passion as if she had been refusing a second profiterole at tea.

From that moment on, Declan Sullivan's entire purpose in life had become shattering that delicious reserve, although, once again, Lane Fallon could not have told you exactly how it had started. An idle speculation, at first, about what it would be like to see that wall crumble and watch her fall head over heels in love with a highwayman or pirate—or maybe a passionate, poetic Irish patriot, torn from the pages of a romance from the Minerva Press. It quickly became a challenge, and soon Declan Sullivan was devoting more of his time and energy to winning the heart of Rose Adair than to unmasking any Fenian conspiracies. Their second night in Jones's Wood raised it to the level of an obsession—no, give thing their right names: raised to the level of raw desire, fanned to a hopeless heat by the unexpected ardor with which she had returned his first kiss.

A *hopeless* heat, he reminded himself, for he had not truly believed he would possess her even then. No, it was not until that night when she had confronted him with an antique dueling pistol and commanded him to save his life, that he had truly seen her as his soulmate, a fiery spirit as reckless and daring as his own, who could threaten to shoot a man as easily as she had just woven the tales of the old pirate Ready-Money Provoost haunting the family crypt in Jones' Wood into the deconsecrated chapel where they were supposed to have been wed by a drunken priest. And as for the way she had coolly bluffed them with her proposed medical exam…

Her eyes were equally cool now, as she appraised him, taking in with painful lack of comment everything from the patched elbows of his coat to his cuffs that had been turned so many times the laundress could no longer stitch them. And suddenly Lane was uncomfortably aware that she was not about to accept any further prevarication, no matter how artfully suggested.

"Alas, I fear the time is come where we must muddy the waters with explanations, unwelcome or inconvenient though they may be," she said, as firmly as if she were questioning several items on a tradesman's bill, rather than discussing her father's assassination and a midnight elopement. "But perhaps it would be easiest if we approach this tangle slowly. So why do we not start with a relatively simple question. What exactly is so important about that chest? Or perhaps I should rephrase. What tale did you spin my father that caused him to covet that chest?"

The truth stung, as she had clearly meant it to. Just as any further truths were likely to hurt only worse. So he might as well accept the small kindness she offered by broaching the simple questions first. "It was not the chest itself," he corrected her. "It was never about the chest. It was what the chest was supposed to contain."

She frowned, puzzled. "You refer to the Greek fire?"

"I refer to the remains of a bridle decorated with silver bells and sea shells, that was dug up in a barrow grave near a shrine that was said to be sacred to the horse goddess Epona." Closing his eyes, he allowed the words to take over, riding on their own energy and sparing him from calculating any further lies or evasions for the moment. "Some said it was ancient, as old as the first Invasion of the Tuatha de Danaan as they rode over nine waves to claim Eire as their own. Some said it dated even before that to the first men, the dark men, the Fir Bolg. Others pointed to the workmanship on the chest, and claimed it was of Phoenician origin, brought to Ireland by those ancient sailors of myth.

"Still others pointed to the fact that the leather of the bridle was still miraculously soft and supple, and suggested even more legendary origins, claiming that it was the bridle of Splendid Mane, the prized mount given by the god of the sea and horses, Manaanan mac Lir, to his foster son, Lugh Macnia, Lug, the warrior-hero, Lugh Lonnbeimnech, Lug the fierce-striker. It is said that the bridle can cause the image of a worker of evil magic to appear beneath the surface of water. Still others say that when brought to the field of a battle where the fate of an entire people lie at stake, it will cause Lugh to rise as he did once in the form of Cu Chulainn, the greatest hero Ireland has ever known…"

His voice trailed off under the force of Rose's gaze, at once incredulous and amused. "And you would have me to believe you talked General Wool out of hanging you with a tale like that?" she demanded. "I of all people am aware you have a quick tongue, but that strains credulity…"

He did what he could to tamp the flush that began to burn his cheeks. "Oh, the bridle is real enough, and its tale is scarcely my doing. The thing has been in the family for years, ever since the first Fallons came to Ireland with John Lackland. Cursed of course, and with it our family, as my old nurse never failed to tell me since I was in my cradle." He met her eye, willing himself to answer the more difficult part of the question. "My own… embroidery on the story had nothing to do with the bridle itself, but rather the manner in which it reached America. A conspiracy of Fenians designed to expose a cabal of wealthy men who were amassing a collection of unholy objects in order to consolidate their power over their fledgling democracy—and, after it, the world."

"You refer to my father and his friends?" she asked, sounding like nothing so much as if she were considering placing them on a guest list.

"Yes," he said, striving, and failing, to match her tone.

"And as for the Fenians involved in the conspiracy, I assume you are referring to the Society of the Horseman's Word?"

Was he? Was he really? He of all people should know the answer to that—for the Society had been his creation in the first place, a tissue of lies cobbled together from a Scottish friendly society and tales of Horse-witchers, with just enough connection to the goddess Epona to whet Adair's interest, and just enough horrifying details to distract anyone from the darker reasons he had come to New York. But for the first time in his life, he wasn't sure how to sort out the lies from the truth any more. So he simply plunged to the heart of the matter, as if he were diving into an icy lake or ripping away a dried bandage.

"I did not lie when I said I was an English spy. I was sent to New York by Her Majesty's Government to uncover what I could about a network of Fenian smugglers selling stolen goods to American buyers. Unfortunately, I stumbled into something far worse. No sooner had I established my *bona fides*, than I was approached by those who wished to launch a Fenian conspiracy against Manhattan. In aid of the Confederacy."

"Now we come to the Greek fire."

He nodded. "It was meant to be one of many explosions—none of them fatal or harmful in themselves. They were merely intended to distract the police while the Confederacy freed the prisoners of war held nearby in order to seize the treasury and armory of New York City."

Her face lit with immediate understanding. "As they so nearly succeeded in doing just this past year?"

"That was a last ploy by a few desperate men," Lane said, with a shake of his head. "The war was lost by then. But had the same plan succeeded before the victory at Gettysburg…"

"But it did not," she said, and he told himself it was his imagination that she seemed to sound approving. "Was that your doing?"

And this was where it grew tricky. She seemed willing enough to forget that the conspiracy in which he played a part nearly cost her father his life, but it was another thing altogether to know how a lady would react to the news that he had been scheming to deliver her father to the hangman. "I went along with their plans to get names, nothing more. I give you my word on that. I was meant to deliver them to the Americans that night…"

"You mean, the names you gave me to take to Jones's Wood," she said. "To entrust to Sammy Nunn in the name of the Society…"

She broke off with a gasp.

"Sammy Nunn! That was his name. Sammy Nunn. I… I couldn't think of why I thought I knew him or recognized the name—in all the confusion, I couldn't manage to think of anything at all, really. But Sammy Nunn was there."

"Sammy Nunn was where?"

"At the hotel, when my father met with his unfortunate accident." She met Lane's eyes. "He was holding my father's desk. And I believe he had just tried to open it."

"Do you think he was trying to steal it? For whom?"

Already, she was on her feet and moving for a bell to summon a porter. "I think that is a question that would be best posed to Mr. Nunn," she said.

"And in the interest of avoiding another scene in the lobby, I think we'd be best on our way before my cousins return."

*****

She was right, of course. Lane was beginning to wonder if there was an occasion when Rose Adair would not turn out to be right. But he would very much have preferred that his initial interview with Sammy Nunn be conducted in private, so he might ascertain how much the old rogue might remember—or have known in the first place. But the wretched luck that had dogged Lane Fallon for the past two years was still holding true to form—so true that he might have been willing to concede that the damned bridle truly had been cursed—and he and his family along with it. For no sooner had they slipped out a side door to discreetly join the throng of gaily dressed people who paraded down Broadway, than true disaster struck in the form of an elegantly dressed woman strolling with her equally impeccable son. Foreigners were hardly unusual in Saratoga, but Cara Butraigo and her son Oscar would stand out in any crowd. Fluent in half-a-dozen languages, Cara was a well-known patron of the arts, as well as the hostess of one of the most brilliant peripatetic salons on the Continent—and a valuable source of information on anything from the latest intrigues at the Hapsburg Court to the more arcane provisions of several recent naval treaties. Her son, Oscar, had established his reputation as both a dealer in antiquities and an art collector—as well as a valuable source of information himself—before he had ever left Oxford, over the authenticity of a score of antique maps in the Vatican archives said to have been drawn by the Lost Sea Kings. One thing was certain: if the Butraigos were in Saratoga, it was not for the racing—or the waters.

It was too much to hope he might slip by unnoticed by the keen eyes of a mother and son who could spot a master criminal as easily as a forged Old Master. Lane put the best face on it he could. But accustomed as they were to avoiding awkward conversations that might well topple governments, both mother and son contrived not to notice his shabby clothes, as they impeccably balanced their felicitations with their condolences upon being introduced to the recently-bereaved Rose as Lane's new wife.

But Cara's eye remained upon Lane, keen as always. "So am I to assume that this happy occasion is what brings your father to Saratoga?"

Or was that a matter for discretion went the unspoken corollary. But Lane was too overwhelmed by this unexpected confirmation of the suspicion that had dogged him ever since the first policeman's punch had cracked his ribs, to formulate something that even resembled an articulate answer. "Oh, you know my father as well as I do. He always has his fingers in half a dozen pies at once," he choked, before he managed to seize Rose's elbow and firmly navigate his leave. For the way his luck was running, the White Wolf was probably waiting for him in Sammy Nunn's gaming hell.

*****

By some faint mercy, the White Wolf did not await them in the grimy little gaming hell that was an unsanctioned rival to Dr. Underwood's far more elegant operation at White's. But Lane was hard-pressed not to imagine his father's unblinking green eyes observing him as he escorted Rose into the shabbily furnished receiving room, with its cheap, tinted lithographs of gods and mortals, nymphs and satyrs that decorated the satin-lined walls. This was no fit place for a lady, let alone one recently bereaved.

The door to the parlor slammed open, and Sammy strode in, his Irish already obvious in the high color that suffused his face, as, ignoring Rose, he addressed himself to Lane. "And what do ye think ye be doing here, ye treacherous English bastard? Ye betrayed the Fenians once. Was that nowt enow for you? How dare ye set foot in one of my establishments ever again?"

Which was, in fact, a vital and necessary question that ought to be hashed out between them. But, for better or worse, before Lane could come up with a convincing lie—or even an honest answer to the question, Rose had already risen from her seat on the peeling settee and said, "I beg your pardon, but your anger is completely misdirected. Captain Fallon has merely been so good as to serve as my escort. I am the one who insisted we come here, for I am in search of answers. Chief among my questions are what you were looking for when you opened my father's desk during that unfortunate incident outside our hotel. As well as who might have put you up to such a nefarious task. My Cousin Preston, perhaps? Did he co-opt you as he attempted to do with my chambermaid at the Union Hotel?"

"Now, miss, I'll not stand her and be accused of violating a lady's chamber…"

"Spare me your righteous protests, and simply tell me the truth, for I am in search of information, not justice," she dismissed Nunn's angry reply with a regal wave worthy of the White Wolf. I simply wish to know what you know; I have no interest in turning you over to the Saratoga police force, such as it is. On the other hand, if you feel my cousin has bought your loyalty, I must apprise you of one fact: Whatever fortune my cousin might have offered you is completely in my hands. He cannot pay you. I can. And I seek to know only one thing. What was my cousin in hopes of finding when he set you on his task? My father's will, I can only presume. Am I correct?"

Lane's jaw dropped; Nunn's brow lowered, and for a moment, the veneer of the gentleman disappeared, and he was as hard-headed a thug as any that had swung a set of brass knuckles at Lane in a back alley. And then he nodded slowly and his face set with mean cunning. "Well, be that as it may, miss, and even supposing that you are right, I will be blunt—even at the risk of offending a lady's sensibilities. I'm a businessman. And as a man of business, I am concerned with only two things: Not loyalty or even love of justice. Just profit and loss. You offer to pay me to tell you what I know. But there are those who may pay me equally well to do just the opposite. So I think the question that faces us right now is, how will your offer compare to theirs? Would you care to offer me a specific number?"

Lane shut his eyes wearily. He had dealt with plenty of men of such low cunning in his multiple ventures, just smart enough to fancy they had an eye for the main chance, and just stupid enough to believe they were the only ones who were. Arguably, he was such a man himself. But he loathed dealing with such men—not out of any fear that they would best him, but rather out of a well-founded fear that they would inordinately complicate the proceedings at as much cost to him as to themselves.

"Listen to me, Sammy Nunn. You may like me or hate me. And you certainly have every cause not to trust me," he said, forcing himself to keep his voice carefully level. "But you must take my word, you are playing a dangerous game—a very dangerous game indeed."

Nunn met his eyes with studied insolence—just as every man of his type did, Lane thought with a sigh. "I will do you the courtesy of assuming that is not a threat," he said, "for given your known choice of profession, I can only think that you of all people would understand my position."

14

Olcott was too angry to even bother to steal a squeeze of Katie's waist as he brushed past her and straight into Sammy's office. "I trust," he snarled, "you had every intention of informing me about Lane Fallon's recent visit, and that the only reason I have yet to receive word is that your errand boy was murdered by a cutpurse in a back alley."

"You yourself said you were in mourning," Sammy protested. "I was observing the proprieties."

"By all accounts, my fair cousin was not," Olcott snapped.

"What would you have me do? Bar the door against them? Throw them out of here bodily?"

"I would have had you think to tell me that there was a chance you might be recognized by Miss Adair."

Sammy shut his eyes. "How was I to know the lass would remember? We only met the once, and then for but a minute. It was just a stroke of ill-luck."

"Ill-luck, indeed." Olcott's face set with such cold contempt that Katie resolved right then and there to never find herself in this man's power, even if it meant scrubbing the priest's wretched rooms under the watchful eyes of the cursed teaching sisters. "I gave you a simple task, Sammy. How could you have failed me so miserably?"

"Mayhap because I'm no thief."

Olcott raised an eyebrow. "The contents of your safe would suggest otherwise."

"That was different! What I did was wrong, for sure, but 'twas nowt at all like…"

Olcott waved off Sammy's choked response. "Spare me your excuses. Just tell me, what did he want?"

"It was not so much *he* as *she*," Sammy protested. "The lady was very forceful."

"My *cousin* should not have been allowed to leave her hotel room. She is in a very fragile state of mind—overset by her father's tragic death to the point where she sees ghosts and conspiracies around every corner. And now that scoundrel Fallon has her in his clutches, and is using her as his catspaw."

"To what end?"

"To recover those papers you stole from him." Olcott's face hardened as he turned toward Sammy's safe, which hung open and unsecured. "And I would suggest it is very much in your interest that never happens. It is said he has a rather cruel hand when dealing with those who wrong him."

Sammy swallowed hard. "Then mayhap 'twould be best that I return them and beg his pardon."

A thunderous pause. Then, without so much as the pretense of asking for permission, Olcott pulled the sheaf of papers out of the safe and held it out to Sammy. "Do you know what's in these papers, Sammy? Do you know what this one says? Please, tell me."

Sammy flushed as he pushed the paper aside. "You play a tune for me, and I can play it back, but never could get my head around reading music. Around reading books either. Better you explain to me exactly what it is you mean."

"So I shall. For such ignorance makes your stupidity understandable if not pardonable," Olcott said with a tight smile, as he spread the papers across Sammy's desk. "These papers contain the names of the Fenians who conspired to terrorize New York City with Greek fire two years ago. Strangely, many of those same names appear on the rent rolls here in Saratoga."

Sammy shook his head. "There are no Fenians in Little Dublin," he said hoarsely. "'Tis the very reason we came here."

"Of course there are Fenians here," Olcott snorted. "For what could be more attractive to such a gang than a racetrack? Money comes, money goes. A lucky winner is indistinguishable from a carefully chosen contact. And Morrissey is an Irishman, is he not?"

Sammy paled. "No. That canna be true. Morrissey may have run with the Dead Rabbits once, but now he cares only for himself."

"Stipulated." Olcott nodded with a tight smile, as if Sammy were a pupil that had unexpectedly stumbled upon the correct answer. "And that is why Lane Fallon is here. The man is a well-known English *agent provocateur*. He missed his chance to engineer a Fenian atrocity in New York City, and he does not intend to fail this time…"

"But why? To what end? The war is over."

Olcott laughed. "The war between the states may be over, but believe me when I say, the war for Saratoga has only begun."

"What war? Saratoga runs fast and loose as its horses, yes, but the people who live here live in peace."

Olcott raised an eyebrow. "Do you really believe the United States Hotel burned by accident? Or that the firemen were truly so helpless against the blaze that they simply retreated to watch the conflagration from a safe distance? Or," he added more softly, "that a cursed chest is responsible for a man's death?"

"Adair's death was an act of God! You were there!"

"I was not discussing Adair—although my fair cousin is already spinning fantastical theories in that direction, and it would certainly be in Lane Fallon's interest to keep her doing so. No, I was talking about the man found dead in Congress Spring. The police are closing in on an identification—and it is common knowledge they are about to uncover a Fenian connection."

Sammy shook his head—mulishly, like a punch-drunk boxer. "You canna be right. To what end such a terrible scheme?"

"Why, to spare the gentlemen of the Jockey Club the trouble of rubbing elbows with John Morrissey. Do you really think gentlemen who buy and sell countries as easily as railways would be content to remain beholden to a shanty Irish bare-knuckles fighter?"

Olcott delivered the insult with a casual contempt that sent Katie's temper as red as her hair, but Sammy was past noticing. "But… what does this have to do with Lane Fallon? Why should an Englishman care about such matters?"

"The English care about eliminating the Fenian threat. And the First Families of Saratoga would prefer to deal with English aristocrats rather than the Irish rabble. Only think how quickly both would come to pass if an English agent uncovered a Fenian conspiracy to destroy the First Families of America that propose to be in attendance in the Grandstand when the race season opens." Olcott swept the papers together and tossed them back into the safe. "Mark my words. There will be a raid on Little Dublin. Those papers will be discovered, and a Fenian conspiracy will be exposed, and the Irish will be driven out of Saratoga—along with Morrissey."

"You mean, the Fenians will be driven out…"

"No, I mean, the Irish. Those colored jockeys can ride as well as the Irish, their musicians and waiters can do anything the Irish can do, and for less money, as well." Olcott paused to allow Sammy to absorb his meaning. "Now you can wait and see whether I am right, or you can do something about it."

The pitcher Katie was holding nearly slipped from her fingers, and she only barely managed to recover and mumble an excuse about seeing to the gentlemen's refreshments. For it had cost Katie time and effort enough to assemble the letters on those pages into words and even longer to arrange the words into meaning, but the nuns had taught her well enough that she knew for certain that was not what those papers said at all. In fact, every word Preston Olcott spoke was naught but a bald-faced lie.

*****

The tired, defeated look on Sammy's face when he at last shambled back into the gaming room, looking more like a gambler begging to play on credit than the establishment's proprietor near broke Katie's heart. Oh, Katie was under no illusions what Sammy was, and there might be those who would say he was as bad as Olcott. There might even be those who would say Sammy was worse. But Sammy had been a father to her, even if he had always taken his cut of what she had earned. Impulsively, she caught his arm and said, "I been thinking, Sammy, and what I think is that Saratoga is no place for the likes of us. Let's go back to Jones's Wood, Sammy. Let's go back tonight. We'll have the old revue up and running soon enough, and I got a little money set aside. It was supposed to be for new costumes…"

And for a moment, Sammy's face lighted with wistful, heartbreaking hope. But then he cuffed her lightly and said, "Be off with you, you girl, lest I send you to the House of Mercy. I'm the Nunn of Nunn's Select Pantomimes and Irish Revue, and I'll be the one who makes the decisions around here."

And with another light cuff, he set her on her on his way, while he turned and headed for his office with slumped shoulders. As Katie watched him go, her stomach sank with a sense of doom worse than the *geases* old Mary would pronounce when the Sight came on her after she had been into the gin at night. But Katie was not a girl to believe such superstitious nonsense. Katie was a girl to believe in the wits and determination that God had given to Nunn's Irish Rose—for they were the only two things that had never failed her in her life.

And so when Sammy slid into his darkened office, only to emerge with a package wrapped in oilskin under one arm, it was but a moment's effort to slip out of the club after him, and follow him to the stable yard where the dark brute of a stable lad was raking out the horses' leavings.

"I got a package for ye," Sammy said. "One I was supposed to deliver it into your hands two years ago."

The stable lad never varied his slow sweeping. "What use is it to me now?"

Sammy drew a long breath. "Perhaps only that ye should know it was never your brother that caused you to flee New York. Perhaps far more." Sammy paused, then added, "In either case, ye should know it was my fault and mine alone."

The stable lad cast him a long look, and once more his eyes flared that curious blue. "Is that the truth, now?"

"Ye know and I know 'tis. Both of us have always known. But the time is come when it must needs be said straight out. The lass delivered both the package and your brother's message clear enough. I knew what he intended for me to do. But I thought to save these for my own profit instead. And so the blood of the souls slaughtered during those cursed riots is on my hands, and I doubt there's penance enough to wash me clean of that guilt."

"If you're seeking to save your soul, you'd best be consulting a priest, not me. As for the rest, the past is the past. What's done cannot be undone." The stable lad's voice gentled briefly, before he went back to his sweeping. "But for what it may be worth, my brother has always had a rather inflated view of my talents. I very much doubt that had you delivered the package, I could have changed anything."

"My soul is my own business, and I'll answer for it in front of my maker when the time comes," Sammy snapped. "But you must to listen to me right now. You be wrong. The past is not behind us. What's been done is far from over. There are those that say there are Fenians here in Little Dublin. Those who might even go so far as to say they plot to set fire to the Grandstand on opening day…"

The broom stilled. "Why would the Fenians want to do a thing like that?"

"Why did they conspire to spark the draft riots?"

The stable lad's eyes grew far away. "Poor men don't have time to conspire. But the Irish, for their sins, have always found time to dream. That is their curse—and that is why the rich and the powerful will make them their catspaw in this, as in all things. Rich men and dreamers. May the Good Lord deliver us from both." As abruptly as the wyrd had come upon him, it was gone, and the dark brute shook his head. "But this makes no sense."

Urgently, Sammy pressed the oilskin packet on him. "It doesna have to make sense. Just… please, take these."

"To what end?"

"I… I don't know. Burn them! Hide them! Feed them to your horses for all I care. All I know is that they cannot remain here in Little Dublin." Sammy's voice crumpled along with his face, and suddenly he was an old man. "Please, Sullivan. I have no power to right this wrong. I see no way out of this for myself, and there'd be those who'd say 'tis no less than what I deserve. But those were terrible times back in New York City, and it mustna happen again."

The stable lad shook his head, his harsh features suddenly tired, as he reluctantly took the parcel from Sammy, and said, "I'll do what I can. But I warn you not to hope for help from that quarter. Ye'd be more likely to see Cu Chulainn himself rise to defend Little Dublin."

15

Jonathan Adair's lawyer and his man of business were scheduled to arrive the next day, but instead of the relief of laying matters in capable hands, the morning's correspondence brought only more bad news. "'Twas not my fault the gentlemen missed the train," Bridie protested, as she handed Rose the silver tray of letters. "I told Mrs. Olcott, I swear it on my mother's grave. I told her as soon as I saw the address on the cables she asked me to carry downstairs. 'That's not right at all. 'Tis Commodore Vanderbilt's railway that runs to Saratoga, the New York Central and Hudson River Railway, not the New York and Harlem River line,' I said. But she would have nowt of it. Said Mr. Olcott's direction was most specific. And when I told her Mr. Olcott could be as specific as he liked, but I was not leaving my young mistress stranded alone with nowt to support her but her poor dead father's corpse over a mix-up any fool could have prevented with a simple glance at a railway timetable, she called me impertinent. Told me she would make it her first order of business to have me sacked when *she* took over as mistress of the Adair household."

Tears sprang to Bridie's worn cheeks, although it was not an uncommon mistake, for the three railway lines that led into New York City, with their three different terminals, were the source of notorious confusion that constantly left baggage and even passengers misdirected and stranded. But Rose found herself curiously unable to comfort the woman. Bridie had always been *her* pillar of strength—scarcely a mother to her, but a brusque source of practicality on everything from her monthlies to the smooth running of the Adair family kitchen.

Fallon, as was perhaps annoyingly inevitable, had no such problem. His voice softened into cadences that had more than a little touch of the brogue that still touched Rose's, even when she knew full well that it was naught but one of Fallon's many clever masks. "Well, then, it can only be all our good fortune that there will be no chance of that pinched, petty woman replacing your own sweet mistress, I give you my word on that. And perhaps there would be no better way for you to assume your rightful place in this household than by answering the knock I believe I just heard at the door."

Bridie's spine stiffened, and her tears vanished. "I believe I can instruct people as to how they should properly behave in a house of mourning."

"Do you believe this is Cousin Preston's doing?" Rose asked Fallon, as Bridie went to answer the door.

"How could it not be?" Fallon raised a shoulder. "It would be nothing short of madness to believe that he was going to take my interference without a fuss."

"Madness," she repeated bitterly. For that would certainly be the word they would give it if the truth about the outrageous scheme she had embarked on with no more thought than as if she were accepting an invitation to step out on the dance floor at one of Union Hall's nightly balls. Sheer folly and excuse enough for Cousin Preston to assume control of both the family fortune and her person if the truth came out. No, not if, but rather when—for how long could she honestly hope to maintain this pretense?

With that uncanny ability he had to read people, Lane immediately sensed her doubt, and laid a hand on her arm. "Please trust me, Rose. I will not allow that blackguard of a cousin to control you, if I have to kill him with my own two hands. You have my word on it."

It was scarcely, she reflected, a reassuring promise. Even less reassuring was his evident sincerity. Had she truly thrown in her lot with a man who could casually promise to kill a man? Or was that yet another of Fallon's masks? Well she knew that Declan Sullivan's wild passion was naught but a tissue of convenient, convincing lies…

She forced a smile. "And we all know how valuable your word is."

Lane had the nerve to look hurt. "Lies are one thing. My word is another."

"Be that as it may," she said, turning firmly toward the commotion at the entrance to the suite. "It would seem we have a guest."

As soon as Rose laid eyes on the man who stalked into their suite, she could understand Bridie's hesitation in admitting him. Dark and glowering, in a coat even shabbier than Fallon's, he looked like a cutthroat.

"Sullivan!" Lane sprang to his feet with balled fists. "If you're thinking to take another swing at me, you best know I'll be prepared this time."

"It's not worth the trouble. Or the damage to my hand," the newcomer snorted. He turned to Rose, his words cultured and courteous, despite the hint of an Irish accent beneath them. "I apologize for disturbing you in your bereavement. But I must speak with my brother urgently."

Brother? Rose glanced back and forth between them. Why yes, how could there be any doubt? The similarity went far beyond their threadbare coats: they had the same lean build, the same wolfish features. And yet similar as they were, they were a study in opposites: Lane coiled and sinewy; his brother, rangy and lanky. And while the spare lines of Lane's face and figure were softened by his russet hair and green eyes, his brother was a stark symphony in black and white, the only hint of color about him a glint of blue in the depths of his dark eyes, which raked over Rose indifferently before he added, "Alone."

Lane raised an eyebrow. "I would happily talk rather than brawl. Indeed, that was my intention when I sought a meeting in the first place. But I'm afraid I cannot accommodate your last request. I am the lady's guest, and it would be the height of rudeness to turn out my own hostess. Not to mention the fact that she has earned the right to meet the true Declan Sullivan, and not the shabby imitation she once believed she had come to care for."

If it were possible, Sullivan's face grew even darker and angrier; then abruptly, its harsh lines cracked into a faint smile. "*Et tu, Brute?*" he asked, the Latin surprisingly easy on his tongue. "Seems like half the world has gone mad over a woman."

"And you have my sincerest hope you will one day find yourself similarly blessed."

"I want no man's blessing, no woman's either." Sullivan spared another moment to study Rose. "Is she the cause of all this trouble, then?"

Lane's face darkened. "Her name is Miss Adair, and I will thank you to remember it."

"My apologies," Sullivan said, with a quick inclination of his head. "Born in a barn, you see. Never raised with all the advantages."

"And whose fault was that, you stiff-necked fool?" Lane asked.

Sullivan's answer was to reach beneath his coat for a thick envelope that Rose immediately recognized. "What does it matter?" he asked, as he tossed it to his brother. "I didna come here to trade family reminiscences. I came here because mischief is brewing in Little Dublin, and, as before, it seems to have followed hot on your heels."

Lane caught the papers reflexively, his speculative gaze never leaving his brother. "And what precisely might that mischief be?"

"Fenians," Sullivan said. "Plotting some kind of rising at the opening day of the Meets—by all accounts worse than the riots in New York City ever were."

"Why would the Fenians do a thing like that?" Lane objected. "It makes no sense."

"Unless it were an English conspiracy to discredit them and John Morrissey along with them," Sullivan said. "So I'll ask you directly, is it one?"

"If it is, it has naught to do with me," Lane told him. "I parted ways with Her Majesty's Service two years ago. But for the life of me, I cannot think why they would wish to embroil themselves in a bloody scheme like this one either."

"Then you must discover who is behind this, and you must needs fix it." If anything, Sullivan's eyes seemed to grow darker. "You owe that much to the Society. No, you owe that much to me."

Lane conceded the point with a nod. "I suppose if one avails oneself of a man's good name, one must be prepared to pay the price."

"A debt is owed. A debt must be paid," Sullivan agreed.

And that should have settled matters. But no sooner had Sullivan turned for the door than he stopped and turned back. "*Why?*" he asked.

A flush stained Lane's cheeks. "It started as a simple matter of convenience. Any good liar knows that it is easier by far to start with a scaffolding of truth and stay as close to it as possible, rather than inventing too many details. I borrowed your biography because it was ready to hand." His jaw set as he strove not to look at Rose—and failed. "It grew into something more complicated."

Sullivan's eyes lit with shrewd humor as they followed his brother's gaze. "Thank you for the lesson on the art of lying and its associated hazards, but what I simply wanted to know was why you had my name and biography to hand in the first place? Why did you come after me, why, after all these years? Why could you not just leave me alone?"

Lane's flush darkened and his eyes slid away from Rose. "Surely you can answer that for yourself," he said irritably. "Our father asked me to find you. And you know as well as I do, he is not a man to be denied."

Sullivan's expression grew even more fathomless, before he spun on his heel. "Your father, never mine," he said. "Now if you will excuse me, I have stalls to muck."

He stalked out, and Bridie hastened to make sure the door was securely fastened behind him, leaving Lane and Rose to linger in awkward silence, before Lane finally drew a deep, angry breath. "And there," he said, "is the man you fell in love with. Not me."

At least Rose thought that was what he might have said. For she was suddenly back on the rocky shores of the East River, with a soft, Irish voice whispering in her ear the secrets of what was said to be the last fastness of the primeval wilderness that had once been Manhattan, where pirates and smugglers had braved the treacherous waters of Hell's Gate to hide their treasures in Jones' Wood and hold their bloody revels there...

"I think you embellished somewhat on the original."

Lane's discomfiture vanished, and his eyes lit with a speculative gleam. "From that, am I given to hope that you find the version I presented you an improvement on the original?"

Her face flamed, and she turned away. "What does it matter?"

"It matters to me," he said. "Very much."

"Why should it? For what was Declan Sullivan, real or imagined, beyond a lark, a diversion, or... how did you put it? A scaffolding of truth upon which to build a lie?"

"And in that you'd be wrong. For I may well say in all modesty that I am the best liar I have ever known—at least, save for one man—but I speak nothing but the truth when I say how I feel about you." Although Lane's tone was light, his words were now suddenly serious. "It is your sad misfortune to have saved my soul, my sweet Roisin, and that is not a debt a man repays lightly..."

"A man can only save his own soul, Captain Fallon," she said sharply. "And my name is Rose..."

Briefly, Lane's face grew wistful, then he lifted a shoulder with careful indifference. "But what does Rosaleen mean but little Rose? In fact the Irish should really be translated, 'Little Rose, be not sad for all that hath behapped thee,' not 'My dark Rosaleen, do not cry, do not weep,'" he said. "Mangan's work was always questionable even when the man wasn't drunk—which was a rare occasion indeed. He claimed that his version conveyed the intricate bardic structure of the original medieval *aisling*, but frankly the man couldn't be dissuaded from using three words when one would do."

She stared at him, flummoxed. Was this the man who had whispered of his passion to save his country back in Jones's Wood? Was this the man who had wooed her with such sweet lies? Was this the man who had just casually offered to kill a man on her behalf? Was this donnish, even pettish, creature, the true Lane Fallon? *Was* there a true Lane Fallon?

"You surprise me, Captain Fallon," she said. "I thought you were a military man, not a scholarly one."

"Does it matter to you?"

If there was a hint of eagerness beneath his words, he hid it well.

"Not in the least," she assured him.

For a moment, she fancied he looked genuinely hurt. And then he grinned. "I never thought you so tart-tongued. But it seems that there remains much I have to learn of you."

"Mayhap because you never really knew me beyond a fantasy of your *aisling* that never truly existed at all."

"Alas, it is said that no man is ever given to know the woman he loves," he conceded the point ruefully. "And indeed, this might be the true key to why he loves her so completely. But I will leave that matter to the poets. For you are quite correct. It is up to me to assume the burden of putting right my old mistakes, not you. And I have no right to cherish any hopes of earning your regard, until I have set matters right and spared you any further involvement in this tawdry mess."

She studied him, still trying to catch a glimpse of the real man beneath the all-too-easy words. "What is it exactly that you mean to do?"

"Whatever proves necessary."

"That is no answer," she said. "And I am no child to be fobbed off with half-truths."

"No," he agreed. "No, you are not. So I will be frank with you. I may not be able to settle this without resorting to methods I would rather you know nothing of."

What kind of methods? Did she need ask? Was not the grim set of his face answer enough?

"Will you give me your word you'll hurt no-one?" she asked.

"No," he said.

16

It seemed that no sooner had Declan Sullivan's footsteps faded away, than a fresh set of boots marched down the carpeted corridor and rapped on the door of the Adair suite with a casual authority that suggested they owned the place. And although the three men were careful to remove their derbies upon entering, it was impossible not to notice the scarred jaws and broken noses that suggested that they were not overly troubled about hiding the fact that they were thugs. Ignoring Bridie's angry protestations that mourning precluded the Adair family from being at home to anyone, they strode straight into the suite's overstuffed parlor, and addressed themselves to Rose.

"Mr. Morrissey sends his apologies for disturbing your peace at a time like this," their leader said, his diction as carefully correct as his clothing. "But Mrs. Morrissey quite insisted that he communicate with you directly. And Mr. Morrissey is not a man to refuse Mrs. Morrissey anything."

"I beg your pardon, but communicate about what? The unfortunate matter of my father's claim to the chest in the hotel lobby? I can assure you, that I have scarcely thought about the matter."

The thug smiled, exposing gapped teeth. "Mrs. Morrissey was certain that would be the case. She would have you know that the chest has been removed from its position of prominence in the hotel lobby, and stored in Mr. Morrissey's private vault until the time comes when you feel prepared to discuss such matters. In the meantime, she did not want it to be placed anywhere where it might cause you distress."

"Mrs. Morrissey is very thoughtful," Rose said.

"Mrs. Morrissey is a fine lady," the thug agreed. "The apple of Mr. Morrissey's eye. She graduated from Emma Willard, you know. Mr. Morrissey fell in love with her the moment he laid eyes on her. Indeed, he's not ashamed to say he intends to build Saratoga Springs into the world's finest resort to provide her with the home she deserves."

"How very romantic," Rose allowed, although her mind was spinning, trying to determine what this conversation was truly about.

In another moment, she had her answer. "So when Mrs. Morrissey heard such shocking rumors about a secret marriage, she prevailed on Mr. Morrissey to ascertain the facts of the matter as discreetly and directly as possible by applying to the interested parties… *both* interested parties."

The weight of the thug's circumlocution seemed to have finally overwhelmed him, and it took Rose a moment to understand his meaning. "You wish to speak with my husband?"

"If it would not be too much trouble."

But the polite words were belied by the look the thug cast toward the closed doors that led to the suite's private chambers that suggested that Mr. Morrissey's power would extend to his men kicking open the doors and forcibly searching the suite if she objected—or otherwise hindered the wishes of the apple of his eye.

"My husband…," she prevaricated.

"Would not have you any further disturbed by these questions," Lane said, stepping out into the room. His eyes narrowed as he glanced at one of the two men who flanked Morrissey's messenger, and his hand went reflexively to his jaw. "So, gentlemen, what brings you here? The recent events at Congress Spring? I'm sure your colleague on the left can attest to the fact that I have already… how shall we put it?… assisted the police in their inquiries into that matter."

"And I would assume you would prefer not to repeat that interview?" the second thug said with an unpleasant smile. "Especially not with a lady present?"

"There would be no purpose," Fallon dismissed the man. He turned back to address himself to the leader. "I can assure you the police were quite satisfied that my presence at the spring that night was naught but an unfortunate coincidence. I was engaged in a private meeting."

"A private brawl is more like it," the leader snorted. "With a notorious Fenian agitator. The same man, in fact, who has just now visited you right here in the Union Hotel. Mr. Morrissey is concerned."

Fallon raised an eyebrow. "I assume you are referring to my unhappy brother, Declan Sullivan. A wild Irish boy, to be sure, whose passion drove him into some unfortunate Fenian entanglements. But I give you my word, he has put those days far behind him, and our meeting was naught but a quiet family reunion."

"Mr. Morrissey would be the last to judge a man by the sins of his past," the thug agreed. "But Mr. Morrissey would also like to make it clear that he wants no such trouble in Saratoga. Bad for business, if you know what I mean."

Fallon frowned. "Are you accusing my brother of bringing trouble to Saratoga?"

"*Someone* has brought trouble to Saratoga—and dumped its dead body squarely in Congress Spring. And that does not make Mr. Morrissey happy. Mr. Morrissey abhors violence at any time, but most especially when his guests are arriving for meet season."

"Bad for business," Lane ventured.

"Exactly," the thug agreed without irony.

"Well, if you truly believe that there is a plot to disrupt Mr. Morrissey's business interests right before the racing season, you have my word Sullivan is not involved," Fallon assured him. "My brother is an idealist at best, I assure you. At worst... well, frankly, I wouldn't be surprised if the milksop turned out to be a vegetarian."

"And yet it is said he has a price on his head in New York City."

A long pause, before Fallon conceded the point. "My fault entirely, I regret to say. Declan Sullivan has never conspired at anything other than winning horse races in his entire life. It was simply his bad fortune that... I found it convenient to avail myself of his name."

"And why might that be?"

Another long pause, during which Rose could see the calculation flashing behind Lane's eyes—as if, she realized to her horror, he was sorting through a rack of lies with no more care than one sorted through bolts of fabric with a dressmaker, holding them up to the light one at a time to decide which was most flattering. And suddenly, she found herself caring nothing for the dangers of the situation that confronted her. Instead, all she could wonder was whether she had ever seen a similar calculation underlying his decision to make love to her?

"Two years ago, I came to America in pursuit of a gang of trouble-makers and belligerents escaped from Ireland," Lane said. "They called themselves the Society of the Horseman's Word."

"Among them your own brother?"

"Half-brother," Lane corrected him. "And I must reiterate, he never had anything to do with the affair. I wronged him by involving him, and I would make up for that mistake now. I give you my word, Declan Sullivan never had anything to do with any foul conspiracies, beyond having a brother who made use of his name, and if you seek any further cooperation from me, you will give me Mr. Morrissey's word that Sullivan will not be further troubled by this matter."

"Mr. Morrissey is unaccustomed to being offered ultimatums," the thug pointed out.

"That truly is a shame," Lane said.

For a moment, their eyes held, two dogs, sizing one another up, before the thug yielded. "However, given Mr. Morrissey's respect for the sacred bonds of brotherhood, let us assume that in this case, he will be willing to overlook any such possible breach of decorum." He reached into his coat and pulled out a penciled sketch. "In the meantime, perhaps you would be so good as to tell me what you know of this man?"

Lane studied the sketch only briefly before handing it back with a shake of his head. "Not a thing."

But Rose had already caught a glimpse of the paper. "I cannot answer for Captain Fallon, but I certainly remember this man," she said. "His name is Cole Washington. He is a rider, up from the South. He… he called on my father down in New York City. Is he now here in Saratoga Springs?"

Suddenly, she was the object of both men's startled attention.

"Are you quite certain?" Lane asked.

"Mr. Morrissey would hesitate to involve a lady…," the thug said at the same time.

"To his credit, of course. Nonetheless, I'm sure the admirable Mrs. Morrissey has provided you with ample evidence of our sex's resilience." Rose bit her lip at the memory of her departure from Washington. She had promised to find him answers. Instead, she had all but forgotten about him. In her defense, she been distracted. But had Washington grown impatient with her efforts? Had he followed her here to demand an answer? "Mr. Washington approached my father in New York City, only a few days ago. He was seeking information about a group of Fenians known as the Society of the Horseman's Word."

The thug cast Lane a sharp glance. "Your belligerents and trouble-makers?"

"I would suggest that is a question better proposed to Mr. Washington directly."

"Mark me, I know my job well enough to do that. But right now, I'm asking you," the thug said.

"And I'm telling you I have no idea what the man might have been doing here."

"Really?" The thug's eyes narrowed. "Then why is it being said that Mr. Washington has been asking after you most particularly ever since he arrived here in Saratoga?"

If Lane was startled, he hid it well. "I trust such things are not a crime here in the enlightened North."

"Murder is a crime, Captain Fallon. So is inciting a riot."

"And both of them bad for business." Lane spoke easily, but it was impossible not to notice the way his entire being had tensed with interest. "Do you have any particular riot or murder in mind?"

"Mr. Morrissey has heard tales that someone proposes to stir up riots in Little Dublin," the thug said. "It has also been suggested that Mr. Washington is a pawn in this foul game. He lost his family to the draft riots in New York City, and has come to Saratoga to avenge himself upon the Irish..."

"No!" Rose said. "He was angry, yes. And very determined. But he sought justice, not revenge..."

"Then he's a fool," Fallon sighed, before turning back to the thug. "And you would accuse me of being the puppet-master who pulls Washington's strings?"

"It has come to Mr. Morrissey's attention that your reputation suggests you might be able to... assist us in our inquiries."

A moment's pause, and Fallon's face set in way that made Rose certain he was once more sorting through his infinite wardrobe of lies, before he finally said, "Perhaps, once upon a time, I might have played such a role; however I have left that game behind me. Still, I might be willing to offer my insights to Mr. Morrissey—as long as it is understood that I am speaking in a strictly advisory capacity."

"Of course."

Fallon nodded, then allowed himself a moment's consideration before he went on, "I came to America because of a Fenian conspiracy—one that looted treasures from Irish tombs and sold them to American collectors—including the chest that so interested Mr. Adair."

"What would you care about Irish treasures," the thug asked. "Do you propose to be an Irishman?"

"My family owns land in Ireland. It's scarcely the same thing."

"For sure it isn't." The thug's eyes hardened, and his brogue abruptly thickened, before he went on, "So then you came to America in order to foil such a plot?"

A long pause. Then Lane said, "You insult me. I did nothing to thwart the plot. Rather, I engineered it."

The thug's fists balled. "Go on."

"What part is unclear? We let it be known that there was a network of Fenians who were willing to sell priceless Irish antiquities to the highest bidder in order to raise funds for their cause…"

"You admit you were a spy?"

"*Agent provocateur* is the usual term," Lane corrected him. "I came to America to expose a cabal of ruthless collectors that included Miss Adair's father, but I soon discovered that many of these men had interests that extended far beyond Adair's monomania. They had come to see the War Between the States as an unfortunate impediment to their plans, and sought to end it as quickly as possible by betraying New York City to the Confederacy. It was suggested that a Fenian atrocity and the subsequent panic it would ignite would be the simplest, most expedient way to accomplish that end. And so I proposed to give them their Fenian atrocity…"

"You conspired to terrorize New York City with Greek fire." The thug shook his head. "And yet you would have Mr. Morrissey believe that you know nothing of a similar conspiracy that threatens Saratoga?"

"The war is over."

"In America, perhaps. But the conflict continues in Ireland. Why should a leopard change his spots?"

Lane raised an eyebrow. "Put quite simply, I found a better prospect," he said. "During my stay in New York City, I was fortunate enough to win the lady's favor, and although I have been told on more than one occasion that I lack even a rudimentary understanding of the mind of the fair sex, I was, and remain, more than a little certain that a lady would hold it against me if I persevered with such schemes as had so nearly ruined her father. Or to put it even more simply, running off with my bride seemed like a far easier approach than risking the hangman. I am nothing if not a practical man."

"And so would you propose that Washington is acting alone?" The thug's eyes narrowed. "Or is it more likely someone has stolen your plans?"

"Imitation is the sincerest form of flattery."

"But you have no personal knowledge of who might do such a thing?"

Again, that pause that suggested Fallon was addressing himself to his wardrobe of lies and half-truths. "I can suggest a possibility," he finally said. "But you must understand that I have no proof, and I hesitate to cast aspersions on any man."

"Mr. Morrissey understands that this conversation is being conducted in a strictly in an advisory capacity."

"Then allow me to advise you that there were others who had an interest in Miss Adair's hand—and still do. In particular, her cousin Preston Olcott resents my supplanting his hopes, and has already tried once to have me hanged…" He cut off Rose's swift gasp with a wave of his hand. "Of course, I cannot prove it. But I can assure you that I planted no Greek fire around New York City. That entire conspiracy was nothing but a ruse to smoke out the offenders. But someone planted Greek fire at Jonathan Adair's party. And who would have better motive to do that than a man who stood to eliminate both a rival for Miss Adair's hand and the man who currently controlled the family fortune?"

The thug tensed. "They say Preston Olcott's an up-and-coming man here in Saratoga."

"Riding on Miss Adair's expectations," Lane said. "And what simpler way to gain control of her money than by engineering a riot in Little Dublin and blaming it on me?"

"And what simpler way for you to eliminate a rival than to do the same," the thug pointed out.

"Of course. Mr. Olcott is rapidly escalating into a nuisance that I would see gone. Permanently." Lane quelled Rose's protest with a sly look that chilled her. "Have no fear, my dear. I can assure you I will protect your interests as if they were my own—for after all, they are."

No. No, that was not true! If there was one thing she knew about Lane Fallon, it was that he was a hopeless liar. This was just another of his harebrained schemes. It had to be.

But instead of reassuring her, Lane Fallon turned back to the thugs. "Come, gentlemen. We are all in agreement about one thing: Riots, like murder and cursed chests, are bad for business. So let us go to Little Dublin and see what we can do to prevent one from occurring, shall we?"

And once more Rose was treated to the spectacle of watching Lane Fallon stroll off in the custody of several burly men, leaving her in doubt as to whether she would ever see him alive again—or wanted to.

17

When Sammy finally stumbled back into the club, the stench of whiskey was enough to tell Katie how he'd spent the hours he'd been gone. And even though Katie had cause enough to know that there was no talking to Sammy when he was like this, she mustered her courage to step into his path.

"Please, Sammy. Sullivan was right. Please, let's just go. Tonight, if we can."

He staggered as he turned to pounce on an easy target to hand. "Oho, is it Sullivan, now? Since when are you personally acquainted with the lad?"

Katie shut her eyes. Why could she never think before her tongue ran away with her? Now was no time to confess to having spied on Sammy, not when his face was bright red in the way that always worried her that the drink and the tobacco would catch up with him and he'd be struck down dead in an apoplectic fit right there in front of her. "He's just the livery stable lad. Why shouldn't I know him?"

But Sammy was off on a tear. "Why shouldn't you? Why shouldn't you? You really think the likes of you can do better with him than with me?"

"I don't know what you're talking about…"

"I'm talking about ye having hopes above your station. Spinning yourself pipe dreams about how he's going to carry you off, if only you bring him old Sammy. I tell you now, ye'll be having none of that!" he snorted. "Gentlemen like that aren't for you."

"What gentleman? He's nowt but a stable lad."

"Oh, and I suppose you'd have me think you believe that. That you haven't found out about his Royal English father and thought to set your sights a little higher than Preston Olcott."

"I never set my sights on Olcott!" Katie protested. "I knew at once what kind of career a gentleman like him might be offering. 'Twas you that insisted I show him some kindness."

"And if you'd played your cards right, the two of us could be sitting pretty, my girl. But instead you propose to get us tangled up with that Fenian. Man's got a price on his head, did ye know that?"

"You mean, because of the Society?"

Her tongue had run away with her once more. Sammy blanched. Then his jaw set. "Ye mind your manners girl, or I'll send you to the nuns. Or mayhap I'll not need to take the trouble. Keep travelling the path you're travelling and you'll chart a course straight to the House of Mercy all by yourself."

The House of Mercy. As if she had actually pursued the career that Sammy was accusing her of. And Sammy, Sammy Nunn of all people telling her she wasn't that good! "I hate you, Sammy Nunn!" she said softly, as she ran upstairs to the cramped sleeping quarters she shared with the other girls. "I hate you! I hate you! I wish you were dead!"

She didn't mean it, of course. It was just her Irish up—same as Sammy's. Flare and forgive, that's how it went—hugs and apologies over a brimming glass of ale—for Sammy had deemed Katie was too young for whiskey yet. How was she to know those would be the last words she'd ever say to the only father she'd ever known?

She stormed up to her room, furiously pulling the coins she had scrimped and saved from their hiding place beneath her mattress, frantically trying to tally them to something close to the price of a ticket back down to New York City. Not that she was going to really buy the ticket—or even venture as far as the railway station. But a girl who'd been on the stage as long as she had, knew well enough how to make an exit so that a man would know she was serious.

But as she flounced down the front hall, making a business of adjusting her hat and her wrap, just as if she were an outraged wife in one of Sammy's comic sketches, her timing was ruined by a colored man who simply ignored the "Club Closed" sign and stepped inside without so much as a knock.

"My name is Cole Washington III," he addressed himself to Katie, "and I would like to speak to Mr. Nunn."

Reflexively, she dropped a tidy curtsey. "Yessir. I'll see, sir. I dinna know if he's receiving sir."

But the door to the office had already slammed open, and Sammy lurched out. "No," he snapped. "I dinna need this kind of trouble. The people of Little Dublin have long memories."

"Then they would do well to recall that it was not my people that started this trouble," Washington said. "Nor do I have any intention of starting any trouble now."

"Then why are you here?"

"My name's Cole Washington III." He didn't waste time holding out a hand that Sammy was sure to disdain. "A man named Sullivan said you might have answers to my questions. He also said he hoped I might be able to save your life. I freely admit, I don't much like Irishmen, so the second is a matter of indifference to me, but it seems like a reasonable enough exchange."

Katie braced against the explosion that was sure to follow. For if Washington's calm composure was not enough to trigger Sammy's temper when he was in his cups, another mention of Sullivan surely would.

"How dare ye?" Sammy breathed. "How dare ye speak to me like that in my own establishment? By rights I ought to call the coppers and have ye removed. So I suggest ye get out. Get out now, before I change me mind."

There was a long moment's pause while Washington studied Sammy. Then he inclined his head and removed his hat. "I see what your friend was speaking of."

"Sullivan is no more friend to me than you are."

"On the contrary, I would suggest he is the only friend you have. And in the name of simple humanity, I would urge you take his advice before it is too late."

"Are ye threatening me! And in my own club too! Girl!" Sammy snapped at Katie. "Go find the watch!"

And Katie gladly seized the excuse to stumble out the door. What did it matter if she spent the night wandering the back alleys or sleeping in Congress Park? She'd done as much before. Surely the streets of Saratoga could be no more menacing than those of Five Points. Or old Sammy when he was on the drink.

But not tonight. She was scarcely a block down Broadway, before she sensed the strange energy that infected Little Dublin, danger whispering from all sides like a living, breathing creature. A passerby muttered under his breath about Fenians; another about Greek fire. A pair of churchmen were heading grim-faced toward St. Peter's, not troubling to hide the shotguns they carried. The nearby innkeeper had begun to draw down his shutters even though it was still hours before closing; the housewives were bolting their doors long before their husbands came back home.

Even Morrissey's casino on the far side of tracks was unusually quiet, the curtains drawn, the doorman examining any new arrival carefully before he allowed them inside. But at least it was open. Katie drew a speculative breath. It was said Morrissey was the most powerful man in Saratoga, with princes and robber barons answerable to him. Was it possible he would listen to the plea of a poor, Irish lass to keep her safe for the night?

She got her answer as soon as she drew near to the gaming house, and felt a hard hand close around her arm. "Unescorted ladies are not allowed at the tables," the doorman said. "Only gentlemen are allowed to place wagers. As for anything else you may be looking to do…"

He broke off, as he caught sight of her hair. "You're one of Sammy Nunn's girls aren't ye?" he asked with a frown. "Everything all right there then? Some said they heard a bit of shouting over that way just a minute ago."

Katie's stomach sank. But she managed to keep her wits about her. "I couldn't say, but I hope not. I'm just on my way back from running a few errands before we open for the night."

The doorman's frown deepened, and his eyes flickered anxiously down the street. "Might be wisest for you to get back there as soon as you can. Not a good night for a lass to be out on her own."

There was no doubting the wisdom of his advice by the time Katie made her way back to Little Dublin. The whisper of danger had swelled into an ugly roar, and more men had gathered with guns and grim expressions, outside the inn, the school, in the graveyard even—their set jaws and angry eyes the same as those that still haunted her nightmares. The danger was no longer a mere whiff borne on the twilight; Little Dublin was about to erupt into a full-scale riot. And the doorman was right: that was no place for even a lass who had raised herself on the alleys of Five Points to be on her own. Temper and drink be damned, Old Sammy had kept her safe enough the last time. She would have to hope he could do so again.

But when she crept back into the club, both the hall and card room were empty. The door to Sammy's office hung open, and a shadow moved in the depths.

"Sammy?" she asked, hurrying over to it. "Sammy, you all right then?"

One look inside, and she knew the answer was no, and that Sammy was never going to be all right again. The safe hung open, Sammy's chair was overturned, and Sammy lay face down in front of it, a trickle of blood spilling from beneath his head.

"Sammy…"

"Step back. This is no sight for a woman." An apparition arose from Sammy's safe—as menacing as the danger that was rising outside. Then it resolved into Preston Olcott, his face pasty and hard.

"What happened?" she stammered. "Did Sammy…? Is Sammy…?"

"It was the Negro. Broke in here and Sammy caught him trying to crack the safe. Hit him across the head with the lockbox…"

No. No, that wasn't right at all. That couldn't be right! Sammy couldn't be dead. Sammy had to protect her…

For… if Sammy wasn't there to protect her, who would? Preston Olcott? To judge from the glitter in his eyes and the reek of wine on his breath, there was small question what price he would demand in return…

Her fingers worked the edges of her skirt, gathering them, as she tried to gauge the distance to the door and whether anyone would listen to her shrieks for help if she managed to make it out to the street.

"That's right," Olcott said. "Ye'd best be out of here, and fast. Get you to the police station, and give them the summons before the Negro can escape. I'll take care of matters here."

What did he mean? Was he giving her a chance to run away? But where? Back out into those mean streets?

What did it matter? She needed to go. She needed to take it. There was nothing left for her here in Saratoga Springs with old Sammy gone. Preston could take over the club and he was welcome too it. She'd simply have to find a way to work her way down to New York City. But that cursed streak of stubbornness, every bit as bad as old Sammy's, took over and Katie shook her head. "But I canna just leave Sammy here."

Olcott flashed her a long look that made her blood run cold. "I'd say that a girl with her head firmly on her shoulders would see that's a far wiser choice than being found alone with him here. Because with no-one else in this house excepting you and the dead man, I don't know what other conclusions the police might jump to about who killed Sammy Nunn." He cast a contemptuous look at her dress, cut lower than was strictly proper for the streets of Little Dublin. "And it wouldn't cost them much thinking to figure out why either. So if I were you, I'd snap to it. Because I'd hate to see a neck as pretty as yours stretch. But the hangman, he most likely wouldn't care at all."

18

Katie only barely managed to stumble down the steps of the club and into the shelter of the nearest alley, before she doubled over, retching up the contents of her stomach. Sammy's death wasn't real, it couldn't be real! Preston Olcott was lying!

Now he wanted her to lie too. And if she didn't, soon enough there'd be copper looking for her on every corner. But if she did? She'd be Preston Olcott's creature for life.

No, she had to run. To get out of Saratoga, and as far away from Preston Olcott as possible. To the Wild West, if need be. Surely there must be opportunities for a girl like her in wicked San Francisco. Or among the Irish in Chicago.

But before she could even wonder how long she might have before Olcott realized she was not coming back to the club and sent the coppers out after her, a rough hand grabbed her arm, sending her purse flying and her meager savings rattling and spinning across the ground.

"Oy! Drunk as a cat, and thinking to ply your trade for more gin. No need for the likes of you to be out right now, ye hear? Now, scat!"

A hard hand landed on her backside, as casually as if she were a cur to be kicked away, as Katie dropped to her knees to chase the few coins that were all she had left in the world, but a second blow followed hard on the first, and this time the man's fist was closed.

With a last, despairing glance at the few bits of silver and copper, Katie snatched up her skirts and ran. She fled blindly, sticking to the back alleys, with no real idea to where she was headed until the stitch in her side forced her to stop. And when she blinked away her tears for long enough to see where she found herself, Katie began to laugh—hysterically, maniacally even. Out of the frying pan and into the fire—it wasn't just a punchline for one of Sammy Nunn's humorous sketches involving several suggestive links of sausage, three wishes foolishly spent by a husband and wife, and a final duel with a pair of frying pans. Katie O'Grady, Nunn's Irish Rose herself, had fled straight back into the arms of the waiting nuns.

This time, when the hand landed on her shoulder, it was gentle, but insistent. "Please, miss. You're in no condition to stay out here tonight."

She blinked up into the tired eyes of the priest, and suddenly she saw herself mirrored as he might have seen her. Giggling, tear-stained, and stinking of vomit, she looked like a gin-soaked unfortunate. But she was not. She was Nunn's Irish Rose. She stiffened her spine and tossed her head. "I apologize. I seem to have lost my way."

"In more ways than one," the priest agreed. "There a lad you might call?"

Sure and there might be a lad she might call. Preston Olcott? Poor, dead Sammy? The treacherous giggles threatened to well up again—and if she weren't careful, they might lead her straight to the madhouse. "No need. Simple matter of a wrong turn. I'll just be on my way."

But the priest wasn't satisfied. "Wait here," he said. "The sisters have barred the door against the trouble, but I'll try to rouse someone."

He hurried down the alley and around the corner—to the front entrance, she was certain. Just as she was equally certain, she was not meant to follow. Unfortunates such as herself were strictly meant to receive their charity at the back door. And at what cost? Katie still remembered the girl at the nunnery, tired and hungry, with Katie's own red hair, but with a distinct bulge in her tummy beneath the homespun shift she wore, as she knelt and bowed her head to the sisters who advanced on her, unable to disguise their greedy anger as they pulled out their cruel steel scissors…

No, Katie would not go back to the nuns—not even if it meant starving on the street. Or worse. She would not stay in such a place, for she wanted nothing of their mercy. Old Sammy had rescued her from such a fate. It would be the worst betrayal of his memory to return.

And what did she have left of Sammy beyond his memory? Sammy was gone. And Sammy was never coming back.

Once more the tears surged. Old Sammy hadn't been much; she had never lied to herself about that. But he had been the closest thing she had ever had to a father. And Sammy had taken care of her, right enough. And the last words she had flung at him had been "I hate you…"

Well, Sammy wasn't there to take care of her now. "A fine head on your shoulders, Katie O'Grady," she scolded the tears away. "Is this how you mean to take care of yourself now that old Sammy's gone?"

For if she couldn't use the wits she was born with, she might as well head straight to the nuns. Her money was gone. And soon enough, the police would be looking for the red-haired lass who had killed old Sammy Nunn.

No, the red-haired lass must vanish, and vanish now.

But not back to the nuns. Never back to the nuns, no matter how kind the priest's intentions. Instead, she ran over to the carts of laundry that were delivered daily from the hotels. Yes, most of it was table and bed linens. But a steady search turned up a sturdy pair of trousers and a serviceable, if patched shirt. She felt a moment's guilt at stealing from a priest, another moment's guilt at stealing from a man who was only trying to help her. But this wasn't truly stealing, she reassured herself. The frock she left in exchange might be crumpled, and the flounce along its hem torn, but it was still more valuable than what she had taken. She would have to go barefoot until she could sneak into one of the hotels and find a pair of boots left out for blacking. Thoughtfully, she ran her fingers through the red-gold curls the nuns would have taken such unholy delight in shearing. There might be some additional use for that blacking as well, but in the meantime, she could make good use of the dirt the good Lord had placed right beneath her feet. Olcott and the coppers would be looking for a red-haired woman, Sammy's Nunn's Irish Rose. No-one was looking for one of the urchins that prowled the streets of Saratoga Springs during the Meets.

Once upon a time, not that very long ago, everyone had said that Katie O'Grady had no small knack for a britches part. It was time to see how good she would be playing one for real.

*****

By the time that Nunn's Irish Rose had been replaced by a grimy lad whose skin was almost as dark as his freshly-chopped hair, Olcott's lies had taken hold in earnest, and the stern citizens of Little Dublin were massing in the streets, their faces as grim as when they had stood guard overnight to protect the steeple they sought raise. Slouching her shoulders, and shoving her hands in her pocket, Katie did her best to slip among them unnoticed, but she was stopped almost immediately by a man whose empty sleeve suggested that he had learned his marksmanship in service of the Union.

"Begone," he said, not unkindly. "This is no place for a lad. There's trouble afoot tonight."

"What kind of trouble?" Katie only remembered to deepen her voice at the last minute, but the man didn't seem to notice.

"Colored man with a grudge against the Irish over the riots down in New York City. He's already killed poor Sammy Nunn, and now they're saying he wants to burn us all in our beds tonight, to make up for what we did to his people."

It was a lie, sure enough, and Olcott's lie at that, but Katie was in no position to argue. Katie was in no position to do much more than thank whatever luck of the Irish still ran with her that Olcott must have long ago left the club to spread his filth—for she had little enough doubt her disguise would survive his gaze.

"Begone," the one-armed man said again.

But where was she to go? Not to the other side of the tracks. And not back to Sammy's club and the coppers. But what other choice did she have? The railway depot? The racetrack—or maybe the surrounding stables...

A stable. Her eyes slid speculatively to the livery stable as she recalled the oilskin-wrapped parcel Sammy had given to Sullivan, the stable lad. There were names in those papers. She could read well enough to know that. Names had brought Cole Washington to Sammy's doorstep. Names that someone killed Sammy over.

Names that someone might pay the price of a passage back to New York to obtain?

There was only one way to find out. Hunching her shoulders, she slid down the street toward the stable.

Only to feel a hard arm close round her throat. "Well, lookie, lookie, lookie what I have caught," a brandy-soaked voice breathed in her ear, as she was yanked into the shadows of the mews. A gold ring glittered briefly, before his lips closed savagely on one shoulder and she could feel his hardness pressing against her back. A rich man, then, and one of unspeakable tastes. Just like Olcott.

What did it matter? His fingers were already fumbling with her buttons, and it was only a matter of moments before he discovered the truth—and Nunn's Irish Rose was discovered fleeing Little Dublin in the guise of a boy after having killed old Sammy.

She twisted. She kicked. She fought.

It only made her captor grunt with pleasure.

She drew in a breath to shriek. Let them find her. Let them hang her. Let them cart her back off to the nuns if it came down to that. If nothing else, she'd have saved them the trouble of cropping her hair.

Footsteps thundered out of the stable, louder than hooves. A shadow loomed—and Katie's tormentor was torn away and thrown to the ground as effortlessly has if he had been a straying stable cat.

"Better ye be the one who learned a lesson," Sullivan hissed. "Play at such things again and the horses will have you. In the name of the Mother of Us all who protects her own creatures against the men that would use them…"

Already his words were threatening naught but the empty air, for the drunken swell was stumbling away, hurriedly buttoning his trousers. And Katie's eyes widened in fear and humiliation as Sullivan turned back toward her.

"Calm yourself, laddie. I'm not of such tastes," he said briefly. "And he'll nae come back for you. Those kinds of coward never do. Still, 'twould be best for you to be off the streets tonight."

"Got no place to go," Katie snapped—which was nowt but the truth. Still it was hard to keep the tears out of her voice as she added, "I meant no harm. No thieving either. Just looking for place to curl up for the night."

Instead of answering, the great brute grabbed her by the shoulder and swung her around to study her face—only to thrust her aside in disgust. "Saints preserve us, laddie, you're too pretty for your own good," he snorted. "Best get thee to a nunnery, and hide behind their skirts until you grow out of those looks. Or beneath their skirts, as ye please."

"I told you. I've got no place else." Her voice caught and she was ashamed to feel the tears well. "Just a corner in the hay. I promise I'll be no trouble."

Which was nowt but the truth, but it made the stable lad pause for long enough to study her curiously. Then, he reached beneath his coat and pulled out a purse. "'Tis slender enough, I admit. But it will buy you a night's lodging, a few more meals," he said, tossing it to Katie. "Take it. And get out of here."

Katie's shock at the sudden, simple act of kindness did not prevent her from catching the purse with a nimbleness born of her days stealing in Five Points.

"A loan, sir," she said. "And I thank you for it. I will repay you one day."

"Too many people waiting to do that already," Sullivan snorted. "Including the Lord God Almighty, it would seem. Take the money, and get out of here while you still can. For there's trouble come in Little Dublin, and you're already too close to its midst."

Katie hesitated. She was tired. Even worse she was frightened. But there was something about this great, glowering lunk of a man that made her feel safe... "I'm an able lad. Been told I have a way with the horses. I only wanted a place to sleep, but I could help out. Work for food and a bed..."

And maybe find a chance to search the place for those papers. Just the thought made her shiver with guilt. What kind of girl was she to repay his kindness with such a cruel trick?

The dark brute's face softened for only a moment, before he shook his head. "It's nae my stable. And even if it were, I'd nae take you on. A boy as pretty as you wants no truck with the gentry. As ye might have just learned. Get on with you. Get out of here. Find a woman who'll pray over you if you can. With a face like that, it won't be long before you find a woman who'll pay you."

"I'd as soon sleep in the gutter," Katie spat. She forced her voice to wheedling. "Please sir..."

A shot and a shout on a far street cut her off mid-plea, then suddenly, men were running everywhere. And Sullivan yielded with a sigh. "Just for long enow to keep you out of trouble tonight. For I meant it when I said, I dinna need the kind of trouble you'll bring."

He hurried them both inside the stable. The horses were snorting and restless, milling and pawing in their stalls, their blood rising as the swelling mob. But Sullivan spoke a single syllable and they calmed. And Katie calmed too. The world might be going mad outside, but in here was nowt but peace...

"There're blankets in the tack room," Sullivan said. "You can make your bed there. You'll not eat there, though. Trouble enough with the rats stealing the hay and grain. No need to give them cause to chew the leather too."

She raised a shoulder. "No worries there," she said. "I've no food with me, I promise."

The lunk drew another sigh. "Then I suppose we'd best settle that matter first."

He dug into his tiny larder and pulled out a pasty, which he carefully cut in half and tossed the larger part to her as casually as he had his purse. He thought for a moment, then dug even deeper and pulled out two pitchers. He poured a mug of ale for himself from the first, then spilled some milk into a mug from the other, and handed it to her with a glare that warned her against suggesting that she was more accustomed to drinking the other.

But Katie had no appetite, for she suddenly found herself consumed by guilt. First it had been the priest. Now it was Sullivan. What kind of sinner was she if she did any man who tried to help her a bad turn?

No, no sinner she. Just a poor lass that was torn between Preston Olcott and the hangman, who was doing what she had to just to survive. But still the memory of the nuns' tales about the torments that awaited her kind in hell made her reach for the lunk's purse and hold it out to him. "I thank ye for the night's shelter, but it must suffice," she said stiffly. "I would prefer there be no further debt between us when I go on my way in the morning."

If such a thing was possible, Sullivan's face grew more forbidding, and he made no move to take it. "'Tis no debt, but rather a gift freely given," he said. "And 'tis the height of insult to reject another horseman's generosity, ye hear? Now finish your milk and do what you can to stay out of trouble until I can find a way to be shed of you and have myself a bit of peace."

19

It had been said that if the Devil was the Prince of Lies, Lane Fallon was his anointed heir. As far as Lane was concerned, that was not simply the truth; it was an article of faith. So what had just happened? The lies about his dealings with Preston Olcott had come to him as fluently as any other tale he had spun in his life. But, as Lane limped out of Union Hall in the company of Morrissey's men, he was assailed by an unfamiliar sense of doubt: Had he gone too far? He had certainly convinced the thugs that he was an opportunist and a cad, a lower form of pond life than even they were. The problem was, how thoroughly might he have convinced Rose Adair as well? And why should she not believe that, of all the masks he had donned, this ugly adventurer was the closest to the real Lane Fallon, when he was half-convinced of it himself?

But regrets were best left for when he had time to wallow in them—and there was naught to do but ignore the voice that whispered that might well be for the rest of his life. Right now, he needed to stay focused on his plan—what little of it there was, beyond a hope that Morrissey's men would prove a better passport to winning the trust of the Irish in Little Dublin than his own English accent. Beyond that, he had no fixed ideas, only a vague notion of finding Sammy Nunn, and using all the persuasive abilities that had suddenly cast Rose Adair in such doubt—along with a few others that he would prefer Rose Adair know nothing of—in order to convince the stubborn fool to see reason. And if the opportunity presented itself, he assumed he owed it to… *someone* to find Sullivan…

But as soon as they set foot in Little Dublin, Lane knew his plans were for naught. When the draft riots had erupted in New York City, he had been lying in a field hospital outside Gettysburg, along with what remained of the Irish Brigade, but the moment he saw the mob that threatened Little Dublin, he knew it was far more dangerous than any Confederate charge could ever be. Already the Irish were talking of massing on Broadway and marching to the colored side of town, their faces set with same grim determination Lane remembered as when Father William Corby stood on a rock and pronounced absolution before the Brigade had launched a doomed attack on a piece of the Gettysburg battleground that would be forever known as the Wheatfield. *Faugh a Ballagh*, the Irishmen had shouted, Clear the Way, as they charged to near certain death. The men massed in front of the brightly lit windows of Nunn's tawdry gaming house looked no less determined.

Even Morrissey's men seemed to lose some of their bullying swagger as they stepped into the crowd and asked, "Now then, Mr. Morrissey would like to know what's going on here."

A spate of shouted replies was enough to confirm Lane's direst speculations. Sammy Nunn was dead. A Negro had killed him, as part of a conspiracy to drive Mr. Morrissey out of Saratoga and the Irish too…

There was nothing left for Lane except to seize the opportunity to slide into the shadows. Sammy Nunn was dead. He had discovered all he needed to know. It seemed there was little left to him here, beyond finding his brother…

"Captain Fallon? I've been looking for you."

A compact man emerged from a nearby alley and immediately held up both hands. "Please. I mean you no harm. I seek only information." He cast a long look at Lane's shabby coat, perhaps comparing it with his own conspicuously neat one. "I am willing to pay a reasonable price for it."

Dear God, Little Dublin was about to erupt in flame, and this man proposed to discuss *price*?

"I have no need…" The instinctive answer died on Lane's lips almost immediately, as he realized how badly he compared to this tidy, well-dressed man. "You're Washington?" he sighed.

"My name is Cole Washington III," the man allowed. "Although in racing circles I tend to be better known as Colonel Farraday's nigger. That was because the Colonel owned me, as surely as he owned his horses. And at least the horses were known by their own names."

Which was, Lane would be the first to admit, a legitimate complaint—legitimate enough that thousands of men had died for it. However, he didn't think he could be criticized for saying it was hardly *germane*. "You need to get out of here. Now."

But Washington just shook his head, his eyes never moving from the mob. "I don't much like Irishmen," he mused.

And Lane knew Washington wasn't seeing the men of Little Dublin at all, but rather another mob, and another building with flames licking from windows. Another mob that Lane Fallon was at least partially responsible for.

But recriminations, like revenge, were best consumed cold. And right now, both of them were likely to find themselves in very hot water indeed. "Then it's your great good fortune that I'm English," he said tightly. "Now can we get out of here?"

But it was already too late. Morrissey's men spotted them and came barreling over.

"You're Cole Washington?"

Just say no, Lane willed him. It was unlikely to do any good, but right now stalling and throwing dust in whatever eyes were nearest to hand was the only option Lane could see.

"I am," Washington said.

"We need you come with us. Mr. Morrissey would like a word."

"In regard to?"

"Mr. Morrissey is not accustomed to offering explanations."

"Unfortunately, explanations are exactly what I have come to Saratoga in search of."

Lane shut his eyes. The cursed fool! Of course, he would play the hero. But if he thought these men would lead him peaceably to a court of justice, he had learned nothing from the draft riots.

The silent stand-off between Washington and Morrissey's men continued. And Lane's gaze turned speculatively toward the steeple of the Church of St. Peter, as he recalled the chaplains of the Irish Brigade. Father William Corby was not alone; while the majority of the Northern churchmen were content to preach abolition from the pulpits and console the Union's widows and orphans, the chaplains of the Irish Brigade had marched along with their countrymen and braved the same dangers. And the Irish returned their church's loyalty with the ferocity of the ancient Fenians.

At least, Lane had to hope that was the case. Ignoring the pain that stabbed whenever he overused his weak left foot, he slid unnoticed into the shadows and raced toward the church. It cost him only a moment's effort to break into the sacristy. It took a moment's more compunction for him to gather up the altar cloths that had been lovingly washed and pressed by the good sisters and spill every drop of oil he could find—consecrated or unconsecrated—onto them. Lighting the tapers cost him another moment's more doubt—should he at least leave a penny for the price of a prayer?—before he tossed them onto the oil-soaked pile. It was scarcely Greek fire, but it would have to serve.

Dashing back out of the church, he pulled out his revolver and fired a shot, then raced back to where Washington still stood facing Morrissey's men. Time to see where Little Dublin's loyalties truly lay.

It was a daring—some would even say a desperate—risk. A gunshot was as likely to inflame the mob as warn them of the danger to their church. And for one brief, despairing moment, he was certain he had failed. Then, the cry went up, "The church! The church! Fire!"

The mob didn't move as one; it was too much to hope that they would have. But Morrissey's men turned away, distracted, and Lane seized the moment to hiss, "Over here! Now!"

Thankfully, Washington at least had the good sense to hurry after Lane down several alleys and into the relative safety of a back street. But then he stopped and stared at Lane, bemused. "Did you just set fire to a church?"

"I've done worse," Lane said. "In the name of far less. But perhaps that is something we could discuss later. You need to run. And run now."

"Run from what?" Washington asked. "I've done nothing."

"And when has that ever saved a man from the gallows?" Lane shook his head. "Please. You need to trust me. Run, now. Run for your life. I'll… try to come up with another diversion."

Washington eyed him. "The Irish aren't likely to be too happy with an Englishman who just set fire to their church any more than a Negro accused of murder."

"Be that as it may." Lane gestured toward his weak foot, which had begun to throb. "I'm not much good in a footrace…"

"Then we'd best come up with another plan."

For the love of God! Lane had never seen such a stubbornly stupid sense of honor unless it was his stiff-necked devil of a brother—who, it could be argued, was the one who got him into this mess in the first place. "Well, if you have a suggestion, I'd like to hear it, because frankly, I'm clean out of them…"

The clop of hoofbeats cut off Lane's furious protest. Moments later, a saddled chestnut mare trotted into view, her reins dragging along the ground. Had she escaped from one of the barns by the track? Thrown her rider on some elegant boulevard back on the other side of the tracks? Wandered astray while her master amused himself in some assignation in the privacy of the parks?

Or had she somehow been *sent*?

What did it matter? Was Lane Fallon of all men one to look what was quite literally a gift horse in the mouth? He seized the mare's bridle and leapt onto her back, then thrust down a hand to Washington. "Here! Swing up behind me and let's waste no more time getting out of here."

A moment's consideration, then Washington looked up, and Lane saw the man was actually grinning. "I accept your offer," Washington said, then paused to reached for his tidy bowler and pull it down hard over his ears, before he added, "With one small adjustment..."

Ignoring Lane's proffered grip, he sprang up in front of the saddle and seized the reins. "You can keep the irons," he said generously. "You'll probably need them. But if you must hold on, grab my belt, not my back."

And before Lane could offer so much as a word of protest, Washington thrust himself up into a jockey's crouch, and then they were off...

The cry went up at the first rattle of the mare's hooves, and the mob surged and ebbed, divided between the burning church and giving chase. Washington showed no such hesitation. Gathering the reins into one hand, he drove straight at them, steering only with his legs, cutting a swathe with the makeshift whip, and kicking out at heads and guns as casually as he might have fought off another horse at the rail. It was the dirtiest, most desperate, most adept riding Lane had ever seen—even on the battlefield. And by God, it was *fast*.

But just when Lane began to hope that the luck that had seen him through Gettysburg might allow him to survive this night as well, a police wagon swung into their path in an explosion of rattles and whistles, and what must have been the entire police force of Saratoga Springs scrambled out and raised their guns. Washington sat the mare back on her haunches, and spun her back toward the seething mob. But how could even the dirtiest, most daring jockey outrun a volley of bullets?

The answer erupted from nowhere in a clatter of heavy hooves, as two mismatched drays, one grey, one black, too old and unfashionable to draw anything more than the morning's milk-cart, but heavy and strong enough to plunge straight toward the line of police, kicking and biting with the ferocity of warhorses…

Faugh a Ballagh, Lane muttered—more a prayer than a command.

Clear the Way.

Another spin, another charge straight toward the line of coppers, and they were through. And the world began to flash by in a series of images like a drunken stereopticon: Washington gathered his mount to leap across the railroad tracks that Lane told himself couldn't possibly be humming with the noise of an approaching train. The cries and shouts of the crush on Broadway as Washington plied his whip and heels past the grand piazzas as if he were threading his way through the pack on the home stretch. And then a brick wall, as high as a five-bar gate, that Washington charged head-on, apparently with every intention of leaping it. And Lane Fallon, who had been on horseback since his father had gifted him with his first pony on his fifth birthday, who had hunted fox and wolves across England and Ireland, and who had even managed to keep his aim steady when his mount had been shot out from beneath him in the middle of the Wheatfield itself, simply gave up and shut his eyes.

20

The Pale Queen, oh, she lost a kiss
 Out in the bonny heather.
The Pale Queen, oh, she lost her mount
When he broke her tether.
The Pale Queen oh, she lost her Knight,
Then came death and slaughter.
The first Queen nurses
The next Queen curses
But the Red Queen is her Father's daughter.

The cracked echo of his poor, daft mother's dying voice had drawn Sullivan into the alley in time to rescue the lad from his attacker. Now, it swelled once more, bringing in its wake a chorus of angry shouts and pounding boots. Sullivan leapt to his feet, tossing the remains of his meal to the lad, along with a terse order.

"Stay. Here."

And he plunged out of the stable, onto the street, to find…

Riastrad. There was no other word for it. The Battle Madness of CuChulainn—a picture grim enough to haunt most Irish children's dreams. The red rage warped CúChulainn into a monster: his bones twisted backward inside his skin, one eye sucked deep inside his head, the other hanging down his cheek. His mouth widened and widened until his gullet appeared, and his lungs and his liver flapped in his mouth and throat…

It was nothing compared to the danger that seethed on the streets of Little Dublin. Eyes narrowing, Sullivan looked around. He could understand what drove horses to a frenzy, the blind panic that caused a herd to stampede. But he still did not understand what possessed good men, ordinary men, and transformed them into the pack of ravening beasts that now howled for the blood of the man who had killed Sammy Nunn.

Sammy. The cracked, insistent singing in Sullivan's head stilled briefly. He hadn't yet had time to absorb the fact that Sammy was dead—let alone mourn him. And mourn him, Sullivan did, no matter that he well knew that Sammy had blood on his hands—as surely as if he had killed 119 people himself and not just sold them out of his own stubborn greed. Indeed, there would be many who would argue Sammy's sin was blacker than that of the raging mob. But in his way, Sammy had been a good man, a kind man, who took under his wing as many as he could of the starving children that were more plentiful than the rats in Five Points—even if he had sought to use them for his own purposes. And he was never without a spare penny to toss to the rest. Sullivan was not one disposed to debate theology, but if he were to believe in a God at all, it could not be in one who would consign a man like Sammy to hellfire...

No, not hellfire. Fire.

Sullivan froze, as he finally put a name to the scent that had been tickling his nostrils ever since he stepped outside.

To a horseman, there was no more terrifying word. To a Saratogan, doubly so, for the memory of the conflagration that had consumed several of the finest buildings on Broadway was still fresh. The United States Hotel had been declared beyond saving in less than an hour. In under two hours it had completely collapsed. Sullivan's stable was made of wood, as were most of its neighbors. How long would it take for the same to befall Little Dublin?

But to release the horses out into the street in the midst of that mob? That would be the same as launching a pack of baying wolfhounds among a flock of sheep. For when horses were in a panic about fire, not even the horsewhisperer that half the world accused him of being could calm the animals enough to save their lives. Or the lives of the men they would trample.

"*The Raven Queen she lost her mount when he broke her tether*," the ugly voice inside his head awoke to agree.

Enough. Sullivan stilled it irritably. He had to think clearly, and he had to think now. By the time the horses caught the first whiff of smoke, it would be too late.

He skirted the stable, around to the yard where the dray horses, solid and uncomplaining, but kinder and more useful than their blooded cousins, spent the night with no more reward than a few forkfuls of hay and a watering trough. Tonight, there was only a mismatched grey and black that drew the morning's milk, and Sullivan's concern relaxed a little when he saw that they had not lifted their heads from their food. There should be enough room here to release all the other horses, if the need arose.

With a quick touch on each flank, he made his way past the drays to make sure the gate was secure.

A shout arose from the street.

And Sullivan at last saw the flames flickering behind the windows of St. Peter's and the untidy line of men organizing themselves into a bucket brigade—just as a lovely chestnut burst out of the shadows, with a dark lad crouched on her neck…

And Sullivan's wretched excuse for a half-brother clinging for all he was worth to the lad's back.

At long last, the fear that clenched Sullivan's gut relaxed. For if it was Lane Fallon who had set the fire—as it did not take the Sight to see it most certainly was—there was little chance of it spreading. Fallon's weapons were lies and illusions, not flames and fists: John Costigan's church was no more threatened than New York City had been by Fallon's Greek fire.

But the men at the church were a different story. Already, they were dropping their buckets and turning to give chase.

"There's Sammy's murderer, for sure!"

"Set fire to the church, too."

"More like the Devil came to claim his own."

"After him!"

"String him up!"

There'd be little enough chance of that, for by God, Washington rode like an angel, even if it was the Devil himself that clung to his back. But even St. Michael couldn't leap his heavenly mount straight over the police wagon that suddenly hove into the view, with the first of the fire engines immediately behind. And Sullivan drew a deep breath, as he told himself this was none of his concern. Lane Fallon deserved whatever fate he had brought down on his own head far more richly than Sammy Nunn ever had.

And Cole Washington? Or the sweet, red mare?

With a muttered oath, Sullivan swung the yard gate open, then turned back to the cart horses. "Now then lads," he said, "I apologize for fashing you during your meal, but the need is come for you see to your Lady. Gently, lads, gently. No cause to harm anyone. But defend your Queen. And if She is willing, defend the Irish against themselves. Bid them save their church and save their souls."

"*The first Queen nurses,*" his mother's voice howled in triumph. "*The next Queen curses…*"

And the two horses, one black, one white, spilled out of the yard and into the street, hooves flying, teeth snapping like Macha's Grey and Saingliu's Black, CuChulainn's own war horses the gift of the Morrigan herself, scattering the line of policemen and driving the men back toward the burning church, as inexorably as the ocean tides that were said to be the white-maned horses of the sea-god, Manannan mac Lir…

"Ye daft fool, what do ye think you're playing at? Ye think the coppers are nae Olcott's men, bought and paid for? They'll shoot ye on sight, ye great lunk."

And Sullivan just had time to wonder why the voice that shouted at him was at once so familiar and so very different, before a shadow flung itself hard into him, slamming him hard to the ground. Moments later, a shot rang out, and Sullivan barely managed to roll his attacker and himself back into relative safety behind the watering trough.

Another moment's tense waiting, but no further shots were forthcoming, and Sullivan turned his attention to the ragged figure that lay face down in the dirt beside him.

And cursed loudly and fluidly and with an inventiveness that would have had his old wet nurse washing his mouth out with soap, Declan Sullivan, no matter that he was a full-grown man, as he recognized the urchin that he had ordered to remain in the tack room, and saw the blood that was seeping from the boy's shoulder.

"Lord, lad, canna you keep yourself out of trouble for even one hour?" he muttered. "I have no time to play at being a nanny atop of everything else."

But it seemed his wyrd was offering him few other options. The lad was limp from shock. Nae, Sullivan forced himself to admit honestly. The lad was limp from taking a bullet that had been meant for him. With a fresh volley of curses, he scooped up the lad and lurched back into the stable, not to the tack room, but rather to the straw-stuffed pallet that served as his own bed. He took heart from the fact that there was little blood on his shirt as he laid the lad down, and looked around for some of the bandages, salves, and ointments he used on sore horses. It seemed the shot had just grazed the boy. Indeed, he was already thrashing and moaning back to consciousness by the time Sullivan got back to the pallet. And when Sullivan reached to unbutton his shirt, the lad was sufficiently recovered to scuttle back against the meager pillow where Sullivan laid his head.

"Relax, laddie," Sullivan said, his voice lapsing into the soothing cadences that could calm the most skittish colts, "I've bound up enow horses that I can most likely bind your wounds with less hurt than any sawbones. Ye may feel a tweak, I'll give you that, but it'll be over soon enow, I promise you that…"

As he spoke, his hands moved to the lad's shirt front, running across the bloody fabric to feel for the wound with the same practiced ease that he'd feel a foreleg for a splint. Only to stop in horror, as his hands moved across the urchin's skinny spavined chest—and instead felt something much softer and fuller—as the cracked and ancient voice rose inside his head in untrammeled glee:

> *The Red Maid, oh, she gave no kiss*
> *To none she did not choose.*
> *The Red Maid, oh, she needs no Knight,*
> *Her maidenhead to lose.*
> *The Red Maid, oh, she needs no mount,*
> *She runs freely as the water.*
> *The first Queen nurses*
> *The next Queen curses*
> *But the Red Queen is her own son's daughter.*

Springing to his feet, he stumbled back across the pile of bandages, as he finally took a long look at the urchin's face. Even in the half-light, he could only wonder what kind of fool he was not to have seen the truth that lay plainly in front of him.

"You're one of Sammy's girls," he said hoarsely. "The red-haired one, is it?"

"And what if I am?"

This time the volley of curses that Sullivan let fly would have roused his wet nurse straight out of her grave. Then he simply began to laugh, shoulders shaking helplessly as he buried his head in his hands. No good deed went unpunished—at least in Declan Sullivan's benighted world. For he had traveled halfway across the globe to flee a curse he never believed in, and still his wyrd had contrived to catch up with him. "By all the saints and all that is holy," he sighed, "please say that you are nae virgin."

The next thing he knew, his world had exploded into pain and sparkling lights. His hand crept to his stinging cheek, as the tears that sprang to his eyes finally receded enough for him to be able to study the creature that confronted him in numb disbelief. For all she looked like nothing so much as one of the stable cat's litters that he had just saved from drowning, right down to the calico hair that seemed to be an unspeakable combination of mud and soft red curls, the lass could land as smart a blow as Morrissey ever could.

21

As if the great lunk of a stable lad hadn't just offered Katie the kind of insult old Sammy would have never stood for, now the daft fool couldna stop laughing. Well, if the reddened patch she had already left on his face was not enough to teach him, then she would give him another lesson in manners quick enough. Ignoring the pain that seized her, she leapt to her feet and snatched a razor from the tidy dresser. "Not one step closer," she hissed.

"Have a care," he said. "I strop that nightly. And you're already bleeding enow as it is."

She glanced down at her shirt, which was rapidly soaking with blood. And damnit if the big lunk seized the distraction as neatly as any pickpocket down in Five Points and simply plucked the razor from her hands, before he said, "I apologize if I frightened you. It was not my intent. But… I confess I was taken by surprise. I took you to my bed, you see…?"

She stared at him. Surely, the poor man couldn't be as daft as all that. Then again, it might explain why a fine figure of man like him was making his bed in a stable. For he was a fine figure of a man when he wasn't scowling or half-pixilated: Tall and strong and with those Black Irish looks that had been the downfall of more than one lass who hadn't kept her wits about her. "In case ye dinna know," she said, "you laid me on your bed. Ye dinna take me to your bed. Not in that sense of the word. And if you're thinking to have plans in that direction, I'll have you know, I'm not that type of lass."

"And I'll have you know I'm not a man to take an unwilling lass, when there have been plenty who'd come to my bed not just willingly, but happily…" His jaw clamped shut, and he forced himself to take a deep breath. "Come now, lass. The damage is already done. Why should we quarrel? I dinna hurt you before. Surely you can trust me now?"

She gathered what remained of her pride along with her strength, trying not to sway as she lurched across the rapidly increasing distance that separated her from the curtain he had hastily drawn to close off his private quarters. "Then I thank ye for your kindness," she said. "But I think it would be better if I am on my way."

"Ye canna," Sullivan said simply.

She stopped. "Why not?"

"Well for one thing, you're leaving blood everywhere you go." His voice was reasonable but there was no mistaking the way he bit his lip, as if fighting down another spasm of daft laughter.

She cast her eyes toward his meagre bed and its stained covers. "If you're that concerned about a pile of old linen, I'll go steal you something better from the workhouse laundry."

"Aye, and I believe you would do just that," he agreed gravely, before he set his jaw and shook his head firmly. "You leave my bedding to me. It's as much of my affair as your rags are to you. But you saved my life, lass. And that puts me under an obligation to you. So if you will be so good as to sit back down before you fall down, and loosen the collar of your shirt a bit, I give you my word I will observe the proprieties and keep my eyes firmly focused on the task at hand."

The room shifted sideways, warning Katie that he might be right about at least half of his prediction. But as she sagged back onto the bed, she caught a glimpse of the dented flask that also lay atop the dresser. "So given I'm no lad," she said hopefully. "Perhaps you'll allow me a drop of that whiskey."

When Sullivan's only answer was to shoot her a sharp glance, she fluttered her eyelashes. "Medicinal, ye ken. For the pain."

His mouth twisted as if once more the laughter threatened to erupt, before he yielded and handed her the flask. "One swallow at a time," he cautioned her. "And make sure you leave me enow to steel myself for the task ahead of me."

With a small smile, Katie took a demure sip. Then Sullivan set to work with quick, practiced gestures that betrayed none of his earlier embarrassment. Now, his hands moved as impersonally as if he were bandaging a sore horse. In no time, he had her propped back against his thin pillow and covered with a blanket, after firmly plucking the flask from her hand.

"Now, sleep," he said. "We'll figure out what to do with ye in the morning, when the excitement dies down…"

"What do you mean, sleep? Here in your bed?"

He raised a shoulder. "No use crying over spilled milk. The damage—whatever it may turn out to be, God help us all—is already done."

"What damage?" Katie's eyes narrowed in sudden suspicion. "What are ye, then? Some kind of priest?"

"I'm sure there's no church that would have me."

And Katie's Irish rose. "Then what's all this talk of taking a virgin to your bed? Do you think I've somehow shamed ye? I'll have you know, I'm Nunn's Irish Rose. And ye are what? A stablehand that stinks of shite?"

He glanced away, but not fast enough that she could see the tell-tale twist of his lips once more. "Strikes me as an accurate enow description," he allowed.

"Then ye scarce need to act like I've seized your maidenhead." She swung herself from beneath the blanket—only to stop as the whiskey and the pain caught her together, and she was forced to wait until the world stopped spinning, before she gathered what dignity she could and said, "I'll thank ye kindly for your concern. And your care. But 'tis probably time I moved on now."

Once more, Sullivan's mouth quirked. "And where exactly do ye propose to be moving?" he asked with careful courtesy.

"Now, that's none of your concern, is it?"

"We've already established that ye've saved my life. Which makes it very much my concern. But even if it were not, you've seen those who are gathering out there on the street. 'Tis no place for a lady."

"And do you think a lady such as myself is accustomed to sleeping in a stable?"

His dark blue eyes glinted with humor as he appraised her. "Why else would such an oh, so proper lady, find herself in a back alley dressed as a ragamuffin?"

Why else indeed? Her cheeks flamed. She might not be a lady, but neither was she that other kind of lass—no matter what Preston Olcott might care to think. She was Nunn's Irish Rose, held to the standards of strictest propriety by old Sammy himself. But the simple, unvarnished truth of what had brought her to that alley would certainly not make her sound that way. "I'll have you know that is my affair and none of yours."

"We have already discussed the reasons I am obliged to disagree." Suddenly, his gaze grew hypnotic, compelling. "So I would have you tell me. What kind of lady prowls the back alleys of Little Dublin in such a kit?"

What kind of lady? One that would cheat anyone—priest, stablehand, or even old Sammy, who was fool enow to show her a kindness. One that still proposed to steal those cursed papers back from this daft stable hand if she was given half a chance. The kind of thief Sammy had died to save her from becoming....

It was all too much. Katie's shoulders slumped. "I came after those papers. I… proposed to steal them back."

Sullivan drew a sharp breath, then pinned her once more with that weird, blue gaze of his. "Why? Why bring trouble on your own head?'

She swallowed hard. "'Twas the only way I could think to save myself from Preston Olcott."

The big lunk's face grew grim. "And what would a lass like you be knowing of a man like him?"

She tossed her red curls, cropped and blackened though they might be. "He took an interest in my career. He told me there was far more open to a lass of my talents than wasting away as Nunn's Irish Rose."

And if the dark lunk of a stable lad's face softened this time, maybe she imagined it. "And did you believe his promises?"

"I'm a singer," she said. "A *chanteuse*, old Sammy called it. Sometimes a bit of a dancer as well. Nothing more."

"That's nae answer to my question," he pointed out.

As if he had a right to be questioning her! "'Tis all the answer you'll be getting until you give me back those papers. They by rights belong to Sammy. And now that he's gone, they're his legacy to me."

A thunderous silence. And then Sullivan muttered something probably best not heard about the bloody logic of the universe, before he said, "And why should I know anything about those papers? I'm just a stable lad who stinks of shite."

"Dinna lie to me. I saw Sammy give you them. I heard him say he couldn't allow Olcott to get his hands on him. Just as I heard him say you were mixed up with a bunch of Fenians."

Sullivan's face darkened. "So you spy as well as steal?"

"A girl's got to take care of herself. No-one else will in this benighted world."

"If you're trying to take care of yourself, you'd best have as little to do with those papers as possible." Sullivan said with a significant glance at her bandaged shoulder. "As perhaps you've already learned."

Once more, Katie's Irish flared. How dare the great lunk lecture her? "You say you're no priest, but you're no different than the rest of those old crows. Lesson learned, yeah? Know my place? And here I was thinking that mayhap you'd be grateful that I saved your life."

He shut his eyes. "I *am* grateful. That's why I'm trying to steer you away from trouble."

"Then 'twould be best if you'd let me see to my own safety and tell me what I want to know."

He stared at her in mute fury for a moment, then gave in with a sigh. "What do you really know about those papers?"

"I know they're what got poor Sammy killed," Katie retorted. "And I know you knew. I heard you trying to warn him."

"More spying?" he asked.

"What does it matter?" Abruptly, all the fight went out of Katie, and her shoulders slumped. "I tried to warn him, too. But he wouldna listen to me any more than you. I told Sammy then it wasn't right. I told him get rid of them. But Sammy wouldna listen, because Sammy dinna truly know what he had—and how dangerous it could be."

"And you did?"

"Those papers had names. Rich men's names. Powerful men's names. Any fool could see that a man like Sammy had no business with such people."

Sullivan glanced at her. "And how did you know that, if Sammy dinna? You'd have me believe you read those papers for yourself?"

His obvious disbelief infuriated her. "I can read and write as well as any shite-stained stable lad, thank you very much. Convent-bred, that's what old Sammy used to say. All his girls were convent bred, and not just Nunn's Irish Rose."

"Sounds more to me like you ran off from a House of Mercy," Sullivan snorted.

It was all Katie could do not to snatch up the razor once more and swing it at his thick head. "And can you blame me? They only schooled us so we could read the Bible and recite their wretched prayers. The rest of the time we spent scrubbing in the laundry. And if you were good enough and worked hard enough one day they'd do you the honor of offering to become one of them and spend the rest of your life hidden behind the convent walls, your only pleasure or purpose tormenting a new crop of lasses whose only sin was to be born without father or mother. Can you blame me for running off?"

Sullivan's eyes glinted with humor. "Sure and that would have been a terrible waste," he agreed. "To think of the world without Nunn's Irish Rose."

"Do *not* mock me," she said fiercely. Just as suddenly, her face crumpled, and her hand went to the muddy mess that had once been her crowning glory. "They would have cut my hair. That's why I ran. And now, look at me. The wages of pride, I suppose. Sure and those dried-up praying bitches were right."

She felt, rather than saw, his hand reach out to touch her, and her own hand moved for the razor. Blinded by her welling tears as she was, she swore by all the saints the cursed nuns had taught her to pray to, she would kill him if he touched her right now.

22

After a gallop that seemed to last an entire night, but probably was finished in less than half an hour, Washington finally pulled the mare up in the safety of the woods that separated Saratoga Springs from its neighbor and rival, Ballston Spa. Lane slid gratefully down from the saddle and spent a long time simply doubled over, remembering how to breathe. When the world finally stopped spinning, he looked up to find Washington had already removed the mare's bridle so she could drink from the stream in which she cooled her hooves, while he rubbed the sweat off her coat with what had once been a neatly pressed handkerchief.

"If you're done there," Washington said, "perhaps you could gather up a little offering of food, by way of a thank you. Try to pull up more clover than grass; it's likely she would prefer it."

Well, if it came right down to that, Lane would prefer to retch up what remained of his most recent meal. But preferences had little to do with anything that had happened that night. With a sigh, he began to gather clover—which somehow seemed to be growing everywhere around him. And when the mare had daintily received his offering with her velvety lips, Lane forced himself to turn to Washington. And sighed once more. The ride had left Lane's clothes sweat-stained, if not shit-stained. Washington, on the other hand, had not only kept his hat on during that entire wild gallop, he had managed to brush it off as neatly as he had the mare's coat.

Lane glanced longingly at the road that led to Ballston Spa, and then at the mare. "I don't suppose there's any chance I can persuade you to get back in the saddle and let her carry you down that road to Ballston Spa and as far beyond it as you can go?" he asked.

"No," Washington said.

Of course not. Lane shut his eyes. "But *why?*"

A moment's pause. Then Washington seemed to come to a decision. He met Lane's eyes and held them, before he said, "Her name was Sarah. She was a free woman and I was a slave, but that didn't matter. We loved each other. And you may not believe in lovers any more than you do heroes, but I can tell you I sought no greater meaning in life than to grow old with her, like Baucis and Philemon." His mouth twisted at Lane's evident surprise. "She was an educated woman. Daughter of a preacher who read Greek, Latin, and Hebrew. She taught me to read English."

He drew a deep breath. "And for a while it was all right. Old Farraday was happy enough to keep me contented, as long as I kept winning for him, and so he allowed us to be together. Even allowed her father to marry us. Sent for his own doctor the first time my wife was taken to the child bed." His face set. "I only saw the truth when the doctor announced it was a girl. Old Farraday slapped my shoulder and said, 'No worries. Plenty of time for you to get me a boy as talented as you. We'll call him Cole and he'll be able to ride like hell, just like you, and just like your daddy, and your daddy's daddy before him.'"

For the first time, emotion colored Washington's voice. "All of them Cole Washington. And all of them slaves, despite their mother having been born free. And the Colonel honestly believed I'd be *grateful* for the opportunity to breed him another." Washington shook his head, recalling himself. "I started making my plans before Sarah started showing the next time. Told her she needed to go North. Told her she needed to keep the children safe."

His jaw set, and his voice grew distant. "And when she refused, when she said she wanted to keep the family together, no matter what the circumstances, I told her I no longer loved her. Told her I'd found a fancy piece down at the track, prettier, younger, and slimmer that she had ever been. Lied to her and hurt her. Didn't care what it took to force her to go North. Go to New York, where she and my children would be free. And safe."

He didn't bother to disguise his irony at the last. Instead, he let it linger, so Lane could feel the force of what was coming before Washington went on, his voice soft with emotion, "They burned down an orphanage—an *orphanage*, for God's sake. They said you could hear the children screaming from a mile away. They tell me Sarah screamed, too, from the second story window where she was trying to throw the babies down to the firemen. She pleaded for their lives. Nor for her life. For the babies. And instead the firemen turned away. There were fires to fight on Fifth Avenue, where the rich men had their homes."

Washington's words trailed off, and Lane felt the stirring of... something he only felt when he looked into Rose Adair's eyes. Which should have been warning enough. He drew a deep breath and forced his voice to reason. "Let me speak frankly, Mr. Washington. Are you looking for justice? Or vengeance?"

"Vengeance would make me no better than the Irish pigs who killed Sarah—along with 118 other innocent Negroes."

He spat the number like a slap—and it stung Lane even harder. It took everything he was capable of, to gather himself enough to say, "The more's the pity. Because that is the only satisfaction you are likely to have." He squelched Washington's angry retort with a wave of his hand. "Because let me tell you frankly what you're up against, Mr. Washington. You are up against the richest men in America. Men who cared no more about the cause of abolition than the shanty Irish they packed off to fight their war. Men whose only god is money, and who are more than willing to make blood sacrifice in that greedy god's honor. Men who profited greatly from cotton, right up here on Wall Street, not down on your plantations. Men whose only loyalty to the North was a matter of geography. Men who would have welcomed a Confederate victory—and arguably even a Confederate army—with open arms.

"Think about the timing of those riots. Lee was marching north, and it began to look like no-one was going to stop him. In the meantime, the Union army was in shambles, the command changing, it seemed weekly. If Lee had not been stopped at Gettysburg, New York was the next place he would march. How much easier it would have been to take that city, if it was already at war with itself. And how much easier to march on New York City, if Lincoln were forced to call out the New York State Militia to defend Manhattan, instead of using it to provide the reinforcements the Union army so desperately needed?

"*Those* are the men you are looking for, Mr. Washington. *Those* are the men who killed your wife. Not a bunch of Irish hotheads riled up by the spies and rumors that those men set loose among them. And those are the men you will never bring to justice. Those are the puppetmasters who sent their agents among the Irish, in the taverns, among the friendly societies, whispering tales of how the colored people were conspiring with the English to squelch the cause of Irish freedom for once and for all, and substitute the Irish for the Negroes as the South's slaves."

A long pause. Then Washington said, "I thank you for that information. I would thank you even more for names."

The stubborn bastard. Had he even listened to a word Lane had said? "You're on a fool's quest, Mr. Washington. Give it up, I beg you. What would it gain to add your life to the 119 that have already died?"

"In other words, you would have me turn a blind eye?" Washington cocked his head to study Lane. "Is that what you did, Captain Fallon? Simply turn a blind eye? Why? To protect your own life? Or your profits?"

Lane shrugged with an indifference he most certainly did not feel. "Take a good look at me, Mr. Washington. Do I look like I made a profit from anything?"

"No," Washington allowed. His eyes narrowed. "Which can only lead me to ask, then why?"

Lane drew a deep breath before he allowed himself to revisit the night that had arguably ruined his life. "When the Greek fire plot failed, I managed to convince the police to take me to John Wool, the commander of the Eastern district of the Union Army, before they hanged me. I intended to do my best to warn him of a cabal that had neither the Union's, nor New York City's, best interests at heart. I could not know at the time whether he took me seriously or not, for I had nothing real to offer him, beyond the name of my brother and a conviction that those behind the Greek fire plot would not wait long to strike again. As it turns out, he never tried to find my brother, and it would have made no difference if he had, for the proof I sought to safeguard by sending it to Sullivan never reached him. But when the Draft Riots erupted, there were 800 troops to hand in New York Harbor, West Point, and the Brooklyn Navy yard, which Wool was able to summon immediately to restore order. I like to think that was because he took my warning seriously, but I have no way of knowing. Just as I have no way knowing how many lives my warning really saved, or how many more might have been if things had happened otherwise…"

His voice trailed off into a shrug.

"In other words, you knew it was a fool's quest?" Washington asked quietly.

Lane sighed. "You're still not going to give up, are you?"

"No."

"Then I can only think of one possible way you stand a prayer of winning this fight," Lane said. "And be warned, it involves you trusting an Irishman."

He heaved himself to his feet, telling himself that the pain that radiated from his weak foot was no worse than any other time he had overused it—then stopped, blinking in bewilderment.

"What happened to the mare?"

For she was gone—vanished as surely as if she had never existed. Even Washington's imperturbable calm was briefly ruffled. Then he shrugged with a faint smile. "She was a Thoroughbred, not a Saddlebred," he said. "Perhaps she feels she has done her part."

He took the bridle down from where it was hanging on the tree, and slung it over one shoulder. "No point in wasting perfectly good tack, though," he said thriftily, before he gestured toward the long, dark road that led back to Saratoga. "So shall we?"

23

It was hard to think clearly when you were cursing yourself as a fool. And Sullivan had just discovered a remarkable fluency and inventiveness in himself for doing just that. How could he not have seen what was so plain in front of him? The ridiculous mud could fool no one, nor could the forced swagger and the hoarsened voice. God help the lass if the stage really were her career, for she had little enough talent. Only a man blinded by the cursed Goddess could have failed to see the lass for what she really was: The kind of trouble Sullivan had no time for right now.

But he could scarce simply throw her back into the street. For all the look of her as a lass who had been hardened and ill-treated worse than a hackney horse, she was clearly an innocent—and for all his sins, most likely a virgin at that. And now she was crying—over what? The nuns punishing her for daring to hold her head high? Instinctively, he reached to touch her chopped, ridiculous hair. Only to be met with the full force of her furious glare from behind the sheen of tears. And he dropped his hand, mindful of the skin that was still stinging from the first time she had slapped him. He had no desire for there to be a second.

Warily, he glanced at the waif again. And suddenly he recognized her. Saw her for the first horse he had ever gentled, the one who had showed him he had the gift. She had been a chestnut mare, untamable and destined for the knackers, her coppery coat covered in shit and sores, because none would venture into her stall to clean her—let alone dare to mount her. He had been a skinny boy who still didn't understand why he had been plucked from a croft to live in this big house with the strange, pale man who claimed to be his father, and the lying, limping bastard who took no pains to disguise his fury at being presented with a brother and a rival. It was for the best, his old nurse had assured him. His father was a rich man. Sullivan would never want for food or a warm bed. And neither would his mother's family; his rich father had sworn to that—buying his own son as casually as the English bought up the Irishmen's land. It was only that promise that had bought Sullivan's loyalty; if it had been for him to choose, he would have willingly chosen starvation, but he could not make that choice for the others, as gaunt and thin-faced as his nurse, for all the old woman tried to sneak her meagre portions to the children. And so Sullivan had grown up with no greater purpose than to remain alive so that his father would feed his family—at least until the mare called to him. She had been calling for help, for an end to her hurt, but it had been she who had saved him.

The mare had only been the first; but she had been the one who had brought him his gift. And now the waif had brought it back to him. Suddenly, Sullivan was filled with a rush of hope as his voice slipped into the soothing cadences he thought he had long forgotten. "And what is wrong with pride? What sin is there in holding your head high? A queen should be proud. I wouldna dare to laugh at a queen. For you are a queen my girl, one of the lost queens of old Eire. A child of the Tuatha de Danaan, the fair folk, the true gentry of our island, who were pushed aside, pushed underground by the Fir Bolg. This is no longer your world, but sometimes one of the Fair Folk will grace this world with visit, in the form of a splendid mare or a woman crowned with red hair. 'Tis great good luck to look on one, but those of this world are too mean and jealous to see them. Or if they do, they will hurt them and beat the pride out of them. So never give up your pride, my Queen, because you wear it rightly. And your hair will grow back, my girl. And when you walk with your head held high, it will stream out behind you like a royal banner."

He talked on and on, his words carrying themselves away and him along with him. It was only when the last echo of the whispers died away, did he notice she was studying him with sharp amusement. "Och, you have a quick enough tongue when you choose to use it."

He grinned back at her, feeling the same as when he'd held out the apple that he'd sneaked from the kitchen to last him on the journey across the moors on the night he had finally decided to run away, and the mare had reached for it with tentative, clever lips, then allowed him to brush her, his words sweeping away the fear and pain as his hands swept away the filth. Then the mare had allowed him to slip up onto her back—saddleless and bridleless in care for her sores, and he and the untamable horse had taken off across the moors, him crouched so low so that his face was buried in her streaming mane, the two of them pulsing as one in the moonlight.

They had run through the night—through the sky, through the stars, the world. And when they returned to the stableyard in the morning, Sullivan had taken a quick mean rush of pleasure in the shock that twisted his father's normally fathomless green eyes, as he whispered, "So Macha Ruad has made her choice."

"Call her what you will, she's under my protection now," Sullivan said, as he swung down from her back. "No man but me lays a hand on her. I'll wash her. I'll feed her. And I'll mount her if she's willing. And I'll kill any other man who ventures to touch her."

Just as this wee lass was under his protection now. "It's said that those that can whisper horses have a way with women as well," he said with a grin. "But I would beg you spare both of us putting it to the test. Cease your needless arguing and get a good night's rest instead. We'll figure what to do with you in the morning…"

He did not need to go on very much longer, for both her eyes and shoulders were drooping with exhaustion. When he was certain she was asleep, he drew the curtain on his quarters and slid back outdoors. He always thought better under a canopy of stars rather than with than a roof above his head.

The fire at the church had been extinguished, and a restless peace prevailed in Little Dublin. A few men still paced the streets warily, but the cart horses were already back at their hay, fresh for their dawn rounds. One white, one black, like CuChulainn's two war horses, foaled the same night he was born: one white, one black. Saingliu the Black and Macha's Grey, her clairvoyance a gift from Macha, the Mother of us all, the Triple Goddess herself. At once the Pale Queen, the Raven Queen, and the Red Queen. Macha, daughter of Ernmas, Macha, wife of Cruinniuc, and Macha Mong Ruad.

Macha the red. Sullivan was not of a bookish turn, but the reverence in his father's voice when he whispered her name had caused Sullivan to seize the first chance he could to steal into his father's study. And forcing himself to a task that was as unnatural to him as his knack with the horses was to most men, he read the truth about the woman that owned his father's soul—and, it would seem, had just claimed his as well.

Macha Mong Ruad, Macha of the Red Hair, daughter of the fire lord, the Dagda himself. the only queen the chroniclers listed among the High Kings of Ireland—and, according to the penciled note in his father's spidery hand, the Sovereignty herself. One who would choose her own mate, as the sons of Díthorba had learned when they tried to claim her, and she had tied them up and carried the three of them bodily to Ulster, where she enslaved them.

Such a story was nothing but another of the high old tales, spun to hold the winter's darkness at bay in front of the smoking peat fire. But the meaning of the pages that Sullivan so painstakingly deciphered went far beyond that, and he pushed them aside with shaking fingers. It was, of course, an open secret that Lord Wolverton fancied himself some kind of druid—as did half the English Court, right down to Her Majesty, the Defender of the Faith herself, whose beloved consort had appeared at Stonehenge for the Solstice Ritual. But the tale that Sullivan could make out from the crumbling manuscripts—the one that bound his pale, distant father—was far more unholy.

This tale was one of another Macha: Pale Macha, Cruinniuc's wife. A fairy woman, one of the Sidhe, the Tuatha de Danaan, who brought her husband untold wealth and power out of no greater reason than love of him—just as Pale Macha, according to his father's scribbled notes—had bestowed her favor on the Fallons—ever since the first Fallons had promised to protect the old ways against the pope and their fellow Normans who sought to bring the Irish church under the heel of Rome. And just as Cruinniuc's wealth had grown, the Fallons grew in wealth and power—their prosperity pledged by the sacred bridle of Manaanan Mac Lir. But just as Cruinniuc had been warned not to speak of his wife to anyone, so the Fallons had been warned not to reveal the secret of their power to anyone. And just as Cruinniuc had failed and his pregnant wife was forced to race the king's horses to save her husband, so the Fallons had fatally revealed their secret to the priests under Henry VIII, and had found themselves cursed by the dying woman as she was put to the test…

Nine generations, she had sworn that the curse would endure. And as she spoke it, so it was. The Fallons began a slow decline, every generation a shade weaker than the previous one, until a son had been born, so pale as to be bloodless—a sign, according to Wolverton's scribbled notes, that the time had come when the final price was due. And that price was nothing less than his first-born son.

A son triply born for the triple goddess, just as her first champion, CuChulainn had been. A son who would defend Her sovereignty with all the strength of CuChulainn. A son who would ride forth in her name and restore to her service the bridle the Fallons so carelessly had forfeited.

The tale made the meaning of the natal charts hidden beneath the manuscript unmistakable. A collection of the names and horoscopes of unmarried lasses in County Tipperary, including that of Sullivan's own mother. Deichtire—an odd name, an uncanny name for all it only meant the tenth: the tenth daughter, of a tenth daughter, it was said. It also meant that Declan Sullivan had been born for no greater purpose than to be sacrificed, got upon a poor, daft crofter's daughter to appease a legend that no sane man would believe in.

Sullivan shook his head as he stared up at the stars, trying to find some answers there. For his mind had gone back to other papers, which now lay buried in the bottom of his dresser. Not Sammy's papers, but letters that were addressed in the same spidery hand as that in his father's private study. Letters that he had thrown aside, unopened for over a decade. Letters that he had left to burn when he had fled Manhattan—only to have fresh letters find him in Saratoga…

His dying mother's cracked voice rose once more inside his head. "He sought to dispossess you. He sought to cheat me of the reward he swore was yours," she said. "But the Goddess will prevail, the Virgin will come freely to your bed, and you will claim your true birthright in her name."

And to his dismay, Sullivan realized that, after all those vows he had sworn so many years ago, his wyrd had finally caught up with him, and that was exactly what he was about to do.

24

The five miles back to Saratoga should have felt endless, especially given the throbbing in Lane's foot. But there was something about the hushed darkness and Cole's quiet self-containment that felt like nothing so much as the peace of a confessional. As he limped along, Lane heard himself begin to speak.

"I was sent to New York City to unmask a cabal whose roots stretched all the way back to the Founding Fathers," he said. "A society who saw the War Between the States as an opportunity to further consolidate American culture and American power in themselves. Men who strove to advance their own interests with no more concern for the side they were dealing with than a common mercenary."

"And your English masters sent you to right that wrong?" Cole asked, not bothering to hide his skepticism. "It was my understanding that the English quietly sided with the Confederacy. They may call it serfdom rather than slavery, or they might even refer to it as bringing Christianity to the heathens, but the South's peculiar institution would seem fairly familiar to the crown."

"The English cared nothing about slavery—or even the future of the Union," Lane conceded. "But the English cared very much about the Irish in America, and so I was sent to ascertain the extent of their influence with these men. I chose to approach Jonathan Adair, for his motives were the simplest. Adair was a man obsessed with the idea of building a museum. A mausoleum of priceless artifacts that would allow his name to live on forever—some said it was even more than his name. Some said the man was a secret occultist who sought to gift America with a collection of artifacts priceless not just for their beauty but for their power. His colleagues, on the other hand, were far more practically minded. And so they approached me."

"In order to do what, exactly?" Washington's voice grew deadly quiet.

"Instead of cooperating with the Fenians to loot the treasures of Ireland, these men sought to create a Fenian atrocity that would destroy the credibility of the Irish Brigade forever and with it whatever Union sympathies remained in New York City. Specifically, they sought to burn prominent landmarks with Greek fire as a distraction that would allow the Fenians to raid New York's treasury and armory, and so end this war that was so inconveniencing everyone.

"The first of the explosions was planned to take place at a soiree, where Adair was going to unveil his latest treasure, as well as signing the documents that would bequeath his fortune to the museum where this treasure would hold pride of place…"

"You mean the chest that contained the magic bridle of your Irish sea god?"

Lane cast Washington a long look. "There would be many who said it was possessed by a far older, far deeper magic than that. For there are many that would say that bridle was brought to the fair isle by its first people: the Fir Bolg, the dark men who settled Ireland long before the Fair Folk, the Tuatha de Danaan." He met Washington's eyes. "Now some would say 'dark men,' is just a figure of speech. But others say the first men of Ireland were truly dark. The race of Ham, some say, the hardiest and bravest of the Phonecian seafarers, in search of a land of their own after enduring a century of vile slavery in Greece. Others said that they were Trojans, led by Brutus, who had been entrusted with the sacred treasures Troy—including the bridle of Hektor Hippodaimus, Breaker of Horses. Treasures that stood surety that a wronged race would see a hero like Hektor arise to fight for his people when they most needed it."

A long pause before Washington asked, "And the point of this fairy tale is… what exactly?"

"Absolutely nothing," Lane said with a sigh. "But when is the point of a fairy tale otherwise? Be it Greek fire or desperate Fenians or magic bridles, what are such tales ever but lies intended to distract people from a truth they would rather not see?"

Washington cocked his head. "It was my understanding that the explosion at Adair's party was quite real."

"It was, for all my sins. But I give you my word, it was never meant to be. The only fire I laid was an *ignis fatuus*, a will o' the wisp, a lie whose only purpose was to smoke out rats. I have no idea who set the bomb inside the chest." Lane's face set. "Although I don't think it takes an overly suspicious mind to ask *cui bono*? Who would have the greatest interest in preventing Jonathan Adair from devoting his entire fortune to his dream of a museum?"

"His daughter?" Washington asked.

"Of course not! Rose would know nothing of such things."

"I see," Washington said.

"I rather doubt it," Lane replied.

Washington eyed him shrewdly. "Then why do you feel the need to tell me this story in order to explain yourself?"

Why indeed? Because if Lane Fallon had had even half his wits about him two years ago, if Lane Fallon had not been blindsided by love, he would have seen what he needed to do immediately, would have been clear-headed enough to understand that there was but one way to put paid to the cancer that threatened Manhattan for once and for all. Instead, he had dithered like a lovesick schoolboy. "Because any farmer knows, there is only one reason to smoke out rats, and that's to kill them," he said with a matter-of-factness he did not feel. "And had I seized the chance to do that, instead of leaving it to Preston Olcott, you have my word I would have succeeded. I had the means and the opportunity to rid the world of this blight, and as for motive—well, hanging is the sentence for treason. And yet I balked at what I saw as cold-blooded murder, and that is the reason your wife is dead. If I had not been unwilling to offend the woman I love by murdering her father and his friends, the draft riots might not have occurred—along with a dozen more plots to try to surrender New York City that cost only poor men and idealists their lives. Never the men who actually instigated them."

A long pause. And then Washington said, "You strike me as an intelligent man, if not a particularly ruthless one, no matter how much you would see yourself as such. Intelligent enough to know that you cannot possibly know that."

"No. I would wager I've every reason to be sure of what I just said. But I'll thank you for that nonetheless."

They walked on in silence for some time. Then, Washington said, "You're not the first who spoke to me of this Fir Bolg."

The night stilled—and suddenly the surrounding woods seemed to be full of strange and secret creatures. "No?" Lane asked with an indifference he did not feel. "Where else did you hear of them?"

"After the war, I came North, to learn the fate of... my people here in New

York." Washington's voice grew carefully distant, carefully neutral. "I had heard the tales of course: A swathe of destruction straight up Manhattan that rivaled Sherman's famous march to the sea. Homes and business establishments burned. Men and women beaten, hanged, torn limb from limb, some witnesses say, all for no greater reason than having strayed into the path of the mob. But I wanted—needed to see for myself."

"Many men do," Lane allowed.

"I discovered quickly enough that what remained of my people had fled in terror to the city of Brooklyn. At first, they would not speak of what happened, bowing their heads and muttering about getting on with their business, just as the slaves did when my master chose to make an example of one of us by administering a beating. It was only after I carefully and painstakingly gained their trust that they were even willing to speak of the horrors," Washington went on. "But, strangely, when I was finally trusted to hear such tales, I also began to hear a strange and unusual new story, mostly from the mouths of children. Stories of a pale and shining man, a white man, who appeared near each of the 119 places where my people had been murdered, to leave a talisman."

Lane drew in a sharp breath, as he yielded to the inevitable and simply relinquished the sad stupid hope that he had ever had any free will in his life. Right now, even falling in love with Rose Adair felt pre-ordained.

"It was the mark, it was said, of the Aos Si." Washington pronounced the Irish flawlessly, as if he had rehearsed the words over and over until he had gotten them exactly right.

Lane forced a smile. "The Riders of the Sidhe? The Tuatha de Danaan, the fair folk themselves? Would you have it the fairies have emigrated to Manhattan along with the rest of the Irish?"

"The gold this man left was no fairy gold turned to dust in the morning light," Washington said. "But good American greenbacks that I admit brought some small measure of comfort to many grieving families."

For a debt was owed, and a debt would be paid. Lane's shoulders slumped in resignation. "But no money came to you?" he asked Washington.

"I was never offered money," Washington said. "Instead, I was offered something infinitely more precious—at least in my eyes. When I discovered the packet addressed to me, it contained merely a talisman, along with some papers that documented the unholy rituals of the Society of the Horseman's Word. Rituals such as…"

"I believe I am acquainted with the form," Lane cut him off. For he in fact knew only well the secrets those papers contained—for he had forged most of them himself. And the rising dawn had revealed that they had at last reached their destination: Congress Spring. "It matters not. We have no more time to waste chatting. Morrissey will be here soon."

Washington's face tightened with suspicion. "How can you know that?"

"Because I took the liberty of leaving an invitation when I set the fire, of course."

"Another English scheme?" Washington asked.

Lane raised a shoulder, suddenly weary of the talk. "Call it whatever you will. Morrissey is the only man who can help you now."

"How can you be sure of that?"

"Because riots are bad for business," a new voice said, and John Morrissey himself stepped out of the shadows. "Just as Captain Fallon's missive stated. But I trust you did not waste your time summoning me here to discuss such an obvious truth."

"In a manner of speaking, yes, I did," Lane said. "More precisely, I invited you here to stand face to face with the man who just barely escaped being lynched for the murder you committed in this very place."

An awkward pause, during which even Washington seemed unsure where to look.

"That's quite an accusation," Morrissey said.

"I was here when it happened," Fallon said.

"And what were the likes of you doing at the spring at such an hour?"

Lane shrugged. "Here to see a man about a horse."

Morrissey snorted. "But instead, you saw what happened?"

"I'm willing to say I did. And mayhap it even is the truth."

Morrissey's gaze grew dangerous. "I've killed men for less."

"But that was in your past. It's said your good wife has cured you of such tendencies."

"I swore an oath to her on the day we were wed. No more prize-fighting." Morrissey's fists balled. "But I am always willing to make an exception."

"On the other hand, you yourself would be the first to point out is that murder is bad for business."

A long pause, then Morrissey said, "A man comes at me to put a knife in my back, I don't consider it murder to defend my life with my own two hands."

"Is that how it happened?" Lane asked.

Morrissey raised a shoulder. "He said he had information about the chest I proposed to give to the Jockey Club. Information that would cement my place with them forever. And he said he wanted to meet alone. I assumed that at best, he would claim the box was stolen and demand a reward. At worst…" Morrissey spread his hands. "He came at me from behind with a knife. I swung to defend myself, as any man would."

"And would any man allow another man to be blamed for a murder he committed?"

"I tell you, it was no murder. 'Twas a fair fight." Abruptly, the fight went out of Morrissey and his voice grew cajoling. "But what does that matter? 'Twill be naught by a nine-days wonder, for such things are not uncommon in Saratoga. And I have no quarrel with your friend. He's free to go. Indeed, I'd be happy to provide him with the funds to leave on this morning's milk train, along with my word that no-one will pursue the issue any further. Your friend will be safe enough. Just not here in Saratoga."

As if Lane had not suggested the same solution himself—with the same prospect of success, he was certain. "Perhaps it might be more profitable for all of us if instead you would consider who might go to so much effort to see you dead?" he suggested.

Morrissey's face hardened with an exasperation that Fallon, if he were being honest, could completely understand. But then the Irishman said with shrug, "I've no shortage of enemies. The Dead Rabbits. The Why-Os. Tammany Hall."

"And the Jockey Club?"

"Why would they have cause to murder me?" Morrissey asked sharply.

"Well, to save their wives the social embarrassment of rubbing elbows with the likes of you," Lane said bluntly. "By all accounts, you're not stupid, man, so think it through. The Jeromes and the Vanderbilts are already angling to secure earls for their daughters, if not dukes. Do you really think they want to take tea with a shanty Irish brawler?"

Morrissey's face hardened. "And what would the English gentleman propose? For me to know my place and be content to run my casinos in Five Points instead?"

Now came the turn of the card upon which Lane had staked nothing short of Cole Washington's future life and happiness—not to mention his own. "I would propose you make your colleagues in the Jockey Club afraid to ever send another man to kill you, even though we all know they will never let you be a member. For you are no fool, Mr. Morrissey, and so must surely recognize that there is no other way for a man like you to deal with such men."

Slowly, Morrissey unclenched his fists. "Mayhap that is true. But what care I of their good opinion? I built this town."

"Perhaps. But men such as your current investors acquire, they do not build," Lane said. "And right now, Saratoga Springs looks like a very desirable acquisition indeed. And you would not be the first who stood in the way of their investments to die conveniently."

He gestured toward the sounds of Little Dublin awakening after a restless night's slumber. "Your business partners engineered the riots that nearly delivered New York City to the Confederacy. Do you think they would do anything less to defend their investment in Saratoga?"

Morrissey's eyes narrowed. "I had nothing to do with Sammy Nunn's dying. Nothing to do with the unfortunate incident involving Jonathan Adair either."

"Be that as it may, they'll say the Irish bring it with them. That it's stamped indelibly in the Irish character. And that there will be no controlling the Irish in Saratoga as long as an Irishman runs the city."

"I know how to keep order in my own town."

"So you say. But what of justice?"

"Why should I care about justice?"

"Common human decency?" Lane suggested.

"Do you believe in such a thing?" Morrissey snorted.

"Then what about a chance to make up for the sins of your countrymen two years ago in New York City? Justice for the men who murdered Mr. Washington's wife and 118 other innocent souls all in the name of their profits. Justice for your countrymen who fought and died for another man's cause, instead of their livelihoods?"

An even harder snort.

Lane's voice softened cajolingly as he turned his trump card. "Then what about the chance to never have to worry about your business partners never sending another man with a knife to plunge in your back. Never having to worry about using your fists to defend yourself again and again, until sooner or later you get old enough or careless enough that one of them finds its way into your back. Or even worse, that of your wife or your son. For that is the future that awaits you if you don't listen to me. A lifetime looking back over your shoulder every step of the way.

"Instead, I'm offering you the chance to build Saratoga into the glittering capital of your dreams," Lane went on, warming to his theme, "and compel those men who would now be rid of you to help you do it. For the riots blamed on the Irish and the draft were nothing short of a seditious conspiracy to betray New York City to the Confederacy, and I have the letters to prove it. Proof so damning it could hang even a man like Vanderbilt or Jerome. Proof that will have these men looking over shoulders for fear of you, instead of the other way around."

A long pause. Then Morrissey asked, "And in exchange?"

"In exchange, I would have you protect Mr. Washington as carefully as your friends would protect you, once they know what I do."

Washington erupted in protest, but Morrissey grinned, exposing a couple of gold teeth. "Well, now, for something like that I would protect this man with my own two fists, even though my sweet Susie has made me swear off fighting before she would wed me." His eyes narrowed, as he turned back to Lane. "But I think you must allow that any reasonable man might ask, if you are possessed of such powerful information, why would you give such a thing to me instead of turning it to your own profit?"

"Let us attribute it to justice for simplicity's sake, although there would be many who would say I was incapable of such a thing." Lane glanced at Washington. "Imperfect justice, I admit. And maybe not justice at all. Instead, I would beg you not to allow the quest for justice turn into a quest for revenge, and allow me to make what few amends I am capable of."

"Words," Washington said, "are easier than feelings."

"And I can assure you that both are easier than atonement…"

"What would an Englishman know about atonement?" Morrissey snorted.

What indeed? Lane raised a shoulder, as he turned back to the Irishman. "Well, I have already received the absolution, from none other than Father William Corby himself, and while I am no theologian, I am given to understand the two go hand in hand."

A pause, then Morrissey said, "So you claim to have stood on the Wheatfield, then? Why?"

"That is my own affair, and none of yours," Lane said.

Another pause, then Morrissey ruminated, "Strange tales came from the Wheatfield. Men said they were hopelessly outnumbered. Any sane man would have turned tail and run, and left the Americans to fight their own damned war. But more than one man said a mysterious rider arose to rally them, a fierce warrior on a milk-white steed. Some even said it was CuChulainn, the Hound of Ulster, the incarnation of Lugh himself, on his mount Splendid-Mane, risen to lead the sons of Ulster to glory."

"Men see what they need to see when the heat of the battle is upon them," Lane said with a shrug. "Just as I would suggest that men see what they want to see when they look at that chest of yours, which has proved so unhappy to so many. So may I suggest you turn its power to a new purpose? May I suggest you present it to the Jockey Club as a reminder that you have names. Names that can destroy even them."

"What names?" Morrissey asked.

"Names that will stand surety for Mr. Washington's continued safety," Lane said. "As well as building the Saratoga you dream of. I will deliver them to you this afternoon, as soon as I clear up a few loose ends. In the meantime, I merely ask that you protect Mr. Washington's person until I make good on my promise…"

Washington's second protest was loud and surprisingly profane. But Morrissey's gold teeth flashed once more. "Riots are bad for business," he said. "We aim to keep Saratoga a peaceful town. It's said the waters in this vicinity are strangely calming. I can assure you that my fists are as well, and that, saints be praised, my sweet Susie, bless her soul, is far more forgiving of my occasional lapses than your Father Corby's god."

25

The streets may have tossed restlessly with the remains of police and fire engines into the wee hours of the morning, but Katie O'Grady slept like a newborn. Still, one night's peace could not erase a lifetime's lessons learned on the street, and she woke the moment the first rays of dawn touched her face—and Sullivan slipped back into his room. She opened her eyes only a fraction, watching him though slitted lashes. So far he had touched her as dispassionately as if he had been tending a sick horse, and he had certainly been unwilling enough to find her in his bed. But any lass who'd slept in either orphanage or streets knew well enough there were those who preferred the excitement of stealing what they wanted—especially in the orphanage.

But Sullivan did little more than glance her way and mouth something that might have been a prayer or might have been an exasperated curse. Then he quietly opened his dresser and pulled out a coat much unlike his dusty shirt and trousers. A quick wash of his hands and face, and he slipped out of the stable.

As soon as he was gone, she pushed herself up on her uninjured arm, touching the shirt he had given her. Like the coat, it was of much finer quality than the clothes she had always seen him wearing: soft linen and carefully laundered. Sewn for him by a loving mother or even wife for his wedding day? Was that the explanation of his monkish reaction when he found her in his bed?

Well, it was simple enough to find out. Even hobbled by her bandaged shoulder, Katie could move every bit as quickly and quietly as Sullivan could when she needed to. It cost her a moment's struggle to pull on the stolen trousers one-handed—but she was outdoors quickly enough to see his lanky figure disappearing down the street.

She slipped along after him, keeping a careful distance, until he at last reached the railroad station. A man immediately emerged from the shadows—and Katie crossed herself instinctively the moment she glimpsed him. His dark clothes blended into the remains of the night, so that his white hair and pale, cruel features, lit by the rising sun, seemed to glitter as dangerously as the ruby on his finger and the silver head of his walking stick. Saints preserve us. The stable lad was treating with Auld Nick himself.

"Two years ago, you sent your son to find me," Sullivan said. "It would seem that his persistence has at last paid off."

"It would be arguably more accurate to say you have at last consented to be found," the pale man said.

"Have it your way," Sullivan said with a shrug. "I did not come here to bandy words."

"Then why did you come here?"

"For ten long years, one of your letters has arrived every Monday, punctual as clockwork, not so much as interrupted by a war, a riot, or a naval blockade. All of them offering the same thing: Money, power, or any other boon it was within your power to grant, if only I would afford you the courtesy of an answer. And so I am here to answer you. And in exchange, I would have my boon."

The white devil cocked his head, studying Sullivan curiously. "Why now? What has given you cause to relent?"

"Necessity, and not forgiveness, you have my word on that," Sullivan said.

"I had no doubt. But what necessity could be dire enough to change a mind as stubborn as yours?"

Sullivan drew a deep breath, then spoke, all in a rush. "There is a lass upstairs in my bed. Injured and friendless. I would have you take charge of her and afford her all the protection you have at your command."

Katie stiffened in startled fury, and not just at his words. Every last trace of the lad's soft, Irish brogue had vanished, replaced by the clipped enunciation of the gentry. For all his talk of queens and dispossession, the bastard had been playing with her all along.

The pale man's cold, cruel mouth twisted in amusement. "I know full well that you think little enough of me. But do you propose that I should descend to snatching children from their beds?"

"It will be considerably simpler if you manage to take her, while the pain has made her... somewhat tractable."

"Tractable." The pale man rolled the word in his mouth, tasting it, just as

Preston Olcott made a show of tasting the wines that Katie brought to his table. "From that I am I to infer that you have yet to apprise the lady in question of your plans?"

"She's no lady..." Sullivan broke off as the white devil raised an eyebrow, then conceded, "She's hurt. And tired. And hungry. And in danger. She'll fight you—I'll give you that, just as I'll allow she can have the mouth of a She-Devil. But she's been tossed around too much to know what she needs any more. Put some food in her stomach, and give her some clean linen, a soft bed, and a few kind words, and she'll turn around soon enough."

As if Katie were naught but another of his horses. Her Irish began to rise as red as what remained of her hair.

Instead of answering, the white devil tapped his finger against his walking stick, setting the ruby flashing. "Ten long years," he mused. "Ten long years you would not speak to me. There must be something special about this lass that would make you break such a deeply cherished grudge."

"She saved my life."

"Ah. So this is nothing but a simple matter of a father fulfilling a blood debt, just as other fathers fulfill tailors' debts or gaming pledges?"

Sullivan's jaw set. "My reasons are my own. All you need know is that I would have you take charge of this lass. Will you do it?"

The white devil raised an eyebrow. "At the very least, I would understand who exactly you propose I take into my household. What is this lass to you? A by-blow? Or the mother of one?"

Sullivan's face twisted with sudden fury, but he swiftly mastered it. "Olcott fears her," he said. "That should be reason enough for you. If nothing else, she should be a useful pawn in your schemes."

The white devil nodded in slow consideration, before he shook his head. "Alas, it is not reason enough for a man such as me," he said with exaggerated regret. "I fear I am driven by an insatiable curiosity to understand what this lass could possibly mean to you that you would put yourself under an obligation to me, after all these many long years."

Something snapped within Sullivan, and his face set with truly terrifying rage. "Obligation? How dare you speak of my obligations, when it is you that owes the obligation? And none of it to me. You are and remain dead to me. And that much will not ever change. No, 'tis my mother to whom you owe recompense. And I am claiming it now—on behalf of the girl that lies upstairs in my bed. I call in whatever ancient troths lie between us as a result of your sin. I'll not be having this lass abandoned and starving and daft, as you left my poor mother—and who knows how many others beside her..."

And for a moment, the white devil's mask slipped. "I scarcely abandoned your mother. Rather I would suggest I fled her—and at no small cost to my soul..."

As quickly as it had flared, Sullivan's rage dissipated and his voice was cold and distant as he spat, "Kidnapped by the Queen of the Sidhe, resisting her every attempt to entice you into being her lover, until you finally bought your freedom by promising to give her a son to serve as Ireland's champion? If you honestly believe that fairy tale, then I strongly suggest you keep it to yourself, before you find yourself locked up for the madman you truly are."

And had Katie been thinking clearly, she would have had the wits to realize that listening further to this conversation might have been very helpful in understanding this lout of a stable lad with his cambric shirts and posh accent and his horror of allowing a woman into his bed. But instead, pride and unreasoning fury took over, and she threw herself between the two men in a royal Irish temper, as she snapped, "I'll thank ye to know that 'tis I 'twill be the one having none of that—and I give not a fig for your opinions in the matter."

Sullivan's face froze with exasperation, then softened with rueful humor, as his voice instantly slipped back into those weird, caressing tones that had soothed her to sleep the night before. "I knew in my heart, you must be awake. But ye must have some talent to fool the likes of me."

"A talent born of the street, where ye never lived a day in your life," she snarled. "So dinna think to ply me with your honeyed words. For I know well enow what ye are, Declan Sullivan—or whatever your true name is."

He froze, then cast a sharp look at the white devil, whose mouth suddenly seemed to be twisted with something that in another man might have been humor. "My true name is Declan Sullivan."

"Mayhap," she sneered. "And mayhap 'tis even true. But what do I care for all your lies, when I can tell ye the one thing I know to be true? You're nae stable lad. You're the quality. And I've had more than enow to do with the quality, I'll have ye know."

"No!" Sullivan protested. "'Tis not what ye think."

"Do not presume to tell me what I think," Katie hissed.

And then she was gone—holding her ears against Sullivan's sudden, startled protest and the white devil's amused query that trailed through the dawn air after her.

"And this is how the lady behaves when she is in a tractable frame of mind?"

26

My dearest Roisin, my sweet, dark Rose,
 When you have finished reading this letter, you will despise me as a coward. And frankly, I already despise myself. But since that is a condition I have long since become accustomed to, I beg you to yield to the logic of efficiency and allow me to take on the full burden of the contempt that is so rightly due my behavior.

 I write this letter so that you can know the truth—a truth that I will never be able to speak to you with my own lips. It is a simple fact that you deserve better than a man who has lied to you and used you from the very start. But it is equally inarguable that if I do the right thing and attempt to explain myself in person, I will instead lie, steal, beg, and cheat in any way I can, in order to win back your heart, no matter what my good intentions. Therefore, I would beg you to instead accept one poor last service that I might offer. Your father's murderer cannot be allowed to walk free—nor can the loss of so many innocent lives in the tragic violence that befell New York City several years ago that remain unavenged. I played my part in both coming to pass, and so it is fitting that I should serve as the instrument of what poor justice I can serve. Indeed, I have staked my life on it. Whether the guilty will reciprocate by destroying me when the final catastrophe is at hand remains to be seen. I am coward enough to admit I hope it will not be so, but you have my assurance that whatever the outcome, you will not be vexed by my attentions any further. If I am fortunate enough to survive, I will flee directly to Canada, and trouble you no longer with my schemes. Instead, I will place your fortunes in the hands of a man far more capable of helping you than I am—as I should have done from the first, instead of yielding to the temptation to love you once more. If I do not survive this day, then I beg you be contented that I did whatever I could to serve justice in my mean way—and, beyond that, I pray you do not mourn me—nor think any more of me beyond knowing that I wish I could have been the hero you believed you loved, the hero you deserve. And know, too, that you made me a better man than what destiny has made me, and that, should I survive what comes next, like the spirit guide that leads the poet in the aisling, *you will be a vision I will strive to follow to lead me to greater goodness for the rest of my life. However, once you have known that, I would beg you forget about me, and walk in beauty and happiness for the rest of your life.*

Forever your devoted,
Tamerlane Fallon

Rose let the letter she had found propped on her dressing table slide from her shaking fingers into her lap. It was the most beautiful love letter she—or any woman—might hope to receive in a lifetime. And it was completely at odds with the scene she had just witnessed between Lane and Preston as they confronted one another across the packet of papers Declan Sullivan had all but thrown at his brother.

She was certain she was not meant to have witnessed the scene, but there was something about the cocky swagger with which Lane had strode across the salon, tucking the papers into his coat, that had made it impossible not to take notice. Carefully, she retreated into the tiny office where she and Bridie had been going over the day's menus, and set herself to listening.

"You will be relieved to hear that I have decided to put an end to this farce," Lane told Preston calmly. "Mr. Morrissey is unhappy about the recent violence that threatened to convulse Little Dublin. Riots are, in Mr. Morrissey's considered opinion, very bad for business. Fortunately, I have managed to convince Mr. Morrissey that the papers that were said to have sparked the upset are a sufficient price to buy my safe passage out of Saratoga—public airing of dirty laundry also being very bad for business. However, I think it is only fair to warn you that he may not be as reasonably disposed to others that cannot afford such a ransom."

Olcott's shoulders stiffened, and he set aside his newspaper with elaborate care. "In other words, you propose to sell him those names that Sammy Nunn once proposed to wield as blackmail."

"You would know more about Nunn's plots than I do," Lane said. "I am, at heart, no such schemer—just a canny enough man to understand when good fortune has fallen into my hands. Or been thrown into them by my brother, as the case may be."

A pause, soft and deadly, before Olcott said, "Sometimes it does pay to look a gift horse in the mouth, and I would suggest this one of those times. For you are aware those papers are what got Sammy Nunn killed?"

Lane raised a shoulder. "Then I suppose I must hope to be far smarter than Sammy was."

"If you were, you would place those letters into my hands, along with my cousin's future and remove yourself from Saratoga as well as this entire business, while you still can." Olcott's face set. "Come, Captain Fallon, let us speak as men of business. You have trifled with a vulnerable young woman's affections—and I shan't begrudge you that hard-earned profit. God alone knows you look like you need it. So let us negotiate, and have done with it quickly. Your price, Captain Fallon. How much will it take for you to hand over those letters and simply go away?"

And much as Rose knew she should be very interested in finally obtaining an honest answer to that question, she found she could not bear the possibility of what she might hear. She threw open the door. "As long as you're entertaining offers," she asked, forcing her voice to what cool disdain she could muster, "am I allowed to venture a bid on my husband's affections?"

Lane's face twisted with indefinable emotion—no, emotion she would not, could not, *dared* not define. "Nae, lass," he said gently, "there's no need for that game anymore. I've put matters in order. A man of business will come. A man I should have turned to right at the very beginning."

"You mean, Declan Sullivan?"

She paid no attention to his stammered response; she simply swept her skirts across the salon and into her room where neither man would dare to follow, slamming the door behind her with unladylike force. The fit of sobbing that followed was similarly unmannerly and similarly satisfying.

Only when she had allowed herself to indulge thoroughly, did she notice the creamy envelope propped squarely in the center of her dressing table.

My dark Rosaleen. My Sweet Dark Rose…

It was the most beautiful love letter she—or any woman—might hope to receive in a lifetime. And it was so enormously *stupid* that she did little but dab away the worst of her tearstains before she exploded downstairs, determined to thwart Lane Fallon in whatever misguided piece of heroic self-sacrifice he seemed currently convinced was necessary…

Only to find herself blocked by Cousin Preston and the doctor, who stepped smoothly into her path as she hurried across the lobby. "Now, now, Rose," Olcott reproached her. "Such displays can benefit no-one."

"You will step aside," she said. "I must find Captain Fallon at once."

"Now, Rose, we well know this is none of your fault," Olcott said soothingly. "The man is a well-known rogue and adventurer who has traduced far less susceptible minds than yours. But for the good of the family, I must insist you leave it to me to repair the not-inconsiderable damage that your folly has wrought."

She tossed her head. "Unfortunately, cousin, I must insist that you leave charge of my own follies—whatever they may be—to me and no-one else."

"You know not of what you speak."

"I know exactly of what I speak. I seek to go the racetrack. I understand Captain Fallon has gone there to meet Mr. Morrissey about a horse."

"A woman attending the horse track in her bereavement?" Olcott sighed. "Scandalous."

"Proof positive, she has no idea of what she is truly thinking," the doctor concurred. "We need to end this for once and for all, without any further display."

For it had escalated into a display, Rose realized, despite the fact that passers-by in the lobby did their best to pretend not to notice. And Rose felt herself waver. Surely, she owed her father's memory something better, if not her family. But she gradually became aware of a pair of eyes that had been watching them openly, if not downright avidly. Cool, green eyes, that reminded her irresistibly of Fallon's.

The man he had promised to send, then?

A tall slender gentleman with a fine sweep of white hair and hawk-like features arose from a deep-sided chair that had concealed all but his slender fingers, the first of them adorned with a ring set with a ruby, folded over the silver head of his walking stick. "How, now, Rose," he said. "Lane described you being as fiery as Mebh, as fierce as Scathach, a worthy match for Grainne O Maille, the Pirate Queen herself. But although he spoke with nothing but admiration, your cousin is right. Perhaps it would be more prudent to take our conversation to a private room." He flashed a smile that exposed pointed, wolfish teeth. "While this is Saratoga after all, I can only plead an Englishman's prejudice against startling the horses."

"What conversation?" Olcott demanded. "Who are you?"

The man extended a hand. "Lord Everett Wolverton at your service. I believe Captain Fallon has already informed you as well as any other interested parties that I am acting on behalf of Miss Adair in this uncomfortable matter of her father's will."

Olcott's face set. "I would like to know on whose authority you propose such a thing. Still, this is not a matter to discuss in public. As you must be aware, the business affairs of the Adair family are in a considerable state of turmoil at the moment. Perhaps we could meet privately at my club later?"

"I am so very sorry I did not make myself clear. I am here to represent the interests of Miss Rose Adair, not the Adair family," Wolverton said. He met Rose's eyes calmly before he added, "And while I will certainly observe the proprieties while we conduct our business, I would appreciate the chance to offer her my bona fides without interference from her family."

"Impossible!" the doctor snapped. "Miss Adair is in seclusion…"

"A woman's head is scarcely fit for such complex matters in any case," Olcott dismissed the idea. "If you have business with the Adair family, I insist you conduct it with me. Although, for the life of me, I have no idea why Her Majesty's government sees fit to pry into our family's affairs…"

"Well, because you were the one who invited us to interfere in the first place," Wolverton said with a gentle smile that belied the predatory glint in his eyes. "As I'm sure you will recall if you cast your mind back a few years. You and I were introduced at a private dinner with a view toward England possibly intervening in a plot by several of the wealthiest men in New York City to hand over New York City to the Confederacy, and so put a swift end to the war. And while England of course had to maintain our neutrality, in order not to be accused of seeking to regain her lost colonies, we sent our best agent to assist you in your quest, one Tamerlane Fallon. Oh, yes, that is his real name," Wolverton answered the angry, unspoken question that burned on Rose's lips. "His only deception was presenting himself as a desperate

Fenian who was willing to rob Ireland of her most priceless treasures in exchange for the money to raise an army against England, and you have my word, that was a necessary one."

And what else had been a necessary deception? The words she had stained with her tears as she read them? Were they nothing but a hasty anodyne, a gentle excuse to take the sting out of handing her over to the English government like a misdirected parcel?

"And what of his bard's songs and auld legends? His high tales of Manannan mac Lir and Roisin Dubh and the hero who would serve her purely?" Rose asked. "Were they a necessary deception as well? Surely, a simple golden hoard of coins would have served Captain Fallon's purposes equally well?"

Wolverton cast her a penetrating glance that suggested he understood the question she really wanted answered. "The tale of the bridle of Splendid Mane is scarcely original with Captain Fallon. It is said that Manannan made a gift of it to his foster-son, Lugh, and it is said that when a man takes the reins of that bridle, Lugh himself will rise within him, as he last rose within CuChulainn. Lugh, the all-talented, the golden god. Or, the philosophers might say, a man's best self. Although there are those who would say that only the love of a woman can do that…"

"I must protest! This is unconscionable!" the doctor burst in. "My patient's delicate condition aside, what gentleman would distress a daughter in mourning over some irrelevant antiquarian legend?"

Rose whirled in him. "I am not your patient. And I will decide what conversations might threaten to overwhelm my delicate sensibilities."

Wolverton's smile grew as sharp as his eyes, as he cut in once more, "Again, I must apologize for not making myself clear. The stolen Bridle of Manannan mac Lir is far from irrelevant. In fact, Her Majesty's Government has reason to believe that this lost treasure was instrumental in the murder of Jonathan Adair."

A thunderous pause, during which even Rose had to wonder about the sanity of this strange, pale man.

"There can be no question of Jonathan Adair's having been murdered. There are plenty of witnesses who can attest to that fact. The unfortunate man has been of unsound health for several years now," the doctor said. "Of unsound mind as well. That is my professional opinion, and I would be willing to swear to it in a court of law."

"There is no question of *proving* he was murdered," Wolverton corrected him. He inclined his head toward Olcott. "I give you credit for that. But that is what you intended when you called in the English to foil this dastardly plot. That is what you offered Tamerlane Fallon the chance to destroy a Fenian conspiracy in order to accomplish. If Adair's death had been attributed to anything other than the curse of an ancient goddess, it would have been the Fenians who would have been blamed. On quite the other hand, Her Majesty's Government dislikes being used in such a fashion, for such tawdry ends. Indeed, as Her Majesty's representative here in Saratoga Springs, I am inclined to take it personally."

"Rest assured you are not the only one," Cousin Preston spluttered. "I have friends, you know! Powerful friends!"

"Who I am quite sure will thank you for embroiling them in this affair," Wolverton observed, before he once more turned his disconcerting gaze to Rose. "Now, Miss Adair, how can Her Majesty's Government best serve you?"

"I would have you convey me to the racetrack in order to find Captain Fallon with all possible haste," she said.

Wolverton raised an eyebrow. "I am forced to point out that the gentlemen are correct in suggesting that such behavior would be deemed scandalous in a house of mourning."

She drew a deep breath. "Lord Wolverton, I have every reason to believe that Captain Tamerlane Fallon is risking his life to put an end to this wretched affair for once and for all. I would suggest that preventing a senseless tragedy arising from his rash decision would be well worth any whiff of scandal." She tossed her head. "Besides, this is Saratoga."

Wolverton studied her with those disconcertingly green eyes, so like Lane Fallon's. "All this for a man who proved himself naught but a ruthless profiteer?"

She matched his gaze. "You are personally acquainted with Captain Fallon?"

Wolverton smiled. "Rather intimately, in fact. Arguably more intimately than he would prefer."

"Well, then, perhaps you should ask yourself, if he were truly such a ruthless profiteer, why is he only possessed of two shirts in this world?"

Wolverton's smile broadened as he conceded the point. "My son has been a sore disappointment to me in many ways," he murmured, as he held his arm out to her, and called for a porter to summon a carriage.

27

So much for the virgin coming to him willingly, Sullivan thought, as he strode the streets of Little Dublin, muttering curses against the first man who harmed but one fiery hair on Katie O'Grady's head and wondering in exasperation how many more red-haired women there could be in Saratoga that he might mistake for her. More like the virgin had just fled him as if he were all the hounds of hell unleashed at once. So why should he not let her? He had tried to help, had broken his own vow to his dead mother, and she had flung it in his face. He owed her no more. So why, by all that was holy, had he instead heard himself utter the two words he swore he would never speak to the man who called himself his father?

"Help me."

"That goes without question," the White Wolf had said. He raised an eyebrow. "As little as you might think of me, I would have done so even had you not asked."

"Then I thank you." Forcing out the words had been as difficult as spitting marbles.

"And I am most sincere when I say it is my pleasure." The White Wolf pulled out his pocket watch to check it. "However, much as I would like to continue this interview, I am sure that you will be relieved to hear that I have urgent business elsewhere. But I give you my word she will be found." He did not quite hide a hint of a smile. "At the risk of trespassing on a fatherly privilege I admit I have yet to earn, might I suggest that when she is found, a humble invitation would be far more effective than snatching her out of her bed in the dead of night?"

"I will talk to her," Sullivan agreed. "And I alone."

With a nod, the White Wolf made to go, then turned back. "I would have you feel yourself under no further obligation to me. But if I you can ever find it in your heart to do me a kindness, I would very much appreciate the privilege of a formal introduction to the young lady who has succeeded where neither I nor your brother could not."

Not to mention a young lady who seemed more than able to elude even the White Wolf's considerable resources. After a morning's frantic searching, Sullivan was beginning to feel the first twinges of panic. She had no bolt-hole, or she would not have fled to Sullivan's stable. But how could she survive even one day on the streets? She had lost too much blood. She was hungry. Light-headed most likely. What would happen if she fainted from exhaustion?

What would happen if Preston Olcott found her first?

That thought caught in his throat and would not release its chokehold even when the coach arrived with his father's compliments and instructions to bear him to Morrissey's racetrack on the other side of town. How had she gotten there so quickly when it was all Sullivan could do not to urge the coachman to take his whip to his horses—or the other carriages clogging the way?

When he sprang to the ground outside the newly-built grandstand, his knees buckled as weakly as Katie's had in his worst imaginings of her sliding unconscious into the gutter. Then, at last, he saw the skinny creature with piebald hair standing at the center of a knot of men who were milling uncertainly—mainly because, he realized in dismay, she was holding a knife on a man. No, not just a man. It was his own cursed brother, Lane Fallon, who she was soundly berating, "Dinna bother to lie to me. You were coming after me just like all the others have been all morning. Did ye really not think I'd notice you? Mayhap you're fit to slide through the shadows at the Opera when the lights are down, but any one of us reared in Five Points learned quick enow to spot the likes of you."

Even more improbably, the quick-tongued bastard who had always come up with a lie for every occasion, looked at a loss for words. But Sullivan felt no such hesitation. Quick as he moved to stop a horse from rearing, he was through the knot of men, and twisting the knife from her fingers. "Nae, lass. This is not what hands such as yours were meant for."

"And who are you to decide what my hands may or may not be meant for…?"

Coward that he was, Sullivan turned away from her furious gaze and concerned himself with the anxious men instead. "I thank ye for your assistance, but I will take matters from here."

They slid away, grateful enough for the excuse. His brother, though, stared at Katie incredulously. "Please say she's no virgin," he demanded.

And Sullivan grinned as he could quite literally see Katie's Irish rise. "A prudent man would find a better way to phrase that, even if I do have hold of the knife now. She tends to take offense on the issue."

"Indeed I do, Declan Sullivan. And I'll have ye know all of Sammy Nunn's girls were convent bred," Katie snapped. "Myself included, I might add. I am not a poor, daft abandoned creature you need to save."

"Peace!" Sullivan stilled her, as he did his best to ignore the incredulous amusement in his brother's eyes. "Indeed, no man in his right mind would ever describe you as such. You're Nunn's Irish Rose, Katie O'Grady. A true Queen of the auld sod. Eire herself. That's what you truly are."

"That's not what you said to your fine English friend!"

Aye, she was a hard one, there was no doubting that. Trouble and strife, and more he was certain that he was yet to discover. Sullivan drew a deep breath, and forced himself to speak the simple truth. Humbly. "My fine English friend is a man I despise—in fact a man I have sworn a vow on my mother's deathbed never to speak to again. And yet I did just that on your behalf," he said. "And in fact, I would bargain with the devil himself for you. And I would you beg you, lass, take that as token of the high regard in which I hold ye."

And if he used a bit of the wyrding voice as he went on, who could blame him? "My fine English friend also told me I owe you an apology for my clumsy attempt to kidnap you last night. And he is right. I can only hope you will forgive the offense of my ever thinking I could force you to do anything—or that you need any protection from me. Instead I would beg you to allow me the honor of being your humble servant, in the name of the Crone who blesses us, the Mother that gives us life, and the Virgin that holds our destiny in her own hands…"

He blinked back to himself to feel both Lane and Katie's eyes on him—Lane's appraising, and Katie's wide with admiration. "Cor," she breathed, "ye ever want to give up the horses you'd have a fine career on the stage."

"Or some would say the Devil's own tongue." Lane flashed Sullivan an odd look. "I'll have you know I never believed such things about you. But I'm beginning to believe that convincing mankind he never existed is the greatest trick Auld Nick played on mankind. For if I had thought, even for one instant…"

If he had thought. But when had Lane Fallon ever thought of anything beyond his own selfish schemes? Suddenly all Sullivan's fear and anxiety this morning collapsed into unreasoning fury at the one target that stood to hand.

"If you had thought, you would have done what? Given even one moment's consideration to who your lies might have hurt?" Sullivan snarled, as he at last allowed the full force of all he had lost to wash over him. "It was not enough that you drove me from Ireland, you must needs drive me out of New York as well? Is there any place on this globe I might flee that you willna let me live in peace? Do you hate me that much? Why?"

"It was nothing like that! It was just a moment's impulse. I needed a name for a glorious hero that would turn a young girl's head, and I availed myself of the closest one to hand."

"I had a life. I had a good life, one I bought myself with my own hard work and not by any man's favor. Were you so jealous that you had to steal that from me?"

A moment's silence. Then Lane's jaw set, and he said tightly, "Then perhaps your need for revenge will be sated by knowing how much you've stolen from me. Or perhaps more accurately, what I stole from myself. For she loved the thought of you like she will never love the truth of me—any more than our father could, when he found his changeling firstborn alive in the cradle intended for you…"

"Is *that* why you believe he sent you…?"

A lifetime's memory of bullying suddenly skewed frighteningly out of focus, as Sullivan's eyes went down to Lane's lame foot. The man scarcely limped now, but why had Sullivan never understood the true pain of the iron brace that had kept Lane indoors with his books, while Sullivan had roamed the moors so freely?

"Of course not," Lane snapped. "And you can give over staring at me as though you would bandage my fetlock, if it would not be too much trouble. I am not here for your… stray. I don't know who may have been following her, but you have my word, it was not I. I came to the track on other business."

Sullivan's anger subsided as quickly as it had arisen, and he seized the excuse to retreat to safer shores. "Washington?" he asked. "Did you manage to get him safely away then?"

"You were watching?" Lane asked. His eyes narrowed. "Was it you that sent the drays…?"

"Don't be daft," Sullivan said. "There's no such thing as a horsewhisperer.

And even if there were, it would have scarcely been necessary. The man rides like an angel."

"Trust me, his skills are far easier to appreciate from a safe distance," Lane said. He drew a deep breath. "But to answer your question, yes, we got safely away. Unfortunately, getting him to stay safely away is a far more difficult question."

"That does not come as a complete a shock," Sullivan allowed.

"But you canna let him come back!" Katie burst out in horror. "Olcott will see him hanged. That… that's why I ran. Preston Olcott would make me lie and say I saw him kill old Sammy. He said that if they didn't hang Washington for killing old Sammy, he'd make sure they hang me!"

Katie's voice cracked on the last two syllables, and all her defiance crumbled. And suddenly she seemed very frightened and very young.

"No-one will hang you unless you drive me to strangling you myself," Sullivan assured her. "I give you my solemn oath."

Lane struggled to mask a smile in a way that reminded Sullivan suspiciously of the White Wolf. "And if such a fine promise is not reassurance enough, you have my word that Mr. Washington has a far more fierce protector than the one you seem to have obtained," he said to Katie gravely. He pointed to the sign that forbade colored people from entering the Grandstand. "And I have taken the liberty of ensuring that this time there is no way Preston Olcott will be able to blame Mr. Washington for his crimes."

Understanding dawned. "One thing to allow a lad to risk his neck riding your winners, another thing altogether to rub elbows with their likes." Sullivan said with a nod, then grinned in sudden admiration. "To be sure you're a cunning bastard, and our father's true son."

An awkward silence followed. Then Lane turned to scan the horses and men who had gathered on the track in front of the grandstand. In a few days' time, the seats would be full of glittering women in lavishly trimmed bonnets, the gentlemen wagering loudly and furiously, with champagne flowing like water. But now it was sparsely populated by Morrissey and a few cronies, gathering to watch one of the private match races that were being run before the meets. "It's only a friendly, informal challenge. So they don't have the stewards to do a regular start by dropping a flag," Lane said, his voice suddenly detached and speculative. "I'm hoping that they'll use a pistol shot instead, especially if a disinterested party offers to fire it. And if Preston Olcott happens to be that interested party, I'm guessing there will be a tragic accident with the starter's pistol—one that most likely will involve me."

"And your plan is?" Sullivan asked.

Lane raised a shoulder. "To hope like hell he's a poor shot."

Sullivan just stared at the limping bully who had made his entire boyhood a torment, wondering if he had ever really known him at all, before his eyes were drawn to a flash of chestnut mane in a distant paddock, and a slow smile twisted his lips, as he said to Katie with careful courtesy, "If we could just persuade Miss O'Grady to be so kind as to stay here and stay out trouble for the next quarter hour, I think I could suggest a refinement on that plan."

28

Even though the formal racing season had not yet started, the road to the racetrack was choked with Saratoga's usual traffic, so when Rose was at last handed down from their carriage, she ignored Wolverton's courteously proffered arm, and dashed straight toward the men clustered near the rail, painfully certain she was too late. She breathed only a moment's sigh of relief when her anxiously questing eyes at last found Fallon, still very much alive, as he made his way across the Grandstand toward Morrissey. For Lane had tossed his shabby coat over one shoulder as insouciantly as if it were an opera cape, leaving his white shirt glinting in the sunlight as if it were a gauntlet he had just thrown down.

"No..." she murmured, quickening her step.

But Wolverton stopped her with a gentle touch on her elbow, and instead turned in the opposite direction, where Cousin Preston stood by a starting line chalked in the dirt, a pistol in one hand. Seconds later, hooves pounded, and the world exploded into chaos.

The lads had been circling their horses, jockeying for position as they eased them toward the line. A hot-blooded colt was the last to slide into place, nipping and snorting at his neighbor, and Cousin Preston raised his pistol.

The colt reared with a shrill squeal, tossing his lad into the dirt. Another horse's nostrils flared, and his panicked lad shouted, "Who in hell let the mare loose?"

All eyes turned down the track, where a chestnut mare cantered gracefully toward the horses, her long, red mane and tail streaming behind her.

"Damme if she's not in season too," someone sighed, just as the starting line shattered. Ears pinned. Teeth bared. Haunches wheeled. Men fell and did their best to roll or scramble out of range of the flashing hooves.

"If you would excuse me," Wolverton murmured.

The Horseman's Word

A shot rang out.

And the mare was gone, galloping off so swiftly, a man might be forgiven for thinking he had imagined her.

In a single fluid move that looked like it had stepped straight out of the Shaolin monasteries of the mysterious East, Wolverton neatly seized the smoking pistol from Preston Olcott's hands—as well as the miscreant himself by the scruff of his well-tailored neck.

But Rose saw nothing. Her eyes were focused on only Lane Fallon—and the sight of the blood that spread with horrific speed across the sleeve of his carefully laundered and mended second-best shirt. Hoisting her skirts, she forgot all questions of propriety and threw herself past a very startled Morrissey, straight into Lane's arms. "Don't you dare die, Lane Fallon!" she shrieked. "Don't you dare die on me! Or run off to Canada either!"

Thrusting Preston into the care of one of the myriad thugs in ill-fitting suits and bowlers that seemed to materialize on every side, Wolverton strode after her. And suddenly, Rose felt herself the subject of not one, but two pairs of amused green eyes. Then Lane's gaze softened into that of the poet who could put down on paper what his lips could never say. "Pray do not upset yourself, my love," he said. "My father is an efficient man, not a bloodthirsty one. Indeed, it is said he hates blood because none runs in his veins. He simply sought to save us all the trouble of searching the entire Grandstand for the bullet that will tangle your cousin up in enough trials for attempted murder to distract him from any further schemes he might have on your fortune or your person." He cast a long look at his father. "Although I must admit, he might have given a thought to the trouble the loss of my second-best shirt might cost me."

Wolverton raised an eyebrow. "You would prefer I ruin your best one?"

"I have no best shirt," Lane snorted. He turned back to Rose, and the glint in his eyes suddenly dulled. "As for my immediate travel plans to Canada or elsewhere, I fear they threaten to be severely curtailed…"

He swayed, and Wolverton caught him, deftly avoiding getting blood on his clothing. "Son," he said, his face twisting with something that in another man might have been puzzlement. "Please. It's only a flesh wound. The merest graze. I made certain of it."

Indeed, the blood was already ceasing to flow. But Lane's face was slackening, his eyes drooping closed.

"What have you *done?*" Rose breathed.

"I'm not sure I know…"

Lane's eyes flew open, and focused squarely on his father. "She called me because she says you have at least earned the kindness of knowing," he said. "She says the debt was long since paid on the Wheatfield, and that I am simply being stubborn and cruel to keep it from you so long."

Then his eyes fluttered shut once more, and he slumped back into his father's arms. And if Rose had been surprised by Wolverton's puzzlement, it was nothing compared to his expression now. He gaped at his son in shock.

At the same moment, Olcott seized the opportunity to wrench free and bolt.

And Morrissey grinned. Then he pounced with a strength and speed that belied his girth and fine clothes. Briefly, he was transformed to the brutal street fighter he was reputed to be in his youth, grabbing Olcott by his hair and sending him to his knees with one swift blow to the face.

Calling for a handkerchief from one on his men, Morrissey dusted his hands with elaborate care before he turned to the stunned on-lookers. "Apologies, ladies and gentlemen," he boomed. "But if there is one thing that will be tolerated in our fine city even less than murder, 'tis startling the horses."

"It was never murder!" Cousin Preston protested through a rapidly swelling jaw. "It was an accident! All of it an accident! I never meant to hit him. Just to scare him. But the bastard grabbed my arm. He made me shoot him. And as for Sammy, I swear to you, he came at me first. A man has to defend himself…"

"Peace! I believe you." Morrissey spat with magnificent contempt. "For you are nothing but a liar and a cheater and a schemer. And while I can tolerate an honest killer, there is no room for your kind in Saratoga."

He snapped his fingers at a pair of policemen who looked little different than the rest of his thugs. "Take this gentleman to the jail and *convince* him he would prefer not to trouble either his fair cousin or this fair city with any of his further schemes. Beat him first to let him know you are serious. Then beat him to make sure you have wrung a thorough confession out of him. Then beat him once more to convince him that he never wants to return to Saratoga or disturb the peace by inciting law-abiding Irishmen to riot. I think a day or two or so should suffice, but try to be done with him before the season begins. Riots are bad for business, you know."

"You cannot!" Preston's eyes widened in outrage. "I demand a trial! I demand a lawyer."

The two men closed in on him, each one roughly grabbing an arm. "We'll make a note of your request."

Cousin Preston paled. "This is America, for God's sake, not some damned Irish bog! There are laws…"

"In Saratoga, my word is the law," Morrissey said. He smiled, exposing several gold teeth, as he knelt and deftly extracted an oilskin packet of papers from the breast pocket of Fallon's coat. "Especially now that I have these."

The papers were miraculously unbloodied, causing Rose to cast a sharp, suspicious glance at Wolverton. Was it possible that Cousin Preston was telling the truth?

"Those are mine!" Preston gasped. "They are stolen property."

"The desk sergeant will be pleased to take the particulars of your case," Morrissey told him, then cast him a meaningful glance. "Although I think it only fair to suggest to you that any information you might be able to provide that would help us in uncovering any further frightful details of this pernicious conspiracy might well serve to shorten your stay with us. I'll instruct my boys to hold their persuasiveness until you reach the station to give you time to consider that option."

He nodded at the two men, who hauled Preston to his feet, none too gently.

"Rose," Preston begged her. "Please, you cannot let them…"

For a moment, Rose was torn by doubt. She loathed Cousin Preston, yes, and the sight of Lane Fallon lying there bloodied, as his father deftly wrapped his wound with a snowy handkerchief, could make her hate him. But was this right? Was this justice?

Morrissey's meaty hand landed with surprising gentleness on Rose's arm. "Please, do not trouble yourself, Miss. For there's nothing you can do to stop me, even if you were of a mind to." He smiled in a way she could only hope was meant to be reassuring. "But have no fear. My boys know their craft, and if I tell them not to kill him, they'll not kill him."

She drew a deep, unsteady breath. "And do I have your word you will tell them that?"

"My word of honor, the very same word I gave my sweet Susie, who you very much remind me of, if I may take the liberty of saying so. No more killings. At least no *unnecessary* ones," he amended himself hastily. "For if there is one lesson I've learned in life, 'tis that dead bodies are bad for business."

29

Lane was at a crossroads—a place of ill-omen, where they hanged thieves and buried suicides. A witchy place, like the sea strand or the gloaming, a place that was neither land nor water, neither dark nor light. A place in between. But, sinner that he might have been, Lane Fallon was neither witch nor suicide, so why was he here, standing beneath a cross, from which three roads stretched…?

And who was this woman who approached him from that way, her fair hair glittering in the sunlight, as she stretched a pale hand to him and said, "And so you have redeemed the price of the bridle. You served and won as my champion, and so the debt that was owed has been paid. Your family is free. And you have won your own choice."

There was part of Lane that wondered whether he'd died and was at last facing the afterlife. But there was a worse part of him that worried that he had done nothing to justify such luck, and instead the daft streak with which his father had cursed his blood had at last won out and he was destined to live out the rest of his days consigned to a lunatic asylum. "What choice?" he asked.

"Three roads," she said, indicating them with a graceful gesture. "One narrow, one broad, one ferny. Which way will you go?"

Lane drew a sharp breath. What was this? Some kind of riddle of the Sphinx? No, he sensed this woman was more powerful, more dangerous than even that fabled creature. But what answer could he make? What answer should he make?

It came to him as a distant melody, borne on the wind.

A Róisín ná bíodh brón…

"I will go back whence I came."

Her eyes flashed, illuminating her hair and skin with green fire. "I can offer endless beauty, endless pleasure. The girl will grow old, as will you. Do you really choose to take that path?"

"Yes," he said.

She inclined her head. "Then I must rescind my claim, however much it pains me. For a debt was owed, and a debt has been paid."

And, placing her long, pale fingers on his shoulder, she drew him close and kissed his forehead. And when she was gone, Lane could only hope that when his eyes opened, his first sight would be Rose Adair. His Roisin.

Instead, it was the White Wolf who sat by his bedside, studying him with his green, unblinking gaze.

It was enough to make Lane turn back to the crossroads. But the White Wolf was too quick for him. "You saw her," he said. "She spoke to you."

Lane shook his head against the pillows. "I have no idea what you mean."

"When you collapsed after you were shot, you came back from… somewhere. You said that 'She' told you that the debt had been paid. I would know what else She might have said to you."

Lane shrugged, costing himself a fresh bout of pain. "'Twas a fever dream, nothing more. I scarcely remember it now."

His father's jaw set, as he drew a deep breath. "She also called you cruel—fine words from one who has refined her cruelty to the same pitch as her falsity. Still, I am forced to allow that there would be those who say you had a right to be. And so, I would attempt to explain the matters that lie between us."

"What matters?" As far as Lane was concerned, all that lay between him and his father was an exasperated bewilderment that the man had not been long ago consigned to Bedlam, and his growing suspicion that the White Wolf had just shot him, no matter how justifiable the cause, was not likely to make him change his opinion.

"Matters that should have been explained long ago, had I not been too much of a coward to do so." The White Wolf's gaze grew distant. "You must understand that she lies even to those she loves best. She cannot help it. It is her nature. But you must believe me that I would have stayed trapped there forever if I had seen what she truly intended."

"Trapped where?" Lane sighed, without any real desire to hear the answer to his question.

"At the crossroads. Where I was offered a choice. Between three roads." Wolverton met Lane's eyes. "I believe you can picture the place. As well as the path she would bid you choose.

> And see not ye that bonny road,
> Which winds about the fernie brae?
> That is the road to fair Elfland,
> Where you and I this night maun gae."

"A scholar of your caliber, and you use a Scottish ballad to explain an Irish family legend?" Lane snorted.

"Thomas of Erceldoune was hardly the only one she coveted. Nor are you likely to be the last." Wolverton's eyes grew distant in a way that Lane was cordially beginning to loathe. "Ours is an old house. Many would say it is one of the oldest houses in Ireland. Many others would say it is one of the most treacherous, for how else could we have managed to preserve our lands through the depredations of the Tudor bastards, the cursed plantations, and the usurper Cromwell with equal success? But the truth of the matter is, we thrived because we were blessed by her—and for no greater reason than her love of our men. But in her very hour of need, we returned her kindness by betraying her to the priests instead. And so her blessing became our curse…

"Nine generations, she swore that the curse would endure. Nine generations, and the bloodline would fade completely—unless a new son was given to her to replace the champion who had so cruelly failed her."

"You?" Lane sighed.

"Only in the coarsest sense of the word." The White Wolf's mouth thinned with distaste. "No, she took me only because she wished me to father her a son. A son triply born for the triple goddess, just as her first champion, CuChulainn had been. I assume you recall the old tale. Stranded while hunting a flock of magical birds, Conchobar and his daughter Deichtine were forced to take shelter in a croft—and as the storm raged outside, a mare gave birth to twin foals, and their host's wife gave birth to a boy. In the morning, Conchobar and Deichtine found themselves in the fairy mound at Newgrange, alone with the two foals and the child. The foals prospered, but the infant died, despite Deichtine's careful fostering. Soon Lugh himself came to Deichtine and explained to her that that was because he wished to gift her with his own son, and CuChulainn was conceived a second time. And a second time, he died, this time ripped from the womb by his mother out of shame. Only to at last arise to his full might as a hero, when he was born a third time to the husband to whose bed Deichtine went 'virgin-whole.' Just as my first born son died, only to be conceived again, and then be born a third time..."

No, the man was mad. He had to be. "For the love of God, man, would you listen to yourself?" Lane snapped. "More superstitious than any bog Irishman, trying to find meaning in a few tales told by the fire and a fever dream."

"Only I was too stupid to see the pattern, until it was far too late," the White Wolf went on as if he had not spoken. "For I swear to you I never would have done it had I known, never would have exchanged your life for my own. But I had watched your mother leap to her death, driven mad by that creature's calling after her child. How could I see that they would save the baby?

"Nay, how could I see that you would be stubborn and strong enough to insist on being born?" the White Wolf correct himself with a smile. "Had I known you then as I know you now, I would have sensed the treachery at once, but I give you my word that I had no inkling until I came back to myself and saw the mark on you. The hoof needing the iron shoe, the mark of the horse goddess' own."

Lane shut his eyes, unable to suppress an angry laugh. "It's called a club foot, father. A simple medical condition that has been recorded even in ancient Egypt. Many men have managed to go through life with such a condition. Talleyrand. Richelieu. Byron..."

"Tamerlane," the White Wolf added to the catalogue. "Timur the Lame. The greatest warrior, the greatest hero the world has known."

"And so you named me. Just as so you bred me?"

"I never bred you! Never named you as such either!" Wolverton shut his eyes and drew a deep breath. "It was supposed to be Declan. It was never supposed to be you. I gave her her damned son, for it was the only way I could see to escape, and damme if I did not think myself clever enough to cheat her..."

His voice trailed off as Lane simply stared at his father. "Do you think that somehow makes it better? Small wonder the poor, daft lunk hates you—if he's even capable of such an emotion."

An odd look crossed the White Wolf's face. "You underestimate your brother's abilities—rather considerably, I might add. Nonetheless, I met my obligations. I sought to raise him with every advantage you had, save one."

"And you did such a good job of it, he fled across an ocean to escape you."

"A fair forfeit for my trying to cheat her, much as I sincerely regret it. Just as the bridle remains a fair forfeit to our house." The White Wolf fell silent before he asked, "What happened to it?"

"I'm sorry to say I don't know. I rather lost track of it. Something distracting about having your horse shot out from under you." Drawing a deep breath, Lane shook his head at a father he never had understood, and was beginning to sincerely doubt he ever would. Nonetheless, it seemed strangely important to at least try to make the man who called himself his father understand. "You asked me to tell you truly what I saw. Very well. Allow me to do just that. What I saw was rich men sacrificing poor men as casually as they would pawns on a chessboard—myself included. I saw myself destroy everything my brother had built for himself for no better reason than to manipulate a man's monomaniacal obsessions. I saw myself deceive an innocent young woman in the cruelest possible manner. And I saw myself justify all of it with the simple conviction that I was serving a higher good."

"Many would argue you were," the White Wolf pointed out. He studied the ruby that glinted on one finger, before he added, "But be that as it may, what, if I may ask, changed your mind?"

"That same young woman whom I so wronged, still condescended to see something worth salvaging in my rotten soul…"

"And mayhap she succeeded." The White Wolf's lips curved into a smile. "Another Scottish ballad. Another Tom. Another rose. And yet many would say one and the same. 'They'll turn me in your arms, lady, into an asp and adder. But hold me fast and fear me not…'"

A long pause while Lane fought down the urge to give ear to what his father was saying, before he snorted, "The difference between you and me is that you actually believe the shite you spin. I only wish I could."

"A father is always entitled to hope." Wolverton got to his feet. "In the meantime, I've taken the liberty of procuring you a change of clothing, for whenever you feel fit enough to join your young lady and me in the salon. As well as an extra shirt to replace your second-best one, which I apologize for having been so careless as to ruin."

30

A single evening's experience of the White Wolf's casual command was sufficient for Rose to entirely understand why Lane resented his father so dearly. When Wolverton finally emerged from his son's sickroom, it was with a list of orders for Bridie, which the cantankerous Irishwoman obeyed instantly and without demur. Then he turned his attention to the wretched chest that had started all this sad business, which had miraculous manifested from the hotel's safe, along with Jonathan Adair's traveling desk. His gaze lingered on its carvings, and the ruby on his finger winked as he reached to trace them. "The bridle of Manannan is gone," he mused. "And yet, there remains the future of this to consider."

"In fact, we need to discuss not just the future of the chest, but the future of my father's entire collection," Rose said. "And I hope you will be pleased to know that I have already given the matter considerable thought."

She had squared her shoulders for a fight, for she had no intention of finally finding herself free of Cousin Preston's interference, only to find herself overwhelmed by this new protector. But Wolverton merely inclined his head to listen.

"My father sought to benefit mankind by amassing objects," she went on, forcing herself to keep her voice steady, and to lay out her ideas as completely and rationally as the catalog entries she had prepared according to her father's exacting specifications. "I have every desire to benefit mankind, but not in such a way. In my mind, my father's proposed museum was nothing but the grandest of mausoleums, with the treasures of the past buried with him like the butchered slaves of Sardanapalus. I personally prefer to see objects, just like lives, put to practical use. However, I would like to honor my father's wishes. In fact, at the risk of sounding overdramatic, I would suggest I consider it a sacred trust. And so I would propose to sell off the objects in his collection and put the money to more practical use—in his name, of course. I thought to begin with rebuilding the Colored Orphans' Asylum."

If she had startled Wolverton, the only sign was that he fell silent for a moment, before he returned his attention to the carvings on the chest once more. "These figures certainly suggest that that might be a very appropriate memorial. For they scarcely look Celtic, do they? Rather, one might argue this confirms O'Brien's hypothesis that the original settlers of Ireland were the remains of a lost sea-going race, some say the Phoenicians, some say the Atlanteans, some say those who escaped Troy, and voyaged first to Carthage and then to the blessed isle…"

"Bearing the lost bridle of Hektor, Breaker of Horses, which legend has it, will bring forth a horseman who can save his lost people at their hour of direst despair?" Rose asked with a weary laugh. "Please, your Lordship, I have already swallowed quite my fill of such pretty tales from your son."

"So cynical then?" Wolverton raised an eyebrow. "I am certain my son wishes to make his explanations to you, and would most likely prefer to do so privately. So it might be best if you and I limit our attention to practical matters, lest I be accused of unwelcome meddling…"

"Practical matters? Is that what you would term this talk?" Lane demanded, manifesting shakily from his sickroom, still gaunt, still pale, as he struggled one-handed to knot the cravat on the fresh shirt that had apparently appeared out of nowhere. Rose wanted nothing so much as to fly into his arms, but with a languid sweep of his hand, his father waved his son to a wing-chair, and Fallon sank into it gratefully, his surge of anger apparently overwhelmed by his surge of pain.

"I apologize if my methods seem a trifle high-handed," Wolverton said to Rose, without paying any further attention to Lane. "I can assure you the fault is none but mine, as many of those who are meant to love me best can attest. Still, I would speak frankly. For, while I find your plans to dispose of your father's collection laudable, and will be pleased to offer you every assistance in the matter—especially in terms of realizing the highest price for each sale, which it is said is rather a gift of mine—I must beg you in the strongest possible terms to allow me to send this particular item to Albany, where it will be shipped down to a waiting vessel that will take it safely back to England—along with a few letters I have extracted from your father's private correspondence. For I sincerely believe that this chest would best serve your purposes in the possession of Her Majesty's Government…"

"You mean, it would best serve as another quiver to your bow," Lane sighed. "Another weapon in your arsenal."

"Quite on the contrary, I would believe the chest's power lies precisely in its *not* being used as weapon—a strategy that your American, Mr. Poe, understood all too well." Wolverton turned the full force of his gaze on Rose. "Brilliant tale, 'The Purloined Letter.' Makes one wonder what genuine secrets might have inspired his fantastic stories, and what role they might have played in his unfortunate death. But be that as it may, just as the fact of the highly-placed indiscretion at the heart of Mr. Poe's tale is unimportant in and of itself, so the fact of a failed conspiracy to blame Her Majesty's Government for an atrocity that delivered New York City to the Confederacy is meaningless in this happy era of peace. But those who hold that secret without acting on it are very powerful, very powerful indeed. And, although I have every confidence that my son is more than capable of protecting your future interests…"

"Recollect yourself, sir! Miss Adair is but recently bereaved and in no position to make any decisions of the heart!" Lane leapt to his feet with a furious protest—only to sink back into his chair, suddenly pale.

"What about engaging a man of business has anything to do with affairs of the heart? Why if you asked me, I'd venture that it is one of the most heartless positions in this world, and I am certain you will be furiously bored in no time. Still, medical wisdom holds that a man recovering from an injury such as yours should avoid excitement at all costs, so it may prove a suitable occupation to distract you during your convalescence," Wolverton said blandly, before he turned back to Rose. "But I would not want to allow there to be even the slightest suggestion that I am acting high-handedly once again. Such a decision could obviously only be taken if it were congenial to you. So, before we go any further, perhaps it's best if we clear the air of any lingering doubts you might have about the role my son played in the unhappy events of two years ago."

"Clear the air? You are physically incapable of doing anything but muddying the waters with a thousand tales and legends," Lane managed to splutter.

"I freely admit that my son is a teller of tales, a weaver of illusions. His weapons are words, dreams, ideas, lies—the gifts of the fair folk, which many have said course through his blood." Regally ignoring another outraged protest by Lane, Wolverton ruminated, "Perhaps there would have been a

The Horseman's Word

simpler way to trace the network of Fenians in this country than spinning wild tales of horsewhisperers and magic bridles, but that is not my son's way."

"No, he prefers to masquerade as a man he is not," Rose said tartly.

"I *would* explain myself to you directly," Lane sighed.

"My son's sense of humor is sometimes a touch idiosyncratic," the White Wolf allowed. "But it is no jest when I tell you that two years ago he unmasked a pernicious conspiracy that involved your father—as well as a group of men that would never be brought to justice, no matter how compelling the case against them. So when my son had amassed as much evidence as he could, there was only one way he could offer the details of the conspiracy to the Americans, and that was by claiming the English had initiated the plot. The plan was that he would be quietly expelled from America in order to prevent a diplomatic incident, and the chest and its contents would be returned to her Majesty's government as a token of good faith, while the Americans would keep control of the names of those Americans the English claimed as co-conspirators. Even in peacetime there could have been no thought of arresting them or bringing them to justice, but the knowledge of those names could be used as... collateral to encourage these men to direct their fortunes and energies toward channels more beneficial to the Union cause—much as I propose that you use this chest now. Unfortunately, my son's rather Byronic tendencies carried him away, and he chose to return to your house one last time before he delivered those names to the Americans." This time there was no mistaking the sheer exasperation on the White Wolf's face as he turned to Lane, and finally addressed his son directly. "I admit myself still uncertain of your motivations. Why did you not trust me to see matters through?"

"Maybe I was loath to leave the lady without making my feelings known."

"You might have trusted me in that as well."

"Maybe," Lane said, "it was too important a matter to trust to anyone else."

And while that was certainly a topic that was far more congenial to Rose than any talk of conspiracies and collateral, the White Wolf dismissed it with an irritated snort. "What you must believe is that the conspiracy my son uncovered here in America is very real and very dangerous. And as your father's heir, you may still find yourself threatened by its perpetrators—especially over your plans to disperse the collection your father assembled in their name."

"I assume you speak of the Society of the Horseman's Word?" Rose asked with a sigh.

"The Society was never real, any more than the Fenian conspiracy with which it threatened New York City was anything but a product of my son's imagination. But other secret societies and other conspiracies are only too real." The White Wolf's face hardened. "Your father was a Yale man, was he not?"

"You would have New Haven a hotbed of conspiracy too?"

"Yale University certainly is and always has been—ever since Ezra Stiles first plotted to replace George III with a Stuart king during the American Revolution," the White Wolf said. "And it is said that the new secret society that has emerged there is on course to become the most powerful secret society not just in the United States, but in the world—with plans that go far beyond delivering New York City into the hands of the Confederacy for economic gain."

Rose shook her head. "My father was a collector, not a kingmaker."

"And that was precisely his importance to the group—as well as the importance of the bridle that my son was so careless as to misplace," Wolverton said. "For however much you may wish to believe that the story of Manannan mac Lir is naught but a fairy tale, I can assure you that your father believed in it—just as he believed in the power of the other objects he sought for his collection. If you will allow me to speak plainly, your father was engaged in nothing less than assembling an occult arsenal to arm these men."

"And *that* is the reason you would have me believe my father was killed?"

"Of course not. Preston Olcott tried to kill your father in order to prevent him from squandering the entire family fortune on this folly—and for that, arguably, we may owe him some measure of sympathy. Your father's collapse here in Saratoga was simply an act of God—or another force." Wolverton's gaze grew uncanny. "For those who would amass such weapons would do well to remember that arsenals have a very unpleasant habit of exploding when least expected."

"By all that's holy, I can only hope that Miss Adair already understands that whatever poor service I might render her is freely offered and freely given. There is no need to frighten her into acceptance," Lane sighed.

"There is every need to ensure that she believes these men and their plans are very real…"

Any further argument was abruptly cut off by a discreet tap at the door. Moments later, Cole Washington was ushered in by a bewildered-looking major domo who seemed poised to seize the slightest excuse to show him the servants' entrance instead.

"Mr. Washington," the White Wolf said, ignoring the major-domo's patent disapproval. "Please sit down and join us. I trust matters in Little Dublin have been smoothed over to your satisfaction?"

Every word that fell from his lips suggested that he considered the matter of the chest as having also been settled to everyone's satisfaction, but Cole Washington was made of far sterner stuff than Rose Adair or Lane Fallon.

"I appreciate the efforts that so many of you have made on my behalf, but I am unfortunately not interested in smoothing anything over," he said, without bothering to take a seat. "Not until I have justice for my murdered wife."

"An honorable man. And an honest one. Unlike me or even my sons. Or any others I have met here in Saratoga, for that matter." Wolverton's gaze grew distant. "You say you want justice for your wife; I would suggest that you will never find it here in the courts of the United States, and you will only waste the rest of your life trying to find it. But I can assure you that the universe has a deeper and truer course of justice than our petty human minds can imagine."

Washington's lip curled. "The mills of the gods grind slowly, but they grind fine?"

Wolverton raised an eyebrow. "Or goddess, many would say. Whatever the case, I would beg you instead to be content in trusting to that balance, and turn your attention to charting your own course instead. There is a sloop awaiting my order to ferry a priceless treasure across the Atlantic. I would beg you to take passage on it as well. For there is plenty of good racing in Paris, and I would suggest you would find the atmosphere more congenial than it is likely to be in the United States for the next few years. It would be my privilege to provide you with a few letters of introduction."

"In other words, you suggest I run away?"

"Quite on the contrary, I suggest that you have played your part valiantly in this fight, and now it is time to leave it to another," Wolverton said. "For your future will never be safe here in the United States—even with John Morrissey's protection, which, you know as well as I do, will not last. For he is, at heart, no better a man than the rivals he now holds in his power. And sooner or later it will occur to him, just as I'm certain it has already occurred to his enemies, that their negotiating position in this standoff is not significantly improved by having a third party privy to their secrets. And knowing that, neither of them will allow you a moment's peace until you are dead—or at least far enough away that you do not pose an obvious threat."

Washington drew a deep breath, then conceded the point. "Be that as it may, there is no other future left to me."

"Ah, yes." The White Wolf frowned, as if he had nearly overlooked a piece of luggage, and he touched a bell by his elbow. Immediately, footsteps sounded in the corridor outside, and the door swung open to admit a fresh-faced maid, leading two children, the boy still round and chubby, the girl already lengthening into the coltishness of adolescence.

Washington gave a muffled cry, but immediately controlled himself. He approached the girl first, taking his time to study her, before he said, "You always had your mother's eyes."

"When she got mad at me, she always said I had your stubborn streak." The girl bit her lip. "Actually, she didn't use quite those words."

And at long last, Cole Washington smiled. "Well, we shall have to see about that, now shan't we?"

He turned to the boy, more hesitant now. "And you are?"

Letting go of the maid's hand, the boy stepped forward and held out his own to his father. "Cole Washington IV," he said gravely. "And my mother made me swear that I should never forget it."

31

Wolverton saw Cole and his children out personally, leaving Rose and Lane alone together in a gesture that might have been carelessness in another man, but coming from the White Wolf, felt like a benediction. The ormolu clock on the mantel ticked off what seemed like an eternity, before Lane jumped to his feet with a violence that made him pale.

"You need not pay him any mind. I'll not leave America until I am sure of your safety, but you need not worry about taking me on as your man of business…" He paused, flushing. "Or in any other capacity—and not only because I am rather certain you are quite capable of handling matters yourself. I… I owe you a debt of gratitude that can never be repaid, but I beg you not to think you are under any similar obligation to me."

"You refer to this matter of my having saved your soul?" She eyed him curiously. "In truth, that sounds more like your father speaking than you. Surely a rationalist such as yourself knows a man is captain of his own soul."

An odd expression crossed his face, reminding her suddenly and irresistibly of that weird scene after he had collapsed in the Grandstand. And then he recalled himself with a quick shake of his head. "Of course. But there remains the matter of my having lied to you as much as I lied to your father. I wooed you under false pretenses. Mayhap I did what I did for the right reasons rather than the wrong ones, but the end result is still the same: You fell in love with Declan Sullivan, not me."

"I remain of the opinion that you improved somewhat substantially on the original. Your brother seems more comfortable in the company of beasts than dastardly conspiracies and secret societies."

"And probably rightly so," Lane sighed. "But that does not make me the man you fell in love with, the man you were willing to betray your family and country to save."

His face was a mask of defiant embarrassment that made her want to throw herself into his arms as shamelessly as she had in the Grandstand. Instead, she cocked her head to study him with a demure smile. "Oh, really?" she inquired. "And what man did I fall in love with?"

"You know as well as I do, you loved the poet. The wild-eyed idealist. Your heart was touched by my Byronic tendencies, as my father was pleased to put it. But those were never my tendencies. They were naught but a sham. A fairy tale as much as all my father's tales of secret societies and occult arsenals."

"Your father said the last two were no fairy tale. And I, for one, believe him."

"We are not talking of secret societies right now. We are talking about Declan Sullivan."

"Are we?" she mused. "For I suppose there's nothing recklessly Byronic whatsoever about a man risking his own life in order to bring a miscreant to justice—in a hare-brained scheme that made about as much sense as J.E.B. Stuart's wearing a white plume in his hat to signal his descent from Mary, Queen of Scots—as well as taunting the Union soldiers with a clear target to fire upon."

"Mine was a calculated risk," he said irritably. "Stuart was a vainglorious madman. I scarcely think the comparison is fair."

She nodded gravely. "And what if I'm in love with the man who could imagine exactly such a vainglorious madman—and then improve upon him. The kind of man who could make Declan Sullivan up?"

Lane's face set in half-hopeful lines that reminded her of nothing so much as a stray cat cadging kitchen scraps while keeping a wary eye out for the cook's swift broom. "Are you?"

She raised a shoulder—perhaps conceding the point, perhaps not. "I am not fool enough not to know that remains to be seen. But I am willing to at least investigate the possibility."

"Is that so?" He stiffened. Then, suddenly, he grinned. "Well, at the risk of being accused of attempting to influence your deliberations…"

And he swept her into his arms, his mouth crushing down across hers in a furious kiss, as once more, time stood still. But a quiet snick of the door opening broke the spell, and they sprang apart in furious embarrassment as Wolverton strolled past them, ostentatiously ignoring Rose's disarranged hair and the fresh blood that had blossomed on Lane's sleeve, in order to pour himself a brandy.

"One supposes when in Rome—or in this case, Saratoga Springs—one must do as the Romans do," the White Wolf addressed himself to the tantalus. "But if you intend to continue your addresses to a woman under my protection, especially one who has been so recently and savagely bereaved, you will do it during appropriate calling hours, and you will do it at her family home in New York City—not this bastard child of Vauxhall and Montenegro."

It cost Lane several deep, steadying breaths before he managed to match his father's careful indifference, and said, "If I were you, I'd have more of a care of Morrissey's fists, if he ever you describe his creation in those terms."

"And," Wolverton went on, turning to cast a terrible look at the bloodstains on Lane's new shirt, "the next time you present yourself to Miss Adair, you will be appropriately attired. Since I would prefer not to face the rumor that will inevitably arise from my son strolling down Fifth Avenue looking like he had only recently escaped from Andersonville, I have arranged for my man at Brooks Brothers to attend you privately in my rooms, where I would prefer you stay until you are fully recovered. It is scarcely Savile Row, needless to say, but he does his best to understand my standards."

The faint hint of uncertain invitation hung between them for what seemed like an eternity. And then Lane relaxed with an exasperated laugh.

"As so many of us do," he said. "I assume you have already made travel arrangements as well?"

"Your train leaves in an hour," Wolverton said. "If you have baggage that needs to be forwarded, I will be happy to make arrangements for it to follow."

"That won't be necessary," Lane assured him. "The Irish Brigade took rather a toll on my admittedly meager wardrobe, as I'm sure you're well aware."

Wolverton raised an eyebrow. "If nothing else, 'tis a preferable explanation to the rumors that reached me about you resigning from the service in order to set up trade as a fur trapper in Canada. I confess I suffered more than a moment's anxiety on that front."

"Alas, completely justifiable. A brutish animal is the mink. John Jacob Astor must have been made of far sterner stuff than most credit him." Lane said, and turned to Rose with a barely concealed grin at the sharp uncertainty that twisted his father's face. "And so I take my leave for now, Miss Adair. And, at the risk of seeming importunate, I beg you to send word as soon as you arrive back in New York City, that I may offer you whatever poor service I can render... as your man of business."

32

Sullivan's stomach tightened in dismay as he returned to the stalls where he had left Katie. Rounding up the mare-maddened stallions had been but the work of a soft whistle and a few words; the mare had required naught but a gentle scratch behind her ears and a whispered thanks. No hope that the redhead that awaited him in the stalls—that he *hoped* awaited him in the stalls—could be managed as easily.

He knew well enough what he must do for her. The bastard who had fathered him could well and truly pay his debt—to the Goddess, to his mother, to a son he had never wanted—by making sure this lass never knew another moment's fear or cold or hunger. By all that was holy, it was a cheap enough price to pay. And if his father decided to kick up rough, well, then his cursed excuse for a brother could put his talents to better use than tormenting Sullivan. Either way, when it came to his family, a debt was owed, and a debt would be paid. But he was well and truly terrified at the prospect of making Katie O'Grady see the reason of his plan.

She leapt to her feet the moment he walked down the row of stalls. "I gave ye my word I'd wait, and wait I did. But now that you're back, I'll take my leave."

"And go where?" he asked, his voice dropping instinctively into a wyrding cadence. "To the club or to the nuns? Neither 'tis a choice fit for a queen."

She glanced up, her eyes as fiery as her hair. "I'll thank you to let me make my own choices. And dinna think to ply me with your honeyed words either. I'll find my own way, thank ye. I'm no daft relict, no object of pity or scorn, no matter what you might tell your fine English father."

Sullivan bit his lip at the memory. He took a step closer, willing her not to shy away.

"I must needs cry your pardon for that. I misspoke—foolish lout that I am. I… I was speaking of another lady altogether." He held up a hand to cut off her furious exclamation. "One that I would tell you about some day. But now, I wish to speak only of you. You are no daft relict, no object of pity or scorn either. You are a true thoroughbred. A *cheval de race*, as the French would have it."

He risked another step closer, and his heart leapt when he saw a flash of a humor light her face. "I'm no horse either, thank ye very much."

One more step, and he would be close enough to lay a hand on her too-thin shoulder, and then maybe trace the fine line of her jaw, as he would do with a spooked horse. The need to do so was almost painful, and yet he forced himself to keep talking. "No, you are not. You are Nunn's Irish Rose. And all I wish is to see you thrive and grow in the warmest sun, the richest soil, nourished by the softest rains…"

She squared her shoulders. "Ye can keep your wishes. I can take care of myself."

"Ye have already convinced me of that, to be sure. That is why I can only ask you for the honor of allowing me to take care of you—and admit 'tis a privilege I scarcely deserve."

"Now you're mocking me."

Her voice cracked and his heart along with it, but he feigned not to have noticed. "Not at all," he said, his voice no longer wyrding, but just his own. "'Twould be a rare man who would be worthy of you, and I never lied to myself that I'm such a man. For you are not Nunn's Irish Rose. Not a queen of Eire either. You are Katie O'Grady, queen in your own right. And you deserve better than a stable lad that stinks only of manure."

She studied him for a moment, then drew herself up to her full height, tossing the remains of her hair as if it were a royal pennon streaming behind her, and Sullivan's heart lifted. "Aye, Declan Sullivan. Aye, that I do. And I intend to have it," she said. "And ye will be the one to give it to me. Sure, and there's no limit to what a man of your abilities can do. Look at Morrissey. The only talent he had was his fists. Now, he owns Saratoga, shares a box with old Vanderbilt himself. There's even talk of him running for Congress."

Sullivan's eyes widened. "Ye propose that I run for Congress?" he asked blankly.

She smiled rosily. "Well, we'll see that as we may. But for the moment, I'd be suggesting that Preston Olcott's barn stands to be offered on very advantageous terms."

Sullivan's face set. "And how do you propose that I would afford even the most advantageous terms on a stable lad's wages?"

She met his eyes calmly. Fearlessly. "You were willing to ask your father for help on my behalf," she said. "I have decided I am willing to accept your kind offer. I am merely stating my terms."

And what terms were they exactly? He began to stammer out his excuses as they crowded in from every side. "Nae, lass. There's still a price on my head down in New York City. And you're right. I'm nothing but a stable lad that smells of shite. Slow and stupid, as most would have it. Daft or pixilated, others would say, fit only to talk to horses. In any case, I'm set in my ways and far too old to wed you…"

His voice trailed off as she laughed. "Rushing your fences, a bit, dinna you think? For who said anything about wedding? I'm not saying it willna come down to that, but I'll have you know you'll court me proper when and if it does. But in the meantime, who could fault a horseman who had suddenly stumbled on good times here in the New World, for sending for his sweet cousin from the auld sod to help him run his stable and home?"

He stepped back, more appalled then when he had first discovered her in his bed. "Ach, who's a bit of a managing female, then?"

"And your great good luck that I am," she retorted. Abruptly, her face softened, as if she was the one to feel sorry for him. "A father's a father, Declan Sullivan, and no matter how right you think your quarrel, 'tis a precious thing to squander. I tell you, if I had had a father who'd stepped forward to claim me at the orphanage, I'd have wasted no time asking whether he'd fought Union or Confederate. I'd have thrown myself in his arms and never let him go. As it was, even Sammy… well, I knew what Sammy was—mayhap better than Sammy himself. But even Sammy seemed like a bit of heaven compared to be all alone in this world."

He stood there in stunned silence, wondering what he was about to unleash on the world—or more ominously, upon himself. "Do ye propose to teach me wisdom as well?" he asked helplessly.

"You could use a bit of improving," she said critically. "'Tis just your great good fortune that I stand willing to take you in hand."

EPILOGUE

The Wheatfield, Gettysburg, July 4, 1863

No colored troops fought at Gettysburg. The blood that was shed by some 50,000 soldiers was all white men's blood. The colored troops were given the far more dangerous task of serving as teamsters, removing the wounded, disposing of the dead, and hauling necessary ammunition, tents and food to the troops, all without the basic benefit of guns and cannon with which to defend themselves.

The horror stories were endless. Teamsters kidnapped from their wagons and tortured into serving the Confederacy instead. Burnings and mutilations of the most appalling kinds when they refused. Mistrust and scant respect from the troops whose goods they hauled. And yet the teamsters served—the Union, the cause of their people? Who knows? They suffered. But they served.

Today, they were there to haul away the dead. A weary task, as weary as the driver and his horse, which once upon a time might have been white, but was now stained dark by mud and blood. This driver had been spared the task of transporting the fallen—many of whom were still writhing and moaning. Instead, he had been assigned the task of scavenging any useful weapons that were no longer needed by the men that had borne them.

But the glint in the mud that caught his eyes was not a gun or even a bayonet. It was a bridle, curiously decorated with sea shells and charms. Not a weapon, and not in the best condition. And how strange it was that no horse nor fallen rider lay nearby. But the teamster hauled himself down to scoop it up anyway, for bridles weren't cheap and there was never a point in wasting. And who could ever know what purpose it might serve in the future?

About the Author

There are three places you can find Erica when she's not writing or teaching courses on mystery fiction and Arthurian Romance at Fordham University: on a hiking trail, in her garden, or at the back of the pack in her local road race. Her favorite kind of vacation is backpacking across Dartmoor or among the hills of Wales in order to find new and exciting legends to inspire her own writing. After she graduated from Yale University, her interest in folklore and story led her to an M.A. in Creative Writing from City College of New York and a Ph.D. in Comparative Literature from the City University of New York, where she published articles and a book about female folklorists of the nineteenth century before she decided she'd rather be writing the stories herself.

Along with their macaw Fasolt and a rotating assortment of cats, she and her husband divide their time between New York City and Woodstock, where they spend far too much time gardening.

CPSIA information can be obtained
at www.ICGtesting.com
Printed in the USA
LVHW051137130919
630971LV00006B/127